THE HAUNTING BALLAD

ALSO BY MICHAEL NETHERCOTT

The Séance Society

THE HAUNTING BALLAD

Michael Nethercott

MINOTAUR BOOKS

A THOMAS DUNNE BOOK

NEW YORK

A THOMAS DUNNE BOOK FOR MINOTAUR BOOKS.
An imprint of St. Martin's Publishing Group.

THE HAUNTING BALLAD. Copyright © 2014 by Michael Nethercott. All rights reserved. Printed in the United States of America. For information, address St. Martin's Press, 175 Fifth Avenue, New York, N.Y. 10010.

www.thomasdunnebooks.com
www.minotaurbooks.com

The Library of Congress Cataloging-in-Publication Data is available upon request

ISBN 978-1-250-01740-6 (hardcover)
ISBN 978-1-4668-5650-9 (e-book)

Minotaur books may be purchased for educational, business, or promotional use. For information on bulk purchases, please contact Macmillan Corporate and Premium Sales Department at 1-800-221-7945, extension 5442, or write specialmarkets@macmillan.com.

First Edition: October 2014

10 9 8 7 6 5 4 3 2 1

To my wife, daughter,
and son: my little club

ACKNOWLEDGMENTS

Many thanks to the first readers of this novel for their input: my wife, Helen Schepartz (first among firsts); mystery fan extraordinaire Cynthia Atwood; and Sir David Lampe-Wilson. David's bookstore, *Mystery on Main Street* in Brattleboro, Vermont, has been a beacon of light for me through many foggy times. And a nod to my dear old friend Crystal Huntington for harboring me on my Greenwich Village research journeys.

Waves of gratitude to my family and friends who've been a support throughout my writing life. Many thanks to my smart and conscientious literary agent, Susan Gleason, and to my sharp and steady editor, Kat Brzozowski. To all the good people of St. Martin's Press. And kudos, India Cooper, on your pugnacious copyediting.

PART 1

O Death

What is this that I can't see
With ice cold hands takin' hold of me?

Well, I am death, none can excel
I'll open the door to heaven or hell.

"O death, o death" someone would pray
"Could you wait to call me another day?"

—*Traditional Appalachian song*

CHAPTER ONE

OUGHLY A MONTH BEFORE her killing, I met Lorraine Cobble, the professional songcatcher, in the smoky, candlelit depths of the Café Mercutio. Actually, *met* is going too far. *Observed.* Yes, I observed her when she stormed over to our table to verbally explode all over the troubadour known as Byron Spires, a handsome young rat if ever there was one.

But maybe I'm getting ahead of myself here. I should first explain why I was perched in a Greenwich Village coffeehouse known for bohemians, beat poets, and folksingers. After all, when you think *bohemian,* five-to-one says you'd never conjure up an image of Lee Plunkett. Free-form poetry and quivering bass strings don't exactly form the backdrop of my life. Sure, as a bona fide private investigator I might be mistaken for the kind of edgy character who dwells on the fringes of society and, as such, holds a great deal of appeal for artists and other fringe-lovers. Well, that's not me, not by a country mile. I don't have the look or the grit. I'm slender as a rail with full-moon eyeglasses that might fool you into thinking I'm some scholar until I opened my mouth, and the only thing edgy is my mood when life's hobgoblins are ganging up on me.

Anyway, what brought me to the Mercutio wasn't business but pleasure. Not *my* pleasure, you understand, but my fiancée, Audrey's. She had a couple of girlfriends who had moved to Manhattan and settled in Greenwich Village. This was the spring of 1957, and the scene there was rolling along with vigor. Audrey had been invited down to partake of the Village life and figured that I should join her that evening so that I might "benefit from the experience."

"You know I try to avoid experiences," I remember saying. "They tend to ruin a fellow's day."

She rolled her eyes. "Oh, aren't you clever."

"I'd like to think the answer is yes. Look, do I really have to travel to beat-land and mingle with the natives?"

"You do. You're badly in need of some culture, Mr. Plunkett."

I tried for a posh British accent. "I'm brimming with culture. Simply brimming."

Audrey eyed me pathetically. "I've seen the extent of your culture. You read pulp novels about three-headed Martians and watch silly TV Westerns."

"They're not silly."

"Sorry, not silly. *Ludicrous.* Big-jawed sheriffs who do nothing but slap leather and fall in love with their horses."

"Hey, don't knock it. There were some good-looking horses back in the Old West."

"Should I smack you now or later?"

"By smack, do you mean kiss?"

"No, I mean slug. Punch. Pummel."

"Then later. Definitely later."

Audrey and I could go on like that nonstop. She was a great gal, no denying, and more than one observer had berated me for stretching our engagement period to the breaking point. We'd made the pledge nearly three years before and still hadn't gotten hitched. Closing out her twenties, Audrey still lived with her parents—pleasant, low-key, working-class folks who didn't mind me at all—whereas I split my time between my rented apartment and my minuscule office. I made a pretty reputable boyfriend and a not-too-crummy fiancé, but I just wasn't sure how I'd fare with the upgrade to husband. So, for one feeble reason or another, our wedding day kept getting consigned to the misty realm of Someday Soon.

Our bouncy little exchange eventually led to us making the ninety-minute drive from Thelmont, our modest Connecticut town, to the fabled Village. Stepping into the Café Mercutio that first time, I felt like a fish out of water. Or, more specifically, a fish yanked out of water and flung into a carnival tent. There was sawdust on the floor, wrinkled old circus posters on the walls, music in the air, and someone akin to a ringmaster—complete with curling mustachios and a long-tailed black coat—who greeted us at the door. This individual turned out to be the owner, one Tony Mazzo, or, as he said upon introducing himself:

"Mazzo—the Grand Mazzo. Welcome to my establishment."

"Why 'Grand'?" Audrey, always direct, asked him.

"I come from a long line of impresarios, dear lady," our host explained. "My grandfather, for example, headed the Mazzo and Morelli Circus. He was from the old country and toured throughout Europe for thirty years, meeting nobility and royalty and all those classy cats. Oh yeah, they really dug Granddad in his day."

This odd blend of formality and jive talk, I would eventually learn, was what made Mazzo . . . well, Mazzo. He looked to be not much older than me—perhaps in his midthirties—but had a premature streak of silvery hair that ran above his right temple. That feature, combined with the handlebar mustache, made for a face you weren't likely to forget. He was tall and a bit blocky but—in the phrasing of some dusty novel I was forced to read in high school—well-formed. I hadn't retained much from my schooling, but I did remember "well-formed" and "the Magna Carta was written in 1215." That's about it.

"Go sink into the scene, *amici miei,*" Mazzo instructed, gesturing us sweepingly into the room before turning to hail his next patrons.

Entering the crowded space, Audrey and I caught sight of her two friends. (I've forgotten their names; they moved away shortly after that night.) They were seated at a corner table, the sole decoration of which was a candle jutting out of a wine bottle. As we slid in next to them, the ladies gave us the slimmest of greetings, transfixed as they were by the young man standing on the small raised stage before them. This, one of our companions whispered reverently, was none other than Byron Spires, up-and-coming folk star. Slight of frame, denim-clad, with an unruly mound of brown curls, he had a waiflike quality that seemed to rivet the young women, Audrey included. He was adequately strumming a guitar that seemed too big for him and singing in a voice both lazy and urgent. His song choice had something to do with mine disasters and obese politicians. The chorus went:

In the end, my friend, who's gonna pay? Not I, not I, the fat men say.

Having known several decent rotund men in my time, I didn't think the lyrics quite fair and tried to share this with Audrey, who *shhh*ed me loudly, her eyes glued on the singer. From cave-ins, Spires shifted to something more upbeat, a nimble tune featuring periodic yelps and yodels that seemed to spur on the audience.

Then, to seal the deal, he slid into a mournful ballad, which I have to admit was downright haunting. Phrases like *the wind that stirred our wounded dreams* and *she was the girl I should have loved were I not so young and lost* seemed to linger after Spires had strummed his last chord. His set finished, he took in the blend of applause and finger-snapping (a modern form of admiration, I was told), muttered a thanks, and sauntered off the stage.

Scanning the crowd, he seemed to take fast notice of our table, stocked as it was with its trio of comely females. My manly presence was seemingly no deterrent, and Byron Spires, guitar slung to his side, made his way to us directly. Three pairs of eyes widened at his approach. Mine—the only non-female set—narrowed behind the twin shields of my spectacles. Right off the bat, I wasn't sure that I really loved this guy.

"Noticed you out there," Spires said to everyone but me. "Like three lovely muses lurking in a corner."

Oh brother. Did this warbler really think he could impress with lines like that? The smiles on the women's faces said *apparently yes.*

"Can I join you all?" Not waiting for any answer, Spires dropped into an empty chair and addressed Audrey's friends. "Think I've seen you two before." Then, turning to Audrey, "You—you're new."

I didn't like the way he said "new." I especially didn't like the way he stared at my fiancée when he said it. Audrey was looking particularly Audrey-ish that night: Her shortish brown hair had a nice little wave to it, accenting her hazel eyes and button nose, and the purple scarf round her neck made her seem both stylish and casually artsy at the same time.

"New . . . New . . ." Audrey rolled Spires' word around on her tongue. "Sure, I wouldn't mind being new."

What the blazes did she mean by that? Now, I should explain that I'm not normally the jealous type. My trust in Audrey was unwavering (at least up to that point). Besides, she was way too much her own person to tolerate an overbearing mate. No, Audrey was nothing if not rock solid. Even my father, who was never particularly impressed with my choices in general, had bestowed upon her high praise: *She's no dizzy dame, that one.* Indeed she wasn't. So her round-eyed gawk that night at the Café Mercutio struck me as uncharacteristic. Troubling, too.

Spires kept on in his lethargic, syrupy tone, his eyes probing Audrey's. "If you wanna be new, then you're in the right place. Just let the music take you." Whatever that meant. "Let it take you and teach you, little beauty."

Little beauty? Back off right there, pal! I thought but didn't say.

The next few minutes were devoted to Spires' half-mumbled reflections on music and life. He ended his monologue with this gem: "Gotta search it out—the music, the memory. Gotta follow the trail. Like a detective, y'know? Hunting the clues, the rhythms . . ."

At this, one of the women (not Audrey) revealed that I was myself a detective.

Spires seemed to notice me for the first time. "Yeah? Like a police inspector or something?"

"Private eye," I stated in a voice I hoped sounded no-nonsense and robust.

"Cool," Spires said, almost interested. "Used to read Dashiell Hammett as a kid. I always dug that Sam Spade. So, are you like ol' Sam?"

Audrey laughed. It was a pretty uncharitable response, I thought—uncharitable, but not unfair. She knew and I knew that my deductive skills weren't exactly the stuff of legend. My father had been the *real* private eye—not just in title, but in temperament—with a tough-guy scowl, a nose for crime, and a mouthful of hard-knock tales. Buster Plunkett packed a gun (which I never have) and a punch (I have fists of clay) and knew his way around the shadowy back alleys of human nature. His death a couple of years back had dropped his sleuthing business squarely in my hesitant lap. I wasn't my father; any success I'd enjoyed as a PI was due largely to a certain clever old Irishman. But I'll get to Mr. O'Nelligan later.

"Sam Spade was fictional," I told Spires with forced dignity. "I'm the real deal." Good God, I was sounding like a fictional character myself—one from the cheesiest sort of hard-boiled thriller. *Keep your mouth shut, Lee,* I mentally instructed myself. No doubt, Audrey was thinking the same thing.

At this point, another young man bearing a guitar walked over to our table. Garbed in a dark green turtleneck sweater, he was slender like Spires but more substantially built. He had a pleasant, open face marked by a tumble of black hair and a slightly upturned nose. He didn't look much out of his teens.

"Hey, Byron, you doing a second set?" The accent was deeply Irish, not unlike the one I'd heard countless times from the lips of the aforementioned Mr. O'Nelligan.

"I don't need to, Tim. Not if you're ready to start. So where are your brothers?"

"Out of town. Mazzo has me going on solo. Guess I'll have to be raucous enough for three Paddies. Or die trying."

"And your delectable lady? Where's she tonight?"

Tim's brow wrinkled. I had the distinct sense that he didn't like Spires referencing his woman in such terms. I could commiserate.

"Kimla's got a gig at the Golden Hut."

"Cool." Apparently, for Spires, everything was in the lower temperatures. "Well, get working, son."

The young Irishman did just that. No sooner had he taken the stage and launched into song than a jarring cry of anger rang out across the room. Tim stopped midstrum. Through the cigarette smoke and candlelight, I saw a tall woman, fortyish, in a red dress hurling toward our table with locomotive speed. Her long blond hair flew wildly behind her, and her face, which normally might have been attractive, was twisted in a furious scowl.

"Spires!" Clearly here was one lady not presently enamored with our pretty boy. "You bastard, you!"

From a half-slouch, Spires straightened abruptly in his chair. "Jesus, Lorraine!"

Then the woman was looming over us, staring daggers, maybe even swords, down at the folksinger. I vaguely noted a

second blonde—younger, shorter, less crazed-looking—standing
directly behind the other. The room had gone silent.

Spires tried to sound calm. "Hey, Lorraine, you need to
relax. Get peaceable, y'know?"

Lorraine's balled fists and murderous glare seemed anything but peaceable. "Who the hell do you think you are?"

Spires drew in a fortifying breath and, for a moment, I
thought he might reply, *Why, I'm Byron Spires, as you well know—
dashing young flatterer of other men's women.* Of course he didn't;
he said nothing.

Lorraine barreled on. "What made you think you could
record 'The Wild, Weeping Heather'? That's my song!"

"Yours? It's a centuries-old Scottish ballad, last I heard."

"*I'm* the one who found it! Brought it into the light, nurtured it!"

"Nurtured it?" Spires smirked unwisely. "Well, guess your
baby's grown up and run loose."

Lorraine let fly something between a scream and a curse
and drew back her arm, fist intact. Before she could strike, her
companion pulled her away from our table.

"Lorraine, stop! Just stop it!" the lesser blonde pleaded.

Lorraine shook her shadow loose and headed for Spires
again.

That's when the Grand Mazzo made a timely appearance,
placing his sizable self directly before the raging woman.
"Enough, Lorraine."

"This is just not cool," Spires declared, unsurprisingly.

"Not cool at all," Mazzo added, making it official. "You
know I don't want any aggression in this place. We're all about
the tranquility here."

That earned a harsh laugh from Lorraine. "Oh really? Tranquility? So, is Byron Spires the great prince of peace?"

Not waiting for an answer, she abruptly pivoted and, companion in tow, made a beeline for the exit. The door slammed behind them like a thunderclap. For a very long moment, the room seemed to throb with a dense, awkward silence. Then Tim, forgotten onstage, called out spryly, "You folks out there should really leave the fighting to us Irish. After all, it's our national pastime."

The audience burst into grateful laughter, and Tim jumped into a rousing upbeat song about a drunken rooster. *This kid I like,* I thought to myself.

Mazzo gave our table a theatrical bow and moved off to resume his hosting duties. Byron Spires shrugged dismissively and said (particularly to Audrey, I noticed), "That was Lorraine Cobble. She collects songs. And enemies."

Then he, too, was up and off, his slung guitar and head of curls bouncing as he strode toward the door. I watched Audrey as she watched Spires.

ON OUR DRIVE home that night, Audrey and I exchanged a few words of review. Very few.

"Well, it's certainly an interesting world in the Café Mercutio," she said.

"Sure, if you like interesting."

Audrey looked at me for a moment before saying, "Maybe I do. Maybe I would."

"Meaning what?"

"Meaning life's a strange thing, isn't it? It can call to you, beckon you, and you might end up . . . Oh, I don't know . . ."

Then she turned away to stare out her window. I had the unpleasant feeling that she was seeing Byron Spires' face out there in the rushing night landscape. My hands tensed on the steering wheel. We said little for the remainder of the ride home.

Of course, on that evening I couldn't have known that my connection with the Café Mercutio had only just begun. It would soon lead me down a road peopled with singers, sinners, desperate lovers, and a killer. As Mr. O'Nelligan once said to me, "You just never know what the world will want of you." Or, he could have added, what darkness you will need to pass through.

CHAPTER TWO

IT WAS AUDREY WHO FIRST informed me of Lorraine Cobble's death. "It happened a little over two weeks ago. She leapt off the roof of her apartment building, and her body was found in the alley below. Dead on impact, the police think."

We were standing in the cluttered backroom of the Thelmont Five-and-Dime, where Audrey worked full-time. It was early spring, four or five weeks after our visit to the Village. We actually hadn't seen much of each other since that night. I'd been tied up with a convoluted case that had taken me out of town for a spell, followed by news that my younger sister had been injured in a car accident in California. I'd flown out to be with Marjorie and ended up staying for nearly three weeks. Now she was recuperating nicely, and I'd just arrived back in Connecticut that morning.

"That wild woman who came screaming into the coffeehouse?" It wasn't an image I'd soon forget. "She committed suicide?"

"That's the assumption. They say she left a note."

"*Who* says?"

"The crowd at the Mercutio."

"Your Village girlfriends moved away right after we saw them, didn't they? So how would you know what people at the Mercutio are saying?"

She blushed—and Audrey generally was no blusher. "I've been going down there from time to time."

This caught me up. "Alone?"

Audrey didn't seem to like the way I said the word. "Yes, alone. I have a valid driver's license, you know, and I'm certainly of legal age to travel without an escort."

I didn't much fancy the sarcasm, so I offered my own. "Nobody said you weren't. I just never knew you were such a fan of sawdust and scruffy warblers."

She turned away and began rummaging through a shelf of household items. I had the strong sense that she wanted to avoid eye contact.

Then it struck me—*Byron Spires.* Could he be the male siren drawing my fiancée to the land of languid bohemians? I didn't say his name and neither did she, but I felt the echo of it bouncing around the room.

After a long, uncomfortable moment, Audrey broke the silence. "Anyway, a suicide always shakes people up. Understandably."

"Sure, understandably," I repeated, feeling shaken up myself—but not, to be honest, by the Cobble woman's death. "So you've been going down there a lot?"

"Not so very much . . ." Audrey snatched a handful of

spatulas from the shelf. "I really need to get back to work, Lee."

That was that. Two minutes later, I was standing out in front of the store, wondering how the ground beneath my feet had shifted so dramatically.

DECIDING TO GO to my office, I climbed into my '52 Nash Rambler, which I had christened Baby Blue on account of its color, and headed across town. Baby Blue was a swell-looking vehicle, but I always thought it looked even better when Audrey was beside me in the passenger seat. So, at the moment, it wasn't as swell as it could be. I'd bought the car off Joe Valish, Audrey's mechanic father, who'd hammered it back into form after the previous owner had slammed it into a parking meter. Since that guy had money to burn, he'd simply bought himself a new chariot, and Mr. Valish had sold me Baby Blue at a discount he only gave to men who planned to marry his daughters. Though, as I've mentioned, I really hadn't held up my end of the bargain.

From the first time we'd ever talked together—side by side at a soda fountain—Audrey and I just clicked. She was twenty back then; I was three years older. Her sister, Clare, and I had been in the same grade in high school, and I had a vague recollection of Clare having a gangly, uninteresting younger sibling. Apparently, in the ensuing years, that sibling had molted: The gangliness had been shed, and Audrey had suddenly become very interesting indeed. The day after our soda fountain encounter, we shared our first bona fide date. There was a movie, strolling, kissing—it was great. Over the next couple of years we had our starts and stops, accounted for by, among other things, my need to travel beyond the borders of Thelmont and the reappearance of an old beau of Audrey's, a navy hero you couldn't help but like. Though Lord knows I tried. In the end, I got some miles under my belt, the lovable sailor returned to the sea, and Audrey Valish and I became a permanent item.

In '54, just after my father took me into the business, I proposed to Audrey. Over the next three years—through my detective apprenticeship, through Dad's death, through my stumbling solo career—she and I held pretty firm, but, as I've said, we just never made it up the church steps. People who knew us thought I was a certifiable idiot for not getting the job done, and they were right. Who'd ever heard of a three-year engagement? Maybe during wartime, but that wasn't the story here. Certainly the fault was mine that we'd stalled on the matrimonial highway. That is, I always presumed so. Audrey had made it clear that she expected to be a married woman before she hit thirty, so it stood to reason that I was the one dragging his heels. However, as they say, it takes two to tango—or, in our case, to stand frozen in the middle of the dance floor. Money woes, timing problems, spats and sputters: Could these all be laid at my doorstep alone? In truth, hadn't many a couple faced the same obstacles and still managed to echo their I-do's at the obligatory moment? Maybe Audrey herself had a hand in the heel-dragging. Maybe she wasn't as gung ho on getting hitched as she made out. Now, into this breach of doubts and delays, had marched a young crooning scallywag named Byron Spires.

I was pondering all this as I shuffled into my office and plopped behind the desk. It was the same narrow space that had served my father before me, with the very same dinged-up desk, creaky swivel chair, battered file cabinet, and framed portrait of Teddy Roosevelt (a "guy among guys," as Dad had often declared). Even the words PLUNKETT AND SON INVESTI-GATORS remained on the office door. My rent was dirt cheap because of some shadowy favor that Dad had once done for the landlord.

This was the first time I'd been here since leaving for California three weeks back, and an orderly stack of letters awaited me on the desktop. This, I knew, was the work of Mr. O'Nelligan, the one person beside the landlord and me with a key to the office. Preoccupied as I was, I wielded my letter opener without enthusiasm. The yield was uninspiring: a sizable number of bills, a few small checks, and a note from an octogenarian thanking me for locating her run-amuck Pekingese—not my most illustrious case.

I was finishing up the letters when the phone rang.

In response to my hello, a breathless young female voice launched into a monologue. "Oh! Mr. Plunkett? Mr. Lee Plunkett? Gosh, I'm surprised to hear a voice on the other end! I've been calling this number for days hoping to reach you. I was beginning to think maybe you'd retired or something. Not that you're old! No, I didn't mean that. Anyway, I'm just glad you answered. I'm hoping so much that you're the person who can set everything right."

"To whom am I speaking?" I opted for professionalism instead of hurling out the *Who the hell is this?* that was on the tip of my tongue.

With a large sigh, the voice slowed itself. "Sorry. My name is Sally Joan Cobble."

"Cobble?" I'd heard the name spoken not an hour before. "Like Lorraine Cobble?"

"My cousin. She . . . She died, you know."

"Someone just told me. My condolences."

"Thanks. I need you to find who killed her."

That stopped me in my tracks. "It's my understanding that she, well . . ."

"Killed herself?" A note of bitterness crept in. "That's what everyone says, but it's just not true. She wouldn't have done that. I know the time you saw her at the Mercutio with Byron she was terribly agitated, but she would never—"

"Wait. How do you know I was there that night?"

"Because I was there myself. I came in with Lorraine."

Now I had a face to go with the voice on the line—albeit a dimly remembered one. This was the short young blonde who had trailed Lorraine over to our table and tried to restrain her.

"I remember you," I said. "How did you get my name?"

"People down at the Mercutio seemed to know who you were. Word gets around if there's an interesting character about."

"Does me being a private eye put me in that category?"

"Oh yes. I heard you were from Connecticut, and I tracked you down. It seemed almost like a sign that you were there that night. Not that I've spent a lot of time at the coffeehouse myself. You see, I live outside Pittsburgh and was just up visiting Lorraine for that week, but I am back in the Village right now dealing with her apartment. On behalf of our family, I want to hire you to find whoever killed Lorraine."

"Whoa now, Miss Cobble," I said cautiously. "I can understand why you wouldn't want to believe your cousin took her own life, but I've heard there was a suicide note."

"Suicide note?" Sally Joan sounded genuinely confused. "I think you've heard wrong, Mr. Plunkett." She paused. "Oh wait! There *is* a note, but it's got nothing to do with suicide. I can show it to you when we meet."

I caught a glimpse of a cart outracing a horse. "When we . . . ?"

"Please, Mr. Plunkett, I'd rather talk in person about all this. Can't we at least sit together and talk?"

I gave in. "Sure, I suppose we could do that."

I suggested we meet the next afternoon at her cousin's apartment. Might as well see the scene of the doubtful crime. Sally Joan Cobble thanked me profusely and gave me the address.

"I'll be bringing a colleague with me," I added.

"Please do!" She almost sounded like we were arranging a garden party.

After hanging up, I sat there for a while reflecting on the weirdness of my life: Within an hour of my hearing from Audrey that Lorraine Cobble was dead, the woman's cousin had contacted me to solve her alleged murder. Here I was, potentially being drawn back into the orbit of the Café Mercutio, one of whose inhabitants might well be stealing my fiancée's affections. What a world, what a world . . .

I shook myself out of my little reverie and rang up Mr. O'Nelligan. Though he claimed to be glad to hear from me and asked about my sister's recuperation, there was a definite tone of distraction in his voice.

"Are you all right?" I asked.

"Oh, I'm splendid," he answered in his rolling brogue, then added hazily, "It's just that this giant marlin has been putting up quite a battle."

"Marlin?" I was struck by a preposterous image of Mr. O'Nelligan wrestling a massive fish across his sitting room. "What the heck are you talking about?"

My friend sighed with gentle exasperation. *"The Old Man*

and the Sea, of course. By the estimable Mr. Hemingway. I'm in the final pages as we speak. Have you read it?"

The reality was that since high school I hadn't read much that didn't come with a lurid cover and a title akin to *Killer Cutthroats of Jupiter.* By contrast, Mr. O'Nelligan consumed books the way a kid gobbles gumdrops, mostly the great classics and other such highfaluting fare.

"Nope, never read it," I said, "but assuming you've landed your marlin by tomorrow, I've got a possible case that might pique your interest."

I repeated the conversation I'd had with Sally Joan Cobble. For an extended moment, there was no response on the other end of the line. I guessed that my friend was sneaking himself another paragraph of deep-sea drama.

Finally he answered, "By all means, Lee Plunkett, I shall attend thee."

"That means you'll be coming along, right?"

"Did I not just say so, boyo?"

HOW TO DESCRIBE Mr. O'Nelligan? There are the facts of his life, of course, which would trickle out of him at odd intervals. You just never knew what fragment of his varied history he'd next reveal. Once, for example, he and I happened to be crossing a cemetery when I paused to comment on the fanciness of a particular mausoleum.

Mr. O'Nelligan nodded appreciatively. "Indeed, the ornamentation is striking. The structure itself appears quite sound as well. I myself built one once."

"You built a mausoleum?"

"I did. It was many years ago, to be sure. Mine was of red brick, being a bricklayer as I was."

"You were a bricklayer back in Ireland? I thought you'd been a teacher?"

"Also a train conductor and a salesman and a stage actor. A man may pursue many callings in his time, may he not?"

You've also been a warrior, I could have said but didn't. Early on, I'd learned not to probe my friend too deeply on that subject. In his youth, back in the '20s, he'd played perhaps his most contrary role: that of the covert rebel and soldier. I knew that he had both faced and dealt death during those days. I knew that he wore his trim gray beard as camouflage for an old knife scar. All this seemed to conflict with the genteel individual that I'd come to know and admire.

There among the gravestones, Mr. O'Nelligan waxed poetic. "Laying bricks has much in common with your chosen art of deduction, Lee."

"You don't say." I in no way viewed my job as an art—I was satisfied just to draw a paycheck on the rare occasion.

"It's true. Just as a bricklayer must work brick by brick, row by row, to raise a solid structure, so must the detective build his case, stacking one observation upon the next until the proper outcome is achieved."

"Never thought of it that way."

"Well, now you shall, yes?"

"Oh, yes indeedy."

At the time of the Cobble case, I'd known Mr. O'Nelligan for about a year and a half. He'd moved to Thelmont from New York shortly after his wife's death and had settled himself into a cozy pine-hemmed little house three doors down from Audrey's family. Audrey and he had become fast friends, and in time I, too, had been won over by the man's quirky charms. On Audrey's urging, Mr. O'Nelligan had begun to aid me on my more complicated cases, and as a result my business (floundering since Dad's death) had been much revitalized. Mr. O'Nelligan was content to label himself my assistant, though that designation fooled neither of us—it was clear who had the true deductive chops in our partnership. Still, despite his invaluable help, the man wouldn't accept a penny from me. Whenever I'd argue the unfairness of that arrangement, he'd wave me off and declare, "Ah, it's fine, it's fine. Assisting you helps fill the hours and keeps my brain well oiled. What more compensation could an old reprobate desire?"

I never did come up with a good answer to that.

CHAPTER THREE

I CONSIDERED LETTING AUDREY know about my appointment with Sally Joan Cobble but decided against it. After all, I hadn't officially agreed to take on the case, and, considering whatever was going on with my fiancée, I figured it best to just see how things shook out. I did place a call to her house, though, and left a message with her mother that I'd be on a job out of town, so Audrey should make her own evening plans. That Friday afternoon—the day after Sally Joan's call—I picked up Mr. O'Nelligan and headed down Route 7 toward the Merritt Parkway.

"A fine spring day, isn't it?" my companion noted. He was dressed nattily in his standard vest and necktie. "A splendid beginning to a quest."

"Listen, this is no quest," I grumbled. "We're just going to meet a potential client. Accent on 'potential.' Why is everything always a quest with you?"

"All life is a quest, lad. One merely needs to recognize it as such."

Somehow in Mr. O'Nelligan's eyes I had maintained my status as lad, even though I'd passed the thirty mark.

"The thing is," I said, "I'm not at all sure that there's even a case here. We may be talking simple suicide."

The Irishman clicked his tongue. "Ah, but suicide is never simple. Back home in County Kerry, there was a miller by the name of Blowick who drowned himself in the River Fertha. It was near the end of March, and he had to hurl into the freezing waters to meet his end. No one could figure the why of it till much later when someone put together that March 29, the day he perished, was the Feast of St. Eithne, and that in his youth poor Blowick had loved and lost a girl named Eithne O'Mara. So, you see, there is oft a hidden complexity to these things. If I might quote Yeats . . ."

"Couldn't stop you if I tried."

My friend always seemed to have handy a quote from his favorite poet and fellow countryman, William Butler Yeats. He now let one fly:

"A pity beyond all telling
is hid in the heart of love."

"No doubt," I responded. "For all we know, maybe unrequited love was the cause of Lorraine Cobble's leap into air. She certainly seemed to me to be chock-full of passion."

"So you were acquainted with her?"

I described my night at the Café Mercutio, highlighting Lorraine's colorful behavior but excluding any reference to Audrey's fascination with Byron Spires. In regard to Audrey and me, I didn't want to put Mr. O'Nelligan in the middle of . . . well, whatever there was to be in the middle of.

My friend *hmm*ed softly. "The late Miss Cobble sounds like she was quite a perfervid individual."

"Did you say 'perverted'?" In the face of Mr. O'Nelligan's ten-dollar word, I felt the need to mock. "Gee, I don't know that I'd go that far."

"Perfervid! It means ardent, of course. Hot in the blood." He groaned. "Dear God, sir, sometimes I think that you and the English language aren't even on speaking terms."

"Listen, no one says things like 'perfervid.' At least no one who hasn't read *War and Peace* a dozen times."

"Three times," Mr. O'Nelligan informed me. "I've only read *War and Peace* thrice."

"Only three times? My, what a lazy scholar you are."

"Scholarship is in the eye of the beholder."

"Then I must have a nasty case of conjunctivitis."

My companion sighed pleasantly. "Ah, Lee Plunkett, you have more wit than one might give you credit for."

I took this as a compliment and let it go at that. Mr. O'Nelligan now opened the thick volume that he'd brought along and read aloud. " 'Call me Ishmael.' "

"Shouldn't I call you O'Ishmael?"

"More wit, I see. Be truthful, is this not arguably the most memorable first line in all of literature?"

"Must be, since I actually know it. *Moby-Dick*, right? Hey, wait a minute, didn't you just read that last fall?"

"I did, but coming off Hemingway's sea tale has inspired me to ship aboard the *Pequod* yet again—for the fourth time, I might add."

"Trading a marlin for a whale . . . that's some hefty up-grading."

"Although still within the nautical realm," Mr. O'Nelligan observed. "For, after all, aren't Hemingway's Old Man and Melville's Captain Ahab both obsessed mariners in pursuit of an elusive leviathan?"

"I was just about to say exactly that."

My comrade smiled and buried himself in his book for the next hour and a half.

As we arrived in Greenwich Village, Mr. O'Nelligan traded literature for history, giving me a brief lecture on the area. In 1822, he explained, a yellow fever epidemic in lower Manhattan drove thousands of New Yorkers north to Greenwich, a village of underpopulated pasturelands. Prior to that, it had been the realm of wealthy landowners who craved a bit of country living. The yellow fever changed all that, and before long the place became a bustling sprawl of grocery stores, coffeehouses, tailor shops, restaurants, banks, and bars. As early as the nineteenth century, Greenwich Village had gained a reputation for its art-ists, radicals, nonconformists, and generally memorable char-acters.

Turning onto West 12th, my friend indicated the oblong granite cobblestones that paved the street. "Belgian blocks. They made their way to America as ship ballast and became the very carpet of the Village. And speaking of ships, down just a ways stands the pier where, some forty-five years ago, the survi-vors of the ill-fated *Titanic* were put ashore."

"Am I going to be tested on all this?" I asked.

"No, Lee. Knowledge is its own reward."

I spent a silly amount of time finding a parking space, but

once I'd docked Baby Blue, we easily located the old Manhattan apartment building where Lorraine Cobble had lived. It was squeezed in between two brownstones, and its lower story (her cousin had told me on the phone) had been a carriage house a century before. The front door was surrounded by black iron in the form of a hanging lantern, a low gate, and a pair of framing columns. As I'd been told to expect, the door was left unlocked, due to the buzzer system having been on the fritz for over a month. We climbed four flights of narrow stairs to our destination. I'd barely gotten a knock in before the door flew open and Sally Joan swept us into the apartment.

"Oh, thank you so much for coming, Mr. Plunkett! I'm so grateful." She looked it. Now that I could fully take her in, I saw a young woman in her early twenties with bright, healthy features and blond curls. She wore a pink and white checkered dress that suggested a good figure without bellowing the fact.

I introduced my partner, and Sally Joan Cobble shook our hands with embarrassing vigor. "Thank you for coming! Thank you both."

She gestured us to a sofa and took the chair opposite. I gave the room a quick once-over. The walls were covered with framed posters of concerts and music festivals come and gone, plus a scattering of photographs, most notably one showing Lorraine Cobble with a group of extremely wrinkled old men, each sporting overalls and a banjo. The room itself was a controlled jumble of books, stacks of paper, and record albums scattered across several surfaces. One long table supported a sizable phonograph and two or three other gadgets that I guessed might be recording devices. A number of stringed instruments— some of which I could even name—crowded every corner of the room.

"The place is a bit of a whirlwind, I know," our hostess said. "Pretty much like my cousin herself."

Getting right into things, I flipped open my trusty notebook. "Were you here in the Village at the time of Lorraine's death?"

"No, I was back home then, but I've been up here since her funeral about a week and a half ago. I've been staying at a hotel—I couldn't bear to sleep here in her apartment knowing that . . ." Sally Joan glanced up at the ceiling, no doubt visualizing the rooftop above. "Anyway, I've been organizing her belongings, meeting with her lawyers . . . Those sorts of things."

Mention of lawyers brought an obvious question to mind. "Who's her beneficiary?"

Sally Joan's face reddened. "I am. Or, I should say, it's mostly me. She left some smaller bequests to other family members and to a few music societies, but she left me the bulk of it. Not that it's a huge amount, you understand. Lorraine spent a lot in pursuing her work, but it's a nice amount all the same."

Mr. O'Nelligan nodded. "Do tell us about her work . . . and her life."

Whereas I was more inclined to aim for the facts of the case, my colleague was always interested in the human angle.

"Lorraine was like . . ." A little smile played across the young woman's lips. "A patchwork. Yes, like that—made up of a lot of different pieces. Kind of a crazy quilt, some people might say. It's really unfortunate, Mr. Plunkett, that you only saw her that one time when she was so . . . Well, you know."

I did know. "Volatile?"

"Yes, she could be very agitated where her work was concerned. You really need to understand, though, that she wasn't just that . . . that nutty woman you saw. She could be very tender and sensitive." Her voice now trembled with emotion. "She was always kind to me."

"We understand," Mr. O'Nelligan said gently. "Every soul is a mix of many things. Your patchwork comparison is a fine one, indeed. So, you were quite close to your cousin?"

"Sort of. Though it's not like we spent tons of time together. She's seventeen years older than I am." Sally Joan paused. "I mean, *was* older. I have three brothers, but I'm the only girl, so I always looked up to her in that way. I think Lorraine thought of me as something of a kid sister. She was living with my family when I was born. Her parents—my uncle and aunt— died in a car accident when Lorraine was a teenager, so my folks took her in for a few years."

"Was she always involved with music?" my partner asked.

"Oh yes, for as long as I can remember. She was already collecting songs when I was little. I remember when I was five or six, she came back from Appalachia and played a dulcimer for me. That one, I think." She pointed to one of the nameless instruments in the corner, expanding my musical knowledge. "That's what her job was—she was a songcatcher."

"Songcatcher?" This was the first time I'd heard the term. "That's a job?"

"Oh, it definitely is. Lorraine would research and gather up songs from all different areas of the country, and Britain, too. Musicology, it's called. I understand that it's really quite a science. I'm not all that up on these things myself, but there's a woman here in the Village named Minnie Bornstein who used to work with Lorraine. She's someone you could talk to if you wanted to know more. She runs a shop a couple of blocks from here. I can give you the address."

"That would be helpful," Mr. O'Nelligan said. "In fact,

perhaps after this interview you could construct a list for us of all those people significant to your cousin. With phone numbers and addresses. It would be useful in our investigation."

I shot my colleague a perplexed look. *Investigation?* We hadn't heard anything yet that warranted an investigation.

Sally Joan continued on, painting a portrait of her cousin as a vigorous career woman who had risen in her field through a combination of skill and bullishness. Early on, Lorraine had apprenticed herself to several prominent scholars in the world of song hunting and had made a name for herself. Along the way, she had briefly acquired and discarded a fairly well-to-do husband whose name she jettisoned after the divorce. The alimony settlement had provided her the means to travel extensively and further pursue her calling. Besides Mr. Moneybags, she had slid through several other short romances in her time, but her true passion was always the music. Despite the glut of instruments in her apartment, Lorraine had been only a passable musician at best. It was in the pursuit and chronicling of songs that her talents lay. As an offshoot of her songcatching, she had identified and promoted a number of promising young folksingers and through that had maintained an ongoing connection with Café Mercutio.

Though I really didn't want to utter the name, I felt I needed to. "What about Byron Spires? What exactly was her beef with him? Something about stealing a song, wasn't it?"

Sally Joan nodded solemnly. "Yes, it was a ballad she'd found on a recent trip to Scotland. I think she got it from an old sheepherder."

"So Spires stole it?"

"Lorraine certainly saw it like that, but to be honest I've never been quite sure how that all works. I mean, one person discovers some ballad that another person sings, and then yet another person sings a new version. It's all kind of a muddle to me. As I say, someone like Minnie Bornstein could explain it much better."

It was time to get down to brass tacks. "They say Lorraine flung herself off the roof of this building," I stated, perhaps a little too bluntly. "That's the official conclusion. So why do you think otherwise?"

"For several reasons." Sally Joan's tone took on a new hardness. "First of all, it just isn't the sort of thing Lorraine would ever do. Not in a million years."

"I'm sure that's what you believe," I said, "but can anyone ever really know what's going on in someone else's mind?"

"Maybe not, but you can know the type of person it is, can't you? You can know what they're capable of and what they're not. Lorraine wouldn't kill herself. She had too much . . . too much . . ." Sally Joan fumbled about for the word. "*Ego*. Yes, that's it. She had way too much ego to throw her life away like that. Plus, she had such vitality and such a hunger for living."

Mr. O'Nelligan stroked his beard thoughtfully. "Could her death have been an accident? Might Lorraine have stumbled off the roof?"

Sally Joan shook her head. "Absolutely not. When you see what it's like up there, you'll understand. The sides are raised all around. They're high enough that you couldn't just stumble off—but you could definitely be shoved or thrown over."

"Or jump," I felt the need to remind her.

"Like I've said, my cousin would never willingly end her life."

"Any idea what she would have been doing on the roof to begin with?" I asked.

"It's just something she'd do from time to time," Sally Joan explained. "Lorraine liked to go up there to look over the skyline and sing to herself. She'd sing and collect her thoughts. She called it her pondering place."

"One might well wonder what she was pondering that fateful night," Mr. O'Nelligan said quietly. "Tell us, lass, how was your cousin dressed when they found her? Bathrobe? Evening wear? Her attire might indicate if she was in for the night or had been out in the world."

"I asked the police that myself," the young woman said. "They told me Lorraine wasn't wearing anything special—just a green housedress."

I moved on. "You said there was a note, Miss Cobble."

She grimaced. "I've misplaced it somehow! When we spoke on the phone, I thought I knew where I'd put it, but it's not there. I spent a long time rummaging around the apartment, but I can't find that envelope now. I'd shown it to the police at one point, but I haven't seen it since."

"Do you remember what this note said?"

"More or less. It was something like 'Meet me at ten tomorrow morning.' It was dated the day before she died."

This was possibly interesting. "Was her body discovered early in the day?"

"No, she was found that night in the alley next door, just before midnight. The coroner figured she hadn't been dead more than two or three hours at most."

I did a quick analysis. "So, almost a whole day of activity had passed between her morning rendezvous and her death."

Mr. O'Nelligan rejoined the discussion. "How was the letter signed, Miss Cobble?"

"It wasn't," Sally Joan answered. "There was no signature,

and the letter was typed, so you couldn't even guess if it was written by a man or a woman. Plus, here's something really odd. Her name was typed on the envelope—just her first name— but there was no address or stamp, so it couldn't have come by mail. Which means it was hand-delivered to her. Why wouldn't the person just call her to set up a meeting?"

"A valid question," my colleague said. "Have you any guesses as to whom your cousin might have been likely to rendezvous with?"

"I really don't. Lorraine knew a lot of people, so it could have been anyone."

"Was there any . . ." Here Mr. O'Nelligan hesitated, and I knew that he was searching for some genteel phrasing. "Any individual to whom Lorraine was recently displaying affection?"

"Like a lover?" The young woman smiled lightly. "That's what you mean, right? If Lorraine had someone on her dance card, she never let on. At least not to me. I'd only visit my cousin maybe two or three times a year, so I certainly didn't know all her comings and goings."

Mr. O'Nelligan went for a different angle. "The downstairs door, has the lock been broken since before your cousin's death?"

"It has," Sally Joan answered. "At least since I was last here over a month ago."

"That suggests that a stranger might have entered the building that night."

"And just happened to make their way up to the rooftop? Gosh, Mr. O'Nelligan, that doesn't sound right, does it?"

"Perhaps not."

"Anyway, I'm thinking the group that hangs out down at the Mercutio might have a better take on things. You should go talk to them."

"We shall," my partner said.

Oh, shall we really? I still wasn't seeing a case here, and I said as much. "Miss Cobble, there's a heck of a lot of details we'd have to shift through to even entertain the idea that your cousin was murdered. You know—timelines, habits, who was last seen with her . . ."

"I'm a little hazy on all that myself," Sally Joan admitted. "You could check in with the police to see what they've already found out. There's a Detective Wilton who seemed to be in charge of the investigation. I'm sure he'd be glad to help you."

I'm pretty certain I kept my eyes from rolling, but it took an effort. Oh yeah, cops just *loved* to share information with private dicks who popped up to second-guess their efforts.

Seemingly oblivious to my doubts, Sally Joan pressed on. "So you'll take the case, Mr. Plunkett?"

I cleared my throat apologetically and glanced over at Mr. O'Nelligan, immediately wishing I hadn't. He fixed me with a look that said, *You're not really going to turn this poor young lady down, are you, lad?* I moaned softly to myself, knowing that my fate was sealed. True, the fee would be welcome, but being in Byron Spires' stomping ground would not.

"Yes," I said to Sally Joan, feeling like I was agreeing to a blindfold before the firing squad took aim. "We'll take the case."

She beamed forth a smile that almost melted my misgivings. Almost.

Mr. O'Nelligan got down to business. "Now, young miss, if you can compose that list of noteworthy individuals for us as soon as possible. Include any other information you think pertinent."

"I'll do it immediately," Sally Joan promised. "Actually,

there are people here in this building you might want to talk to. You can start with Mrs. Pattinshell, who lives one floor down. I can write up the list while you're there. I've already mentioned you to her."

Apparently, this was all a done deal before we'd even stepped into the apartment. "Who's Mrs. Pattinshell?"

"She's one of the people that Lorraine helped set up in this building. She even chipped in with her rent, I think. Like I said, my cousin had a kind-hearted side that not everyone got to see. Of course, Mrs. Pattinshell has a certain skill that Lorraine was very interested in, but even so . . ."

"What skill is that?"

Sally Joan offered an embarrassed smile. "Look, I'm not saying I believe it, but I know Lorraine did. Mrs. Pattinshell is a ghost chanter."

That raised my eyebrows. "Come again?"

"A ghost chanter. It's what she calls herself. It means she can sing songs that dead people teach her."

"Can't wait," I lied. "I never met a ghost I didn't like."

CHAPTER FOUR

NO SOONER HAD WE STEPPED out into the hallway than a ghost appeared two doors down. At least he looked like a ghost—rail-thin, dressed all in white, and stooped over a gnarled walking stick. His narrow face, impossibly wrinkled, turned slowly toward us, and his pale lips parted to deliver his unearthly proclamation.

"Good day, gents."

I was struck dumb by the sight of this apparition, but Mr. O'Nelligan wasn't so afflicted. "A good day to *you*, sir," my partner returned.

The ancient man nodded, tossed us a little salute, and vanished into his apartment. Once the door had clicked shut, Mr. O'Nelligan gave a wry chuckle. "It's not often I'm made to feel like a young stripling!"

"How many years do you figure that old guy has racked up?"

"I couldn't say, but I'm sure he's earned every one of them."

We descended to the fourth floor, and I rapped firmly on the door that Sally Joan had specified. After a moment, it was opened by a slender woman in an austere navy blue dress. Her graying brown hair was tied tightly back, giving full display to a long, sharp nose and tightly drawn lips that, I'd venture, didn't spend much time in smile mode. Whatever the heck a ghost chanter was, this lady looked right for the part.

Her greeting was hardly warming. "I don't know you men."

"True enough, good woman." Mr. O'Nelligan, ever the diplomat, politely explained the who and why of our presence, ending with "Whatever assistance you might render would truly be appreciated."

I wouldn't exactly say that Mrs. Pattinshell softened her bearing, but she did unclench it slightly. "Oh, that's right, the Cobble girl mentioned that someone might be making further inquiries. Come in if you must."

Stepping inside, we were met by the smell of previously burned incense. In contrast to the near chaos of the apartment we'd just left, Mrs. Pattinshell's living space was precise and uncluttered. The low-lit room we now entered had been set up with a round table draped in black lace, behind which stood a high-backed chair, upholstered in plush red. In response to our entrance, an ominous-looking Siamese cat catapulted itself off the seat and scurried across the faded Persian rug straight out of the room. Three simple wooden chairs, pushed into corners, seemed to be the only other furniture. The walls were a bleak burgundy, and the one decorative touch was a painting that depicted several barely human figures struggling to extract themselves from a swirling mist.

"Very cozy quarters," Mr. O'Nelligan offered.

I would have traded "cozy" for "creepy," but I kept that thought to myself.

Mrs. Pattinshell dragged two of the wooden chairs to the table, gestured for us to sit, and settled herself in the plush one opposite.

My partner got the ball rolling. "Tell us of your skills, madam."

The woman studied him for a moment. "Your accent suggests that you hail from Ireland."

"Indeed I do."

"Ireland is a ghost-ridden country. I imagine my work would be intriguing to you—even beyond your investigative interests."

Her style of speech was refined and exact, but I knew Mr. O'Nelligan could hold his own with her.

"I'm sure I *will* find it intriguing," he said. "Not to mention enlightening. Much can be learned from the metaphysical sciences."

Mrs. Pattinshell nodded noncommittally. "My abilities as a ghost chanter first revealed themselves when I was a child. I'll tell you of my earliest experience. My father made his living as a lawyer, but in his leisure time was a member of a barbershop quartet . . ."

My partner smiled. "Ah! A crooning barrister."

"Rather incongruous, I know," said Mrs. Pattinshell, "but that's how it was. Anyway, one evening Father and his friends were practicing in our parlor, while I was in the adjoining room working at my school lessons. Partway into their rehearsal, I heard a high, wispy male voice—higher even than my father's tenor—mingling with the other voices. The quartet was practicing 'Sweet Rosie O'Grady,' but the fifth voice was singing an entirely different song. From what I could make out, the lyrics had something to do with a baker's daughter and a hungry suitor. When the quartet finished singing, the other voice ceased as well. I hastened in from the other room to catch a glimpse of this new singer, but there was only my father and his three friends. When I asked where the fifth man was, they all looked confused and claimed that there was no such person. As I became more insistent, my father grew quite angry and banished me from the parlor. I learned from then on never to speak to my parents of these matters."

I tried to interpret her story. "So you're saying, Mrs. Pattinshell, that the extra singer was—"

"A spirit, yes," she finished for me. "Someone who has passed beyond the veil. Of course, I didn't know that at the time, although as these experiences persisted and intensified, I came to understand the truth."

"This must have all been rather overwhelming," Mr. O'Nelligan said.

The woman gave him a razor-thin smile. "Only the weak allow themselves to be overwhelmed."

"Still, for a child to encounter such things . . ."

"Sometimes I think I was never a child," Mrs. Pattinshell said, pride evident in her voice. "To continue, over my lifetime numerous spirits have sought my ear to pass on songs that were significant to them when they lived—songs from their work or play, songs they may have learned as children, or perhaps even composed themselves. I never see these spirits, mind you, but I do hear them. Sometimes I know exactly who they are. I can make out a name or get a sense of who they were in life. Other times, I've no idea who's singing to me."

"Why songs?" I heard a smirk creep into my voice. "Why not plays or lectures or naughty limericks?"

Mr. O'Nelligan's eyes flung a warning shot across my bow, but it was too late. Our hostess' face had turned into a mask of contempt.

"You're a self-assured young whelp, aren't you?" she said to me. "Tell me, do you really know how the universe works? We are surrounded by mysteries you cannot begin to comprehend. A strident mind is a foolish one."

My strident, foolish mind searched for a proper retort but came up short.

Mrs. Pattinshell continued. "To answer your rather impertinent question, I'm not sure myself why only songs come to me. Perhaps it's because during my first year of life we lived next to an opera house."

Now, that *really* struck me as ludicrous, but I sure wasn't going to say so.

Much to my annoyance, Mr. O'Nelligan still clung to the topic. "So, madam, once the deceased have offered up their songs to you, what do you do with them?"

Mrs. Pattinshell shrugged lightly. "That depends on the situation. Sometimes I simply listen and let them pass. Other times, as when a client requests to hear a song from a loved one, I'll write it down or record it as I sing aloud."

"Quite fascinating," my partner said. "So you can actually summon a particular spirit to sing to you?"

Sure, if the price is right, I wanted her to say. *For a tidy sum, I'll hear Napoleon whistling "Dixie."*

Instead, she said, "Yes, with great concentration I can sometimes connect to a particular singer."

"How do you acquire your clients?" Mr. O'Nelligan asked.

"I place advertisements from time to time. Additionally, Lorraine, bless her, would aim people my way."

"Right. Lorraine . . ." I reentered the fray. "We understand that she helped set you up here. Even paid your rent."

The woman's haughtiness drained away, and she suddenly looked frail and flustered. "She helped some, yes . . . but only partially, you understand! You mustn't think that I'm some sort of . . . I'm a widow, you know. I don't have the resources that other people—"

"Don't distress yourself, dear lady." Mr. O'Nelligan's voice was as soothing as a lullaby. "Certainly, a widow's life is not always easy. How long ago did your husband pass away?"

"It's been thirteen years, come November." Having regained her composure, Mrs. Pattinshell now offered a sour little smile. "Has he even once in all that time sung to me? No, he has not."

I let that slide. "But Lorraine . . ."

"Lorraine treated me well. I, by way of exchange, provided her with a good number of songs."

"She requested you contact certain deceased persons?" Mr. O'Nelligan asked.

"No, she just accepted whatever songs I thought might be of interest to her. She was always very eager to receive a new one."

"I imagine that Lorraine's passing must have been difficult for you," my partner said.

"Of course. We shared much common ground, she and I. Neither of us suffered fools lightly." Here, Mrs. Pattinshell favored me with a glance. "Lorraine was a strong, talented female. The world is often unreceptive to such as us."

Mr. O'Nelligan nodded just right. "So true, madam. Now, you are aware that the younger Miss Cobble suspects wrongdoing in the death of your friend?"

"I am."

"Do you share that viewpoint?"

Mrs. Pattinshell took a moment to answer. "It does seem queer to think of Lorraine as a suicide."

"Uncharacteristic, perhaps?"

"Oh, yes, I should say so. Then again, what man knoweth the things of a man, save the spirit of man which is in him?"

"First Corinthians, is it not?"

"Why yes, I believe it is! You know your Good Book, Mr. O'Harrigan."

"It's O'*Nelligan*," my friend calmly corrected. "As to my biblical erudition, I know more than some, less than others. Tell us, on the day Lorraine Cobble died, did you have any contact with her?"

"None whatsoever. I've been over this all with the police."

"We understand, but we're obliged to make our own inquiries."

"I suppose. Of course, if there *was* some wrongdoing regarding Lorraine's death, then I hope you get to the bottom of it. Alas, I'm afraid I can't offer you much in terms of information. I'm a very private person, you see, and my interactions with Lorraine were fairly limited. I hadn't seen her for perhaps a week prior to her death."

"Did she seem to be her normal self at that time?"

"She did."

I felt like we'd run our course here. "Well then, thanks for your time, ma'am."

"Yes, thank you," echoed Mr. O'Nelligan. "Perhaps as things unfold, we'll have occasion to contact you again."

"If you must."

Mrs. Pattinshell stood and led us to the door. Then—weirdly, I thought—she extended her hand, palm down, to my partner, who automatically took it in his own and planted a kiss. She didn't make the same offer to me, I noticed.

As the door shut behind us, I turned to my friend. "What was that last little bit of flourish?"

"Mrs. Pattinshell appears to have rather classic sensibilities, as do I. An extended feminine hand requires the appropriate attention."

I was about to question the femininity of that spooky old dame but realized that she might well be listening behind her door. We made our way back to the upstairs apartment, where Sally Joan met us with a hastily composed list of her cousin's contacts.

"I've jotted down some names and numbers from Lorraine's address book," she explained. "It includes some of the Mercutio crowd. You can go down there directly and see who's hanging around."

I looked over the list. "You've got here another tenant who lives on this floor—Cornelius Boyle. You wrote 'Civil War veteran' next to his name." I suddenly remembered our hallway ghost. "Is that true?"

Sally Joan smiled. "Mr. Boyle is one hundred and five years old! Isn't that amazing? He was a drummer boy in the war. Lorraine would get him to sing old soldier tunes to her. She arranged for him to move into the building."

"So your cousin liked to collect people who could give her songs," I said.

The young woman frowned. "That's not the kindest way to put it, Mr. Plunkett. Nor accurate, really. Like I've told you, Lorraine had a charitable side."

"Sure, it just seems that—"

Mr. O'Nelligan cut me off at the pass. "Does Mr. Boyle live alone here?"

"Yes, he's amazingly self-sufficient," Sally Joan said. "Plus, he does have a granddaughter who comes by nearly every day to see to his needs."

"I believe we glimpsed the gentleman in the hallway not twenty minutes ago. Perhaps we might stop in to see him now."

Sally Joan glanced up at a wall clock. "Oh, it's past four. Lorraine told me that he always takes a nap promptly at four, but maybe you can catch him tomorrow. As you'll see, he's still very sharp considering his age."

We went over a few more details and arrived at an agreement regarding our fee. Sally Joan gave us a quick tour of the rest of Lorraine's living space—basically more jumble with a musical theme. Then I asked to see the rooftop.

THE THREE OF us stood in the last place where Lorraine Cobble had drawn a breath. The flat roof was a tangle of chimney caps and exhaust vents, surrounded on all sides by the Village's sea of buildings. I could make out the Hudson River in the near distance. Just as Sally Joan had described, the edges of the rooftop were bordered by a sort of low wall, about two and a half feet high. Even a blind man wouldn't accidentally step off here into thin air. If Lorraine hadn't thrown herself off, then someone had definitely assisted her plunge.

A vigorous wind forced Mr. O'Nelligan and me to clamp down our hats as Sally Joan silently led us over to one edge of the roof. Staring into the alleyway below, we saw nothing but trash cans and a crate or two, but all of us were no doubt picturing the sprawled, shattered body that had lain there two weeks before.

Mr. O'Nelligan was the first of us to step away from the edge. When I eventually turned, I saw him paused in the middle of the roof, framed against the cloud-streaked sky. He stood there alone, eyes shut and lips slightly moving, and I realized that he was offering up a prayer.

And, knowing him, a vow.

CHAPTER FIVE

FTER LEAVING OUR NEWLY minted client, we decided to track down Minnie Bornstein, the dead woman's former associate, since her shop was only a few minutes' walk from there. First, though, I wanted to talk with the detective who had investigated Lorraine's death. Of course, I could have made the call from the apartment, but I preferred not having Sally Joan's big earnest eyes trained on me as I did it.

"Well, what think you?" Mr. O'Nelligan asked as we walked on in search of a phone booth. "Based on what we've heard thus far?"

"I think I should have firmly begged off of this case, that's what I think. But no, I had to cave in like a mine shaft. My guess is we'll poke around for a couple days, learn a whole heap of nothing, and report back empty-handed. What the hell, I suppose we'll get to pocket a few bucks for our troubles."

Remembering my friend's refusal to accept compensation, I added, "At least *I* will."

"Ah, now, I know you're not as mercenary as you make out, Lee Plunkett. Do you truly see nothing of merit in Miss Cobble's speculations?"

"What speculations? All I heard was a kid cousin's reluctance to accept her idol's suicide."

"I'm not sure that Sally Joan quite idolized her. After all, she did acknowledge her cousin's shortcomings."

"Yeah, well, it'd be hard not to. From my limited observation of Lorraine Cobble, I'd say she was one difficult woman."

My partner smiled ever so slightly. "I see . . . a damsel who distressed."

I hopscotched over his wit. "Anyway, the theory that she killed herself—for whatever reason, knowable or not—seems like the path of least resistance."

"True, but what glory has ever been gained by such a path?"

I tossed up my hands. "Glory? Look here. Quests, glory, shining knights . . . that's all your department. Me, I'm strictly the no frills, no thrills type."

"An uncommon description for a private detective, isn't that?"

"Uncommon, but in my case accurate."

"Come now, lad, I know the true hero that lurks within your breast."

"Then you know that he's real content to just stay there and not stumble out into mayhem. So what makes you so certain there's a homicide here?"

"I'm not certain at all, but I do think there's cause for exploration. I was taken by Sally Joan's depiction of her cousin as someone with a grand passion for life. A valid argument can be made that such a woman would not simply throw her life away."

"People do impulsive things all the time—especially hot-blooded people."

"Quite true," my partner admitted.

"Okay then. Couldn't that be the story here?"

"It might well be. I'm merely questioning. Such is the nature of man—to ever question."

"Then mark me down as the last of the unnatural men. There's nothing I love more than a big, fat, uncomplicated answer that I don't have to probe for."

This got a laugh from my Irishman. "Ah, dear Lee! Ever the jester."

"Yeah, that's me all over. Mr. Chortles of 1957." I sighed. "All right, I did sign up for this, come what may, so bring on the parade. Complete with Civil War drummers and ghost chanters."

"Ah, yes, Mrs. Pattinshell . . . She certainly makes an extraordinary claim."

"Which your haunted Irish heart no doubt embraces."

"Not necessarily."

"Just for the record, I don't think we got anything at all from that one—except maybe the heebie-jeebies. Sally Joan didn't offer much more. As for evidence . . . well, there isn't any."

"There's the letter."

"Sure, the one that can't be found," I said. "Not much help, is it? Besides, the fact that Lorraine Cobble had a meeting that morning might have nothing to do with her death twelve or thirteen hours later."

"It might or it might not. Now, in addition to that letter, there's also a second significant piece of correspondence. The one that does not exist."

"By that you mean . . ."

"I mean a suicide note. Or, more specifically, the lack of one. Frequently, in cases of self-inflicted death, the deceased has left a note stating reasons, regrets, or apologies."

"Frequently, but not always. Certainly not when the suicide was spur of the moment."

"Quite true."

I stopped in my tracks and caught my companion by the elbow. "Then what are we arguing about?"

Mr. O'Nelligan raised his eyebrows. "Is it arguing we're engaged in? I see it more as healthy discourse."

Glancing across the street, I noticed a drugstore—a good bet for finding a telephone. "Let's go get the official lowdown on all this. That is, if the local Dick Tracy's in a sharing mood."

A minute later, wedged in the store's phone booth, I consulted Sally Joan's list and dialed up the police station. "Is Detective Wilton in?"

The cop at the desk shouted out, "Is Smack Wilton here? Anybody seen Smack?"

Smack? Why did that ring a bell?

Soon a hoarse, impatient voice came on. "Wilton here. Who's this?"

I gave him my name, profession, and home base.

"Plunkett?" Wilton's voice lifted slightly. "From Thelmont? Wait, are you related to Buster Plunkett?"

"He was my father."

"Goddammit!" he responded merrily. "Sonuvabitch was a pal of mine. We were flatfoots together back in Hartford before he decided to go solo. Had the right idea, your old man. Shoulda become a private dick myself, but I ended up down here with the dope fiends and bureaucrats. Remember me, kid? Smack Wilton?"

"Definitely," I said, by which I meant *not really*. After all, my father had a small legion of cronies with names like Lefty and Loopy and Bazooka and—sure, why not—Smack. Judging by his sandpaper growl, I imagined Wilton to be one of the big sloppy palookas that Dad so delighted in.

He plunged on. "Yeah, I used to come over to Thelmont sometimes for Buster's poker games. Remember those?"

"Sure do." In truth, I'd tried to forget those drunken, deafening, borderline violent soirees that Dad had hosted in the years following my mother's death.

"I remember you, too, kid. You were a scrawny little runt. Beefed up, have you?"

"Not so you'd notice. Listen, Detective Wilton—"

"Make it Smack. You and I go back a ways."

"Smack . . . I've been hired by Lorraine Cobble's cousin to look into her death. She suspects foul play."

"Cobble, oh yeah. The dame who went skydiving without a parachute, right?"

Jesus. "Yes, that's the one."

"Listen, pal, there's nothing there."

"Probably not, but her cousin—"

"Yeah, I remember the cousin," Smack said. "Cute little number, sweet disposition and all, but she just couldn't accept the facts. Believe me, there wasn't a damn thing that pointed to anything murky. Seems the Cobble dame just decided it was *arrivederci* time and took the leap. Not unusual with these artsy types down here. They're all so goddamn high-strung and mopey, with their poetry and black clothes and depressing songs. Christ! You want songs? Listen to some Glenn Miller, for God's sake. Put on a little 'Chattanooga Choo Choo' and you won't be wanting to fling your ass off a roof."

Clearly, the man was a philosopher. I let Smack ramble on for a minute about music and mental health, then asked him what ground he'd covered in his investigation.

"We talked to the neighbors, which was a bust," he told me. "A number of them were away when she made her big exit, including the ones on her floor. Those tenants still in the building that night didn't notice a thing. I even went down to that coffeehouse where she used to hang out. Again, nobody there had much to give. How she spent her day? Who saw her last? Had anybody threatened her? Nobody I talked to had a clue."

"Or they did and weren't saying."

"Yeah, well, I don't think that's the case here."

"How about alibis?"

"Nobody seemed to know where anybody else was the night she died. It was a Sunday, and seems like everybody was off on their lonesome. That would've been a headache if I thought there was something that needed alibiing, but this was a clean open-and-shut deal."

"There was a letter, right? Something about a morning meeting?"

"Yeah, but she didn't die in the morning. She jumped well after dark. Like I told you, there's nothing to uncover. By all accounts, Lorraine Cobble was a real firebrand—had a temper and knew how to use it. I just figure, in the end, her temper imploded."

"There's been no hint of why she'd want to commit suicide?"

Smack huffed. "Like I say, these Village types are an odd-ball lot. Who the hell knows why they do what they do? The silly damned broad has a great big woe-is-me moment, scampers up to the rooftop, and does a swan dive. End of story."

Suddenly I felt very uneasy. Wilton's harsh flippancy had made me ashamed of my own. This was, after all, a human being we were talking about, not an inconvenience or a passing, snide anecdote. No one deserved to end up as a broken rag doll sprawled among the trash. As to the official inquiry into her death, it seemed to have been limply conducted at best. I was about to say as much but held my tongue. Smack might be someone I'd want in my corner one day.

I tried to sound casual. "Well, guess I'll just poke around town a little, seeing as I'm already on the time clock."

"Sure, kid. I don't begrudge you making a few bucks on this thing, but I just wanted to give you the heads-up. It's a fool's errand, plain and simple."

"Understood," said I, the fool. "Can I get in touch with you if anything comes up?"

Over the line, I could almost hear Smack shrug. "Sure, why not. Hey, it's nice to see you've taken up your dad's business. I sure liked that sonuvabitch. I know Buster died a couple years back, but never heard how. Was it on the job? Did he go down swinging?"

"No, he died over a bowl of beef stew. Heart attack."

"Aw, that's too bad. Tough old bastard shoulda gone down in a hail of goddamn bullets."

With that tender image, I said good-bye and rang off. Stepping out from the phone booth, I found Mr. O'Nelligan standing at a magazine rack, reading one of the periodicals. Was he perusing some highbrow literary journal? Looking over his shoulder, I saw that the periodical in question was a copy of *Detective Comics,* its glossy cover adorned with a picture of Batman surrounded by boomerangs, or, more specifically, "The 100 Batarangs of Batman!"

"That's not *Moby-Dick,*" I observed.

My colleague continued reading. "True, but it does possess all the elements of high adventure. Not to mention mythology."

It wasn't the first time I'd seen the old scholar engrossed in a comic. In fact, Audrey would regularly set aside a stack of them for him down at the five-and-dime. While my fiancée saw my penchant for pulp novels as juvenile, she found Mr. O'Nelligan's funny-book fixation downright charming. Not fair at all.

"I feel I should point out," I said, "that just because it's called *Detective Comics* doesn't mean it offers practical sleuthing tips."

"I'm aware of that. A little recreational reading helps keep the brain limber between bouts of high activity."

Mr. O'Nelligan paused in his limbering while I gave a quick rundown of my conversation with Smack.

"Not very helpful, was he now?" my partner noted. "Well, don't be dispirited. We'll just have to do better than the local gendarmerie, won't we?"

"Hey, Pops!" From behind the store counter, the big, grumpy proprietor wagged a cigar at us. "Looks like you already read half that thing. How 'bout you buy it?"

Calmly, Mr. O'Nelligan closed the comic book, marched over to the counter, and plunked down a dime. "I'll hereby enact the purchase."

The big guy grunted and scooped up his bounty. "Kinda old for superheroes, ain't ya?"

My partner took a deep breath and intoned:

"I am of a healthy long-lived race,
and our minds improve with age."

That drew a confounded gape from the proprietor.

"William Butler Yeats," Mr. O'Nelligan added as, purchase in hand, he led us from the store.

Back outside, I asked, "You're not going to conduct interviews while clutching Batman and Robin, are you?"

Just then, from around a corner, appeared a scruffy little fellow of perhaps ten, a shoeshine box tucked under one arm. Without missing a beat, Mr. O'Nelligan pressed the comic into the boy's free hand.

"For your leisure reading, young friend."

Paused before us, the kid mumbled a surprised thanks. My companion nodded and strode on as I hurried to keep up.

"Fear not, Lee," he said cheerfully. "I'll do nothing to sully our professionalism."

I actually felt bad for separating him from his funny book. "I'll buy you another one later."

"No need. I managed to finish the lead story back in the store and now possess a thorough understanding of Batarangs."

I grinned. "Great. Maybe that'll come in handy during our investigation. In case we run into any rough characters. Thugs hate Batarangs."

"So goes the common wisdom," said Mr. O'Nelligan. "Now onward! Onward to adventure!"

CHAPTER SIX

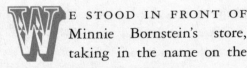 E STOOD IN FRONT OF
Minnie Bornstein's store,
taking in the name on the
large gilt-lettered sign: TUNES AND PANTALOONS.

"What the hell?" I muttered.

The front door was bordered by two large display windows, each presenting a different assortment of the shop's
wares. The one to our right offered a fanned-out collection of
sheet music, as well as several instruments including a tuba
and what I think was a cello. The left window featured several
male mannequins attired in stylish three-piece suits. Entering
the store, we saw that the split-themed motif continued inside:
music to the right, men's clothing to the left. From behind a
rack of music books, out popped a rotund woman in horn-
rimmed glasses, her brown bangs framing a smiling full-moon
face. She was squeezed into a yellow dress studded with blue

and red polka dots—a daring choice considering her size and her age, which I put on the flip side of fifty.

"Oh, hello, fellas!" she said brightly. "We were just closing, but if you know what you want . . .'"

From the clothing area, another figure appeared—a thin, balding man in a crisp gray suit. "Which is it, Minnie?" he asked dryly. "Songs or garments?"

"I'm thinking they're yours, Abe," the woman called out, her eyes traveling down my rumpled overcoat to the worn cuffs of my pants. "At least the young fella here. Looks like he could use some nice new things. Now, *you* . . . !" She had noticed Mr. O'Nelligan, he of the natty coat, vest, and tie. "You look fine! I can tell by your deep eyes that you're a man of the arts. What do you play? Piano, right? I've got all the best music, from Bach to Broadway. How about *My Fair Lady*? You look like Professor Higgins himself!"

"Alas, madam, my piano playing is subpar," my colleague said. "Though, most certainly, I've logged my time on the stage."

"An actor! An Irish one, right?" Minnie gambled. "If you could make your accent a little more English, I'm *sure* you could play Henry Higgins."

On the likelihood of passing himself off as an Englishman, the former Irish rebel offered no opinion. Instead he noted, "An interesting enterprise you have here. With an even more interesting name."

Minnie's grin widened. "You're not the first to say that, mister. See, here's the deal. My Abe here and I came into a bit of money about two years ago, and each of us had always wanted to run a little shop."

"But not the same shop," Abe added.

"That's right. I wanted a store where I could sell sheet music and musical instruments. Abe wanted one where he could sell clothes."

"Men's fine apparel," Abe clarified.

"Right, but since we didn't have enough money for two shops, we agreed to go with just one and split it down the middle—trousers for Abe, music for me. Tunes and Pantaloons. Get it? The name was my idea."

"And you're welcome to it," her husband said in a cranky singsong.

"Oh, don't be such a grumbler, Abe. After all, you could have ended up with a wife who didn't have my creative streak."

"I should be so lucky."

"You know I bring panache to the business."

Abe gestured to his wife's dress. "*Panache?* You call all those polka dots panache? They make me dizzy just looking at them."

"Hey, you've got to have fun in life! That's why I dress like this. You stick to your grays and browns, Abe. As for me, give me a little razzle-dazzle."

Abe gave us the stingiest of grins. "Listen to her! At her age she wants razzle-dazzle." He tossed up his hands. "What do you do with such a woman?"

I felt like I was watching a vaudeville show. Seeing the two of them engaged in their easy, pleasant quarreling made me think of Audrey and me. Or, at least, the "Audrey and me" that I'd known. I wasn't sure exactly what the updated version looked like.

Just when I'd thought that my partner and I had been forgotten, Minnie turned back to us. "So, like Abe asked, what is it—songs or garments?"

As succinctly as I could, I laid out who we were and why we'd come.

Minnie's natural bubbliness subsided at the mention of Lorraine Cobble. Now, aware of our purpose, she gestured distractedly toward the door. "Lock up, will you, Abe, while I talk to these fellas."

Leaving her husband to his duties, she led us to a small back room where stock from the two halves of the business seemed to overlap. Among stacks of pressed trousers and music books, we sat tightly together in a little circle of folding chairs. Minnie Bornstein expelled a deep, weary sigh and rested her hands in her lap.

"It makes me sad to think about Lorraine," she began. "Very, very sad. That girl had such promise. I met her when she was still in her twenties, you know, and in a way that's how I still think of her. It's hard to imagine her dead and in the ground." She gave a little shudder. "Lorraine was so full of life. Not to mention chutzpah! God knows she had chutzpah. Way too much for her own good, if you ask me. Now, I know you're not supposed to badmouth the dead, but honesty's the best policy, don't you think?"

"Yes, indeed," Mr. O'Nelligan answered for us.

"I mean, why should we pretend that someone's personality was all bells and roses just because they're deceased? I sure wouldn't want anyone to pretty up *my* memory. I've told Abe, 'At my service, when you're standing by the grave, I want you to step forward and declare, *My wife was stubborn and flighty, and she ate way too many pastrami sandwiches.*' God love him, I know he'll do just that."

"We understand you share some history with Lorraine," Mr. O'Nelligan said.

Minnie gave a knowing little nod. "Oh, right. You're detectives. Of course you want to learn all about your suspects."

I tried to protest. "No, that's not it. We're just—"

"Don't worry, I'm not offended. You just said that Lorraine's death could be suspicious. That means you're looking at people whose feathers she may have ruffled. Certainly, you'd have to put me in that category. Though, to be quite frank, I'm just one among the many." She paused. "Let me tell you how we met. It was back in '41, just before the war. I'd moved down to North Carolina and was doing some transcribing work for Olive Dame Campbell. I don't suppose either of you know who that was?"

"A prominent collector of American folklore," said O'Nelligan the Great Know-it-all.

"That's right!" Minnie looked glowingly at my partner. "You *are* a man of the arts. Forty years ago, Mrs. Campbell published a very influential book on Southern Appalachian folk songs. She really was the queen of the songcatchers, so, of course, Lorraine had to ingratiate herself with her. Lorraine had already starting collecting by then. She'd been to Appalachia on her own, and I think Mrs. Campbell saw something of herself in her. She hired her on to work with us."

"So were you a song collector then, as well?" I asked.

"Yes, I'd done some gathering of old Yiddish songs and such, but once I'd started working for Mrs. Campbell, I got this whole different idea. I wanted to head out west and collect work songs from Navaho and Apache women. Now, I know what you're thinking—what would a roly-poly Jewish lady from New York do with herself out on the plains? Honestly, I was just really keen to take it on."

My partner unleashed his civility. "I'm sure you'd make the best of any environment, Mrs. Bornstein."

She dismissed the compliment with a snicker and a smile. "So what happened then is that Mrs. Campbell put me in touch with some well-to-do folks from Arizona who said they'd sponsor my project. I was ecstatic! This was a few months after Lorraine had joined us, and she and I had become friends—or so I thought. She offered to help me follow up on organizing things and ended up being in contact with the benefactors herself. Long story short, Lorraine Cobble somehow talked them into sending *her* and not me out to the reservations. In the end, she didn't gather that many songs, but she sure squelched my dreams."

"That's real lousy," I said, and I meant it. "Did you ever call her on it?"

"Of course I did, but she just insisted everyone thought she was the best choice for making the trip—because of her collecting experience and her youth. Anyway, that's the kind of person she was."

"Did you have much contact with her after that?"

"Not at first. I ended up moving back here not long after and didn't see Lorraine for almost a decade. Then we both found ourselves living in the Village and would run into each other from time to time. I was still dabbling in song collecting, and every once in a while she and I would overlap on some project or other."

"You'd still work with her after what she did?" I asked.

"Well, I'm the forgiving sort—though I made sure never to put my full trust in her again. To be honest, she was one of the few people around who I could talk with about obscure

Ozark ballads or the history of Northumbrian pipes." Minnie laughed and smoothed out her lapful of polka dots. "Oh, don't get me going on Northumbrian pipes!"

I didn't. "You said there were other people Lorraine Cobble had done wrong to. Such as?"

"Well, you could talk to the gang down at the Café Mercutio. She spent a fair amount of time there and had a number of run-ins, I understand. Talk to Tony Mazzo who owns the place."

"Mazzo, right." I remembered him from my last visit.

"He's quite a character," Minnie said. "Fancies himself a big patron of the arts and a renegade, to boot. He likes to brag how three or four years ago he told the anti-Communist committee to take a giant hike. So, yeah, go talk to Mazzo. Talk to the Doonans, Byron Spires—all those people."

I revisited my least favorite topic. "About Spires . . ."

"Sure, he and Lorraine had a run-in or two."

"There was something about him stealing some Scottish song from her. Did you hear about that?"

"I wouldn't call it *hers* really. That song goes way back, but it's true, she did collect it—at least that particular version. You have to understand that there's no such thing as a single authentic version of a folk ballad. Each time a different singer gets hold of a traditional song, it just naturally undergoes changes. There's one theory that song variations are like Darwin. Survival of the fittest, you know? Over the course of time, as a particular ballad passes from one singer to another, the best lyrics survive and the lesser ones drop away."

"Leaving the hardiest version?" Mr. O'Nelligan asked.

"Yes, that's it. But despite the changes, the main storyline of the ballad stays intact. What I like to call 'the spine of the tale.' You can add whatever meat you want—whatever variations—but the main story, the spine, still remains." Minnie slapped her knee and offered a satisfied grin. "That, fellas, is my own little contribution to the terminology."

Mr. O'Nelligan smiled back at her. "A fine contribution it is, madam. So, Lorraine had quarrels with Byron Spires . . ."

Minnie nodded. "Sure. Oh, and ask about . . . now what was the name? Crimson? Yeah, I think that's it . . . Crimson Somebody. Strange name. Funny, I can't remember if it was a guy or a girl."

"Who's Crimson?" I asked.

"A folksinger who Lorraine screwed over—pardon my language. Abe says I curse like a stevedore, but I think that's an exaggeration. Anyhow, the story I heard is that this Crimson person had shared a pile of songs with Lorraine, let her record them and everything. Then one night at one of the coffeehouses—I forget which one—Lorraine signed on to do a set just before Crimson was scheduled to perform. Now, mind you, Lorraine was no virtuoso, but she could strum a guitar and sing a tune well enough. So what she does that night is get up and perform all of Crimson's set. Each and every song! Of course, that left Crimson nothing to do—didn't even bother to take the stage. Crimson confronted Lorraine later, and I guess there was hell to pay. Though, like I've said, this is all just what I've heard. You'd have to ask around to get the full story."

"Lorraine Cobble sounds like quite the piece of work," I said.

Minnie shook her head ruefully. "Not exactly a mensch, that lady. I will say this much—there *is* something, in a way, that I owe her. If she hadn't done me such dirt back with the

Arizona fiasco, I never would have ended up returning to New York and meeting my Abe. We wouldn't have had our three fine boys, each as sweet as their father."

Thinking it best not to question the sweetness of Abe Bornstein, I simply nodded. "When was the last time you saw Lorraine?"

The woman's brow wrinkled. "Let me think. A month ago was it? She stopped in here to pick up a book she'd ordered."

"How was her comportment?" Mr. O'Nelligan asked.

"You mean how was she acting? Like Lorraine Cobble—no more, no less. She was in a hurry. Lorraine was one of those people who always seem to be in a hurry, even when they're not. I do remember she said that she'd just passed someone in the street who looked exactly like Groucho Marx, only much shorter. Funny, isn't it? You know a person and suddenly they're dead, and when you think back on your last encounter, all that sticks out is something silly like that—a tiny Groucho." Minnie Bornstein paused, a look of contemplation crossing her face. "I guess if I up and died tomorrow, all they'd remember about me is sheet music and polka dots." Then she laughed gaily. "Hell, it could be worse!"

AFTER TAKING LEAVE of the Bornsteins, Mr. O'Nelligan and I grabbed a quick dinner at a nearby cafeteria. My Irish comrade found the corned beef and cabbage "profoundly lackluster," but my hamburger did me just fine.

"So, what think you of Minnie's reflections on Lorraine Cobble?" my partner asked between forkfuls.

"What think I? I thinketh Miss Cobble did stinketh." I actually giggled at my little rhyme.

"Rather cheap." Mr. O'Nelligan sounded unamused. "Cheap and fairly unkind."

"Unkind? Unless I heard wrong, Lorraine Cobble was the unkind one. Like Minnie said, honesty's the best policy—even where a corpse is concerned. From what we're learning, Lorraine made a hobby out of unkindness. Where other people collect stamps or seashells or flypaper, she collected nasty deeds."

Mr. O'Nelligan paused midbite. "One moment—*flypaper?* Who collects flypaper?"

"Just me," I mumbled. "When I was eight."

"Go on . . . I'm intrigued. Were the flies still affixed?"

"It doesn't matter," I grumbled. "Are we discussing the investigation or my childhood?"

My so-called friend grinned. "When a childhood is apparently as piquant as your own, one does feel compelled to review it."

"Lucky for you I don't know what piquant means. Anyway, Lorraine Cobble seems to have had a knack for making enemies."

"True. Which, of course, makes us wonder whether that knack led to her untimely demise."

"You mean it makes *you* wonder. My mind's still open to the suicide theory."

"An open mind is an admirable thing."

"Then admire to your heart's content."

After dinner, we reclaimed Baby Blue from her nearly boxed-in parking spot and headed across the Village for the Café Mercutio. In the reddish haze of the deepening sunset, streetlamps had begun to pop on, turning the roadway into a corridor of dappled light.

"Do you miss the city?" I asked my friend.

"Well, the Gotham life did have its allure. Although, after Eileen died, I was more than happy to abandon the fast pace for the pleasures of a small town. Thelmont suits me quite nicely."

"Still, it must have been—Christ!"

Suddenly, from my left, a figure dashed into my headlights. Man, woman, child?—I couldn't tell. All I saw was the swirl of a dark overcoat and the flailing of limbs. I slammed on the brakes, jolting my passenger and myself forward. In a flash, the dark figure had leapt from the road to reach the opposite sidewalk. When I looked around to see who it was I'd almost struck down, all I caught was a glimpse of the overcoat vanishing around a corner.

I let out a deep groan. "Inches! I missed running them over by inches."

A half-forgotten memory came rushing back, one from about seven years before. It wasn't long after I'd returned to Thelmont from my travels and had gotten back together with Audrey. One summer evening, we were out on a double date with another couple on our way to the movies. I still remember the main feature: *Sunset Boulevard* with William Holden and Gloria Swanson. I remember it because everyone says it's a great film, though I never did get to see it because of what happened. Ernie, my counterpart, was the one driving, and even though it was still fairly light out, he just didn't see that bicycle. It wasn't really his fault; the boy came barreling across the street out of nowhere, like the overcoated figure just now. Ernie was able to swerve enough so as not to strike him dead-on, but he couldn't avoid him entirely. I know "sickening thud" is a cliché, but there really isn't a phrase that works better here. Seconds later, we were all standing on the side of the road gathered

around the boy, a pudgy kid of about thirteen, who lay
sprawled beside his bike. There was a bloody gash on his head
where he'd hit the pavement, and his limbs were twisted at
various angles. I knelt beside him and clasped his hand.

"Hang on. You'll be okay." It seemed the thing to say, even
if I didn't know it to be true.

Ernie was staggering around like a marionette, cursing and
running his hands through his hair. His girlfriend stood next to
the car, as glaze-eyed and motionless as a mannequin. I glanced
around to look for Audrey, but she seemed to have disappeared.
Then I saw her on the front porch of the nearest house, rapping
tenaciously at the door. When it opened, a man stepped out and
Audrey pointed toward us, giving him quick instructions. The
man nodded and vanished back inside.

Audrey sprinted over and knelt beside me. "Someone's calling for an ambulance." She leaned down close to the boy's face.
"Don't worry, we're here with you."

She asked him his name, where he lived, how he felt—all
the time gently stroking his hair and comforting him. I continued to grip the kid's hand and echo Audrey's reassurances.

At one point, the kid whimpered, "I'm scared. I'm so
scared. . . ."

I squeezed his hand. "It won't be long now."

Audrey managed to summon up a little smile for him. "I
know this is kind of scary, but you want to talk *real* scary?
Teeth-chattering scary? You should have seen me yesterday.
I'd been swimming at the town pool and forgot to towel my
head off afterward. When I got home and looked in the mir-
ror, boy oh boy, I nearly jumped! My hair was all tangled up
and sticking out in every direction. I looked like Medusa. Do
you know who she is?"

"Snakes," the boy said softly, accepting the distraction. "She had snakes for hair."

"Exactly! Since my hair isn't very long, it looked like I had a head full of stubby little baby snakes. Yikes!"

That actually got a small laugh out of the boy, and he looked grateful for the story. In the course of the ordeal, our companions proved useless, having detached themselves from the ongoing drama, but Audrey was focused and solid throughout. Before long, the ambulance arrived and whisked off the boy (who, we later learned, had sustained a mild concussion and some nasty bruises). As the ambulance was driving away, siren wailing, Audrey and I met each other's eyes. I think, at that moment, we were both sharing the same thought—we made a pretty good team.

Mr. O'Nelligan returned me to the present. "Are you all right, Lee?"

"Yeah. You?"

"Shaken but not shattered."

"He . . . she . . . just came out of nowhere."

"Aye. Like life itself, one might say."

"Or death," I said.

The car behind us began honking insistently, reminding me that we were paused in the middle of the road. I shifted and kicked in the gas, and we shot forward into the twilight, two raddled knights resuming their quest.

CHAPTER SEVEN

FTER PARKING, WE STILL had a couple of blocks to walk to the Mercutio. Now firmly in the heart of bohemia, we navigated through a stream of locals, many young and casually dressed. There seemed to be a disproportionate number of them in black, and several were sporting sunglasses—despite the fact that the sun had gone down. We passed bookstores, record shops, magazine stands, restaurants, and cafés. Leaning against one stretch of brick wall, a dozen paintings, framed and unframed, formed a sort of impromptu art gallery. Most of these works were vivid, chaotic explosions of color, all with price tags affixed. A little ways beyond, standing outside a storefront labeled FOLKLORE SOCIETY, one young man was playing a harmonica while another juggled a trio of alarm clocks. Yes, alarm clocks.

Just as I had a month before, I entered the sawdust-strewn,

candlelit Café Mercutio to the strumming of a guitar and the greetings of the Grand Mazzo.

"A thousand welcomes!" Mazzo called out. "First time for you gents?"

"Indeed, for me it is," Mr. O'Nelligan answered, "but not for my companion here."

Our host looked at me without recognition. I mentioned my last visit and informed him of the reason for the current one.

"Ah, Lorraine . . ." He shook his head slowly. "She could be a jumbo-sized drag at times, but she had a spark, you know? A fairly hep duchess when she wasn't going all ape."

Figuring I got the gist of that, I asked if he could spare a few minutes to talk with us.

"It's Friday night and the joint's starting to fill up. But sure . . . a few minutes." Mazzo turned and called across the room. "Hey, Ruby!"

In response, a bohemian princess appeared before us, one hand balancing a tray of mugs and the other resting on her hip. She was slender but curvy, decked out all in black—sweatshirt, scarf, and tight pants—with straight jet-black hair that hung almost to her waist. Her lack of makeup made for a clear view of dark deep eyes, high cheekbones, a slightly crooked nose, and an old scar that curved under her left eye in a perfect half-moon. Somehow this combination of features worked well for her. If she wasn't exactly beautiful, she was in close proximity to it.

"What do you need?" Her voice was languid and compelling.

"I've got to go converse with these gents for a few minutes," Mazzo told her. "Toss out a welcome to anyone who comes in, will you? I'll be out back if you need me."

"Your wish is my command," Ruby responded, though her tone suggested anything but.

As we followed Mazzo past the small stage, I caught a glimpse of the performer—a young Negro woman seated on a stool, swaying gently in place as she plucked her guitar and sang. Her husky voice seemed much larger than her petite frame would contain. The lyrics followed us as we left the room:

"Who can tame the wild tides?
Tell, who can brave the storm?
Oh, if I had the answer, child,
I'd keep you from all harm."

Mazzo ushered us through a small room with a couple of old couches—the musicians' hangout, no doubt, now empty—into a back room that looked to be a cross between an office and a museum. Surrounding a nondescript desk and a few chairs, the walls were lined with shelves chock-filled with various odds and ends: knickknacks and paperbacks; bells, shells, and gnarled chunks of driftwood; glass bottles filled with marbles, brass buttons, dice, and doll's eyes; numerous statues that seemed to hail from the Orient; and, most abundantly, old shoes. Lots and lots of shoes—men's, women's, and children's—scattered among the other objects. Somehow, I found that unsettling.

Mazzo gestured us into two available chairs and perched himself on the edge of the desk. Gazing down at us, he lazily twirled his large, curled mustache, looking every inch the impresario.

I started things off. "How long have you had this place, Mr. Mazzo?"

"Going on three years. Before I got here it was a shoe repair shop."

That explained the footwear. One mystery solved, my mind could now rest easier.

He gestured around the room. "I found a bunch of the leftovers in the basement and decided to put them in my little temple of art."

"Shoes are art?" I needed to ask.

"*Everything* can be art, my friend," our host informed me. "Shoes, buttons, bow ties, plastic eyeballs . . . the breath from your lungs and the sweat from your brow. All art. Get it?"

I hoped my strained smile registered as a resounding yes.

Mr. O'Nelligan joined in. "How did you arrive at the name of your enterprise here, good sir? I ask because, in my youth, I had the fortune to play Mercutio with a touring troupe. His Queen Mab speech is sublime—

"She is the fairies' midwife, and she comes
In shape no bigger than an agate stone
On the forefinger of an alderman."

Mazzo nodded. "Yeah, Mercutio's my favorite character in *Romeo and Juliet.* He's one worthy cat—full of dreams and derring-do. As to how I landed on that appellation, well, not long before I bought this place, Joe McCarthy's boys came after me . . ."

"The House Un-American Activities Committee?" I asked.

"Not exactly, but it was a couple of McCarthy's lackeys pressuring me to turn Judas on some friends of mine. Anytime they pushed me for a name, I'd just give them some character from Shakespeare. *Oh, yeah, it's Mercutio you want. Brutus, Portia,*

Othello—those are the Commie creeps you're after. After twisting their brains in knots, I basically told those apes that if they dragged me in front of some Red-baiting committee, I'd cause them havoc and hellfire. I guess I made my point, 'cause they backed off."

"Thus sparing your friends further trouble," Mr. O'Nelligan noted.

"Unfortunately, somehow they still got at my friends. I take some solace in knowing that Edward R. Murrow finally took McCarthy down. I've heard that old Tail Gunner Joe has drunk himself nearly to death and is on his last legs at the Naval Hospital in Bethesda. Anyway, I figured 'Mercutio' was fitting for what I wanted to set up here. Fiery and lyrical, you know?"

"You have a passion for music and poetry, then?"

"Music, poetry, revelry . . ." He paused and grinned. "And debauchery when the mood hits me."

"I see." If Mr. O'Nelligan had an opinion on debauchery, his tone didn't reveal it.

Mazzo pressed on. "Yeah, these days I'm mingling with the muse—and, be advised, she is one jealous chick. It's not like I haven't put in my time on the great American treadmill. Along the way, I've been a bread baker, a soda jerk, a machinist, and an encyclopedia salesman. Plus I did my stint with ol' Uncle Sammy. At Guadalcanal, back in '42, I had a mortar shell slam into a tree just a foot from my skull. Not long after that, I acquired *this* little memento." He pointed to the white shock of hair above his temple. "I always thought it was a myth that a scare could turn your hair white. Apparently not."

"You might consider it as a badge of service," Mr. O'Nelligan suggested.

"Sure—or a symbol of me being scared utterly shitless." Mazzo shifted his gaze from my friend to me. "How about you, man? You look the right age. Were you in the big one?"

"I wasn't." I left it at that, not wanting to haul out the fact that my poor eyesight and unimpressive physique had landed me a 4-F designation.

My partner took on the questioning. "Did you know Lorraine Cobble well?"

"As well as anyone around here, I suppose," Mazzo said. "Which is to say, not well at all. Lorraine wasn't a lady who cuddled up to whole lot of folks. Kept her own counsel, dig? She was hot for the music, that's for sure. She started showing up not long after I opened the place. We got along well enough, and she steered a lot of singers over to me, which I appreciated."

"Have you any knowledge, Mr. Mazzo, of her activities on the day she died? Of, for instance, a morning meeting she partook of?"

"A police dick came poking around a while back and was asking the same things, but no one here had seen her for at least a couple days. Which wasn't unusual. She'd just kind of float in and out. Like a phantom, you know?" Mazzo stared off for a moment. "I guess that's all she is now—a phantom. It's a lousy shame."

"Who else at the café did she have a connection with?"

"Well, the musicians. Byron Spires, the Doonans, Kimla Thorpe, Manymile Simms . . . those are the ones who've played here a lot, and Lorraine was mainly interested in. If you stick around, most of them should probably be showing up tonight."

I flashed on Minnie Bornstein's story. "How about a singer

named Crimson? We heard that one night at a coffeehouse Lorraine stole all Crimson's songs and performed them as her own set."

"Crimson? I don't think I know any Crimsons. Is it a cat or a chick?"

I wanted to say *neither fish nor fowl* but settled for "We're not sure."

"Well, it didn't happen at the Mercutio or I'd know about it."

"What about your staff? Were any of them connected to Lorraine?"

"My staff tends to be a fairly transient lot. Wandering wenches who put in a month or two of work, then make tracks. None of the girls that were here when Lorraine was alive are still around. That is, except for Ruby Dovavska, the one you saw a few minutes ago. Ruby's been here awhile. She waitresses, but she'll also take the stage now and again."

"As a singer?" I asked.

"No, Ruby gives out with the verse. Poet girls in black— that's one of our bumper crops here in the Village."

"Let me ask you this," Mr. O'Nelligan said. "Do you know of any individual who would be inclined to take Miss Cobble's life?"

"That's a weighty thing, taking a life." Mazzo paused. "I know because I've done it."

That widened my eyes. "Oh?"

Mazzo continued. "When I was in the Pacific, I shot at least two Japanese soldiers that I know of. Shot them dead. Now, maybe they were vicious, bloodthirsty sons of bitches . . . or maybe they were just poor dumb kids like I was, doing whatever their generals told them to." Mazzo pushed off from his desk and walked over to one of the shelves. He reached up and took down a statue of a dragon made of shiny green stone—jade, I guessed—and cradled it in his hands.

"This comes from Japan, and all those, too." He nodded back toward the row of statues behind him. "I was never one of those guys who went in for battlefield souvenirs. I never purloined a pistol or a bayonet, or pried out the gold fillings from a corpse. After I came home, though, I started to collect these Japanese statues. It's sort of my way of saying to those two dead cats, 'Hey, I'm damned sorry I had to kill you, but I keep a little bit of your world on hand to remember you by.'"

I wasn't sure what the heck to think about that, though I noticed Mr. O'Nelligan was nodding thoughtfully beside me. Knowing something of his history, it suddenly occurred to me that I was the only one in the room who hadn't slain a man in battle. It was a sobering thought.

Mazzo replaced the dragon on its shelf. "Got a little off track, didn't I? You were asking if I knew of anyone around here who could kill Lorraine. Well, my first impulse is to say 'hell no.' It's one thing to find somebody annoying and aggravating; it's another to actually hurl them off a roof like you're suggesting. On the other hand, if I slap on my philosopher's cap, I'd have to admit that the world can be one cruel, crazy playground—Guadalcanal taught me that—and dark things happen, man."

"Yes, indeed," Mr. O'Nelligan said. "Dark things do happen. The question here is did they happen in this particular situation."

"Either way, the answer's yes, isn't it?" Mazzo gave a bitter little laugh. "I mean, whether Lorraine jumped or was pushed, it wasn't exactly a big beautiful moment of splendor, now was it?"

"Of course, you're correct," my partner said. "The loss of life, in whatever circumstances, is always a regretful affair."

Mazzo pushed on. "Anyway, I don't buy into the homicide angle. Though, to tell the truth, I'd almost rather it was murder than suicide. I was pretty ticked off at her when they said Lorraine had done herself in. Death will chase you down soon enough, Jack. There's no need to do the bastard's job for him."

"A sound point of view," Mr. O'Nelligan said.

Mazzo shifted gears. "Hey, so you're Irish, yeah?"

"Is it not obvious?"

"You'll definitely want to meet the Doonan Brothers. They're like walking shamrocks, those boys."

"Is that so?" My partner's tone suggested that this image didn't wholly appeal to him. "Then I shall look forward to our imminent encounter."

Mazzo whistled. "You have yourself a poet's tongue there, don't you, dad? Plus you've got that brogue to back it up. We Italians know food and *amore,* but you Irish trump us with the wordplay."

"Don't sell yourself short," Mr. O'Nelligan said. "After all, you can boast Dante and Boccaccio as your national treasures."

"Yeah, those cats could definitely wield a quill pen, but for free-form babbling I tip my hat to you sons of Erin."

Their ping-pong game of admiration was interrupted by Ruby, who stopped in to announce dryly that the Mercutio was filling up and that Mazzo's presence would be highly appreciated. Or more specifically, "It's getting busy. Don't let me drown out there."

After she exited, Mr. O'Nelligan turned to our host. "That young lady is certainly no meek subordinate, is she?"

"God no." The impresario smirked. "Ruby ain't subordinate to nobody."

"Somewhat like Lorraine Cobble?" I suggested.

"Two entirely different specimens. Whereas Lorraine would combust, Ruby just . . ." Mazzo searched for a word. "Simmers."

"In more ways than one, maybe?" I said, hoping I didn't sound too lascivious.

Mazzo narrowed his eyes and grinned at me. "Fancy her, *amico mio?*"

I sputtered out something that was meant as a denial, but it only caused his grin to broaden.

"No shame, man," he said. "If I went in for chicks, I'd probably fancy her, too."

"Oh," I replied.

"Well, I've got to get back to work," Mazzo continued. "You gents, too, I guess. Just don't nut out my clientele, okay?"

I assured him that no nutting out was planned. By God, we were professionals.

CHAPTER EIGHT

ETURNING TO THE CROWDED main room, Mazzo told us to find a seat and settle in; he'd introduce us to various musicians as they showed up. As our host went off to his duties, my partner and I nabbed a corner table directly under a large circus poster of acrobats leaping over several enraged lions.

I indicated the gaudy image. "Not the healthiest pastime, is it?"

"Ah, but is it not an allegory for the human condition itself?" Mr. O'Nelligan mused. "Do we not all, at times, find ourselves vaulting perilously over the savage beasts of life?"

"Sure. What's an allegory?"

Mr. O'Nelligan let out one of his patented soul-weary sighs, the ones he seemed to reserve just for me and my denseness. "Oh, lad, you're an astounding fellow."

I guessed that a "thank you" wasn't the appropriate response.

The same performer as before was still onstage, midway through a song, and I was able to take more note of her now. She had a light brown complexion, a close-cropped halo of dark hair, and a gentle expression—calm and thoughtful, with maybe a touch of soft sadness. In contrast to the black garb favored by many in the room, she was dressed in a white blouse and a lavender gypsy skirt.

Ruby approached our table and asked for our order. I went for coffee since it was, after all, a coffeehouse. Mr. O'Nelligan, of course, had to be different.

"I hope requesting tea is acceptable, dear miss, since coffee is no doubt the paradigm here."

I winced. Did he really have to use one of his triple-jointed words on this young beauty?

Our waitress ran a hand through her long black locks and smiled mildly. "It's fine. Coffee hasn't been paradigmatic at Mercutio's for eons."

Obviously, Ruby wasn't intimidated by a flashy vocabulary. She pivoted and resumed her rounds.

After the last guitar strum and the accompanying applause, the singer onstage offered the crowd a Mona Lisa smile. "Thank you so much. Now here's a song from Madrid. It's about love and loss."

She sang the forlorn ballad sweetly, performing much of it in its language of origin. Next came a Dutch children's ditty about a candlestick maker. As the last note trailed off, a male voice, strident and Irish, called out from near the front door.

"Grand stuff! Sing us another ten or twenty, won't you?"

Heads turned, including my own. The speaker was a barrel-chested man of under thirty with a broad smile and a head full of tight black curls. Flanking him were two other young men who appeared to be his juniors. The youngest-looking I recognized from my last visit—it was Tim, guitar in hand, the kid who'd been onstage when Lorraine Cobble exploded so memorably. The trio clearly shared a common bloodline, and all wore the same dark green turtleneck sweaters. Here, no doubt, were the Doonan Brothers.

The central Doonan called out again. "Keep at it, lass! God knows, no one wants to hear *our* rough-hewn voices."

The singer onstage answered pleasantly. "Now, Patch, you know that's not true. Everyone's eager to hear you boys."

"Ah, Kimla, you're the soul of charity," Patch replied.

The young woman turned back to the audience. "I give you now the Doonans from Galway. Patch, Neil, and Tim."

She stepped off the stage, and the three Irishmen marched on. Without ceremony, they launched into a rambunctious song that had something to do with whiskey and the devil. Tim handled the guitar work, while the one who had to be Neil added a pennywhistle between stanzas. The raucous Patch contented himself with belting out each and every line and punching the air sporadically.

I whispered to my friend, "Does this bring you back to the old isle?"

"We could well be burrowed into a cozy little pub down some country lane."

The Doonans delivered a half-dozen songs—some boisterous, some poignant—on a variety of subjects including fair young maids, disrupted wakes, dispersed rebellions, and plucky highwaymen. Their last number was done a cappella with Tim taking on the solo part. As I'd noticed on my previous visit, he had a strong yet angelic voice that rang every drop of emotion out of a slow ballad. He did particular justice to the present lyrics:

"Down by the salley gardens my love and I did meet;
She passed the salley gardens with little snow-white feet.
She bid me take love easy, as the leaves grow on the tree;
But I, being young and foolish, with her would not agree."

Mr. O'Nelligan seemed transfixed by this song. "Yeats," he said under his breath, and over the subsequent applause, he could be heard calling out, "Exquisite!"

Announcing that there would be a break, the Doonans left the stage and commandeered a table next to ours that had just been vacated. The young woman singer came over and took a seat beside Tim, who leaned over and gave her lips a brief but tender kiss.

"Nice set," she said to him.

Tim returned the compliment. "You did a lovely set your-self, Kimla."

She bestowed on him her gentle smile. "Were you even here for it?"

"Only caught the last song," Tim admitted sheepishly. "We would have been here for the whole thing if it weren't for Patch."

"Aye, I fully accept the blame," Patch said. "I insisted we stop in at the White Horse for a nice jar of ale. As these things go, one jar became three."

"Only for you," Tim contradicted. "Neil and I stuck to the one."

Patch gave a mock scowl. "Well, I'm the oldest. I have to take on the brunt of things, don't I now?"

Neil, whom I took to be the middle brother, rolled his eyes and muttered, "A true saint, this one."

As crowded as the room had become, our two parties were now almost squeezed together. Up close, the family resemblance among the three Doonans was even more evident. All had pleasant oval faces and thick dark hair, though Patch's mane was curlier and faintly tinged with red. Only in the nose department did each Doonan firmly go his own way. Tim's was slightly upturned, giving him an appropriately boyish look, while Neil's was straight, precise, and practical. As for Patch, his snout was a flat, puggish affair that made me wonder it hadn't been introduced to a well-aimed fist or two.

Mr. O'Nelligan now leaned over and addressed our neighbors. "May I offer you my compliments, gentlemen—and to you, young lady—for your performances." Then, turning to Tim Doonan, he added, "Mr. Yeats would unquestionably be pleased by your rendition of 'Down by the Salley Gardens.' A grand poem, and a grand song you made of it."

Tim's "Thanks" was overridden by Patch, who thrust a finger at my partner and exclaimed, "A fellow Celt! I hear the Kerry countryside tripping off your tongue, though there are other shades in the mix, I'd venture."

"Quite true," said my particular Irishman. "My years on the stage and in New York have colored my accent a bit."

"Well, it suits you!" Patch declared. "Gives you a spot of style. Plus, with that fine gray beard, don't you bring to mind Saint Paddy himself?"

"That, young sir, would be a stretch," my partner said.

Names were exchanged and hands shaken all around.

"How long have you been in the States, Mr. O'Nelligan?" Tim asked.

"Twelve years now. How about you lads?"

"Patch and Neil came over three years ago in '54, and I arrived the following spring."

Patch addressed my partner. "You say you've done some acting? I've put in a bit of time on the stage here myself. Oh, but don't these Yanks love to hear a brogue being bandied about when the curtain rises? For my first part in town, all I did was stagger about the stage cursing humanity and bellowing for a drink."

Tim snickered. "Oh, and weren't we all shocked that he could land a role so contrary to his own sweet self?"

Ruby now reappeared, bearing her tray. "What would you all like here?"

"What would I like?" Patch reached up and slipped an arm around her waist. "I've got a lively answer for that, my girl."

Ruby shook herself free of him and asked once more for our orders. It was coffee all around except, again, for Mr. O'Nelligan and his tea. Ruby nodded and strode off.

Patch studied her retreat. "Glory! A well-constructed female, that one." He clicked his tongue.

"For God's sake," Neil grumbled. "Enough already."

"Enough of what? Artistic appreciation? I was just honoring the sturdiness of her backside."

"Quit your vulgarities!" Neil demanded. "Have some respect for Kimla here."

Patch turned to the young woman. "Ah, Kimla knows me for a harmless clown. Don't you, love?"

Kimla smiled in her calm, easy way. "I'd say that you're your own worst enemy, Patch."

He wagged a finger at her. "You're a keen girl, y'know.

Brimming with insight. Our Tim here best beware or you'll turn him inside out with all your clever witchery."

Tim placed a protective arm around Kimla. "Leave her be now. She's just too polite to tell you to get stuffed."

The Grand Mazzo suddenly appeared and stared down at our gathering with a satisfied look. "Cool! You all found one another."

"We Irishmen are drawn to each other like bloody magnets," Patch said. "Just couldn't resist the pull of Mr. O'Nelligan here."

"You boys should drag him onstage to join you in a tune." Mazzo paused, his mind hunting for a joke. "I know! You can sing 'When Private Eyes are Smiling.'" He laughed freely at his own wit, then hurried off on his hosting rounds.

Patch furled his brow. "Private eyes? I don't get it."

Clearly, it was time to state our purpose for being there. Mr. O'Nelligan did the honors, laying out our mission succinctly and delicately. The musicians listened without interruption— even Patch.

Finally, after a moment of quiet, it was Tim who spoke. "Lorraine Cobble was a feisty lady. She won't be soon forgotten, God rest her soul. But as to murder . . . That's what you're speaking of, isn't it? Someone flinging her off that roof?"

Beside him, Kimla gave a notable shiver, and Tim drew her closer.

"It's just so terrible," she said softly. "A suicide . . ."

"They're saying it *wasn't* a suicide," Tim corrected. "They're saying that some flesh-and-blood villain did her in."

"That's a strong claim," Neil added.

"Yes it is," I agreed. "Though we're not actually making it.

Not yet. We're just trying to see if anyone knows anything that might steer us one way or another."

"Well, I for one never bought into it," Patch said. "Her suicide, I mean. Lorraine wouldn't snuff out her own flame. She was just too damned ornery."

"Jesus, Mary, and Joseph!" Neil sputtered. "Respect the dead, can't you?"

"Who's not respecting her? I believe ornery to be an admirable trait."

Tim chuckled lightly. "I'm sure you do, Patch."

"How long did you all know Lorraine?" I asked.

"A year maybe?" Tim guessed. "She was in the audience one night when we were just starting to make a go of it. We were seeing, y'know, if we could earn a bit of a living doing what we like to do anyway. This singing thing, I mean. It wasn't here we were performing, but at a dive across town called the Duckbill."

Patch groaned. "Oh, but what a dungeon *that* place was."

"It's true." Tim stared off and lapsed into a sort of reverie. "But when I think of that gig, what I most remember is Lorraine Cobble. I can still see her there—a handsome woman, really, with her long blond hair and fine features—sitting up front, watching and listening to us so intently. Truly *getting* us, if you understand me. Swaying a touch with the gentle tunes and tapping away with the wild ones. After our set, she collared the three of us and wanted to know all about the songs, their origins and all that."

"What *I* remember from that night," Neil said, "was how intimidating she seemed. With those great piercing eyes of hers."

Tim nodded. "Aye, she could fairly nail you to the wall

with those eyes, but she always struck me as someone who truly *embedded* herself in life. Or at least that part of life that interested her. The music, y'know. It was the music that seemed to connect her to the world."

Patch slapped the tabletop. "Brilliant, Timbo! Now, aren't you our own wee Aristotle? You with your deep thoughts and ruminations."

Tim frowned. "Oh, push off, why don't you? I'm just trying to give these fellows a sense of the woman."

"Which we appreciate," I said.

Ruby returned with our beverages, which she distributed quickly before Patch could get into anything with her. When she'd moved off, Patch dug out a small silver flask from his pants pocket and poured a liberal dose of its contents into his coffee.

"It curbs the bitterness," he insisted. "The stuff they brew here is a touch rugged."

I tasted my own coffee. It was fine. Patch offered the flask around, but there were no takers.

I now turned to Kimla, who had kept largely silent since sitting down. "How about you, Miss Thorpe? How long did you know Lorraine?"

Her reply was unhurried and subdued. "Not as long as the boys here. I've only been in the city since last summer. Of course, it's so very sad."

"Most certainly it is." Mr. O'Nelligan matched the softness of her voice. "A very sorrowful thing. Did you have much of a connection with the woman?"

"Oh, we talked about music a little. She'd come in and take note of some song I was singing and ask about it later. Like Tim says, music was what she most cared about. I just don't like to think of how she, well . . ." She looked down into her cup and went silent.

Tim reached over and squeezed her hand. "I know, Kimla. It's not a very nice thought for any of us."

Patch lifted his mug of whiskey-fortified java. "To the poor woman's memory! I drank to her when she died, and I'll drink to her now."

Then he did. I'm pretty sure it was a duty he didn't mind discharging.

"Death is a curious creature, isn't it?" Tim said to no one in particular. "It takes hold of whatever you were and whatever you hoped to be and swallows it all whole."

Patch became suddenly solemn. "Aye, it swallows you and, God willing, doesn't spew you back out. There are tales aplenty of the dead returning, all vapory and restless, to harass the living."

Neil gave a grunt of agreement. "Especially when they've had a turbulent death."

"Right you are," Patch said. " 'Tis said those are the hardest ghosts to put to rest."

Mr. O'Nelligan blew the steam off his tea. "Perhaps it's up to us the living to help such spirits find their repose."

"How, sir?" Neil asked.

"With truth," said Mr. O'Nelligan. "With simple, unflinching truth."

CHAPTER NINE

THE DOONANS TOOK THE stage again for a few more songs, mostly loud, raucous ones that precluded any conversation at our table. When they returned to us, I got back on course, trotting out our standard inquiries: Had Lorraine Cobble been seen just prior to her death? Did anyone know about her meeting that morning? Besides her incident with Byron Spires, had there been any other recent altercations?

Only that last question drew a noteworthy response, as delivered by Patch Doonan, who gave out a long, loud sigh—foghorn loud—and cast his eyes heavenward.

Tim smirked. "Go on and tell it, Patch. It's a tale that shows you in all your glory."

The dour Neil actually cracked a smile. "Don't leave out the bit about your trousers."

"If I *do* tell the tale," said their older brother, "it wouldn't be for the amusement of you two blackguards. It would be to assist these gentlemen in their investigation." He indicated my partner and me with a magnanimous sweep of the hand. "By providing a snapshot, as it were, of the deceased."

"For which we would be immensely grateful," Mr. O'Nelligan said soothingly. "Please proceed."

Patch leaned back and lit himself a cigarette. "It was last month, about three weeks ago, I'd say."

"So, a week before Lorraine died," I clarified.

"Maybe only a few days before. We'd just put in a set here, the boys and me, and were kicking back a little. Herself was in attendance, sitting off on her own, giving a good listen to the next singer. Manymile Simms it was. So Lorraine's there keeping her own company, as was her preference, when this little weasel Loomis scurries over to her table."

"Loomis—would that be a person?" I asked.

"In a manner of speaking," Patch said. "A twitchy, toady breed of person, but, yes, technically a human being."

"You're being cruel, Patch," Kimla said quietly.

"Oh, come now, girl! Don't tell me you'd want to cozy up with that sort. Him with his gambling and slick ways and filthy gossip. Always sniffing about for a bit of dirt to dredge up on some poor soul or other. Is that a class of scoundrel you wish to defend?"

"She wasn't defending him," Tim said sternly. "Back off now."

Patch softened his tone. "No offense, Kimla. I know you've got a good heart, but don't let it bleed itself out on riffraff like Loomis Lent. The man's a barnacle. I should know; I had to share the stage with him last winter. He somehow wormed his way into a play I was in. He filled the role of third imbecile, I believe."

"He's awkward," Kimla countered. "And he's lonely. Lonely people can be difficult like that."

"True enough," Tim said. "As for the gambling, if I remember right, Patch, you've taken a wager or two off him yourself."

Neil nodded. "Sure, you're just bitter because you've lost a few dollars to the man."

"Blessed Mary!" Patch barked. "Are you going to let me tell the damned story or not?"

"Tell it and be done," Neil said.

"So, as I was saying, Loomis strides on over to Lorraine's table—"

I snuck in a question. "Why would a guy like Loomis be hanging around a place like the Mercutio?"

"He fancies the music, I guess," Patch said. "Even a barnacle can fancy music. Anyway, he plops himself down beside the formidable Miss Cobble, uninvited and undesired. When Lorraine was intent on listening to a tune, she hated to be distracted. Especially by Loomis."

"Though those two did have a bit of an alliance," Tim added.

"Sure they did," Patch conceded, "but only because he provided her with spiteful tales of their fellow beings. Lorraine wasn't above reveling in gossip herself, God rest her soul. To continue, Loomis starts in to jabbering about some nonsense or other, and it's more than obvious that Lorraine wants him to vacate. Dense as the man is, he just keeps babbling on like a bloody brook. So here I am witnessing this all when a lovely notion comes to me. Promptly, I get up and find the waitress . . .'"

"Ours?" I asked. "Ruby?"

"Nah, Ruby wouldn't have put up with it. No sense of high comedy, that one. This was some other girl that's since come and gone. So I arrange for her to deliver a bottle of wine and two glasses to Lorraine's table. Plus a little note I jotted off that says *Take your leisure, sweet lovers—the night is young.*" Patch grinned at the memory. "A nice touch, I thought that was."

I looked for clarification. "They weren't, though? Lovers, I mean."

"God, no!" Patch guffawed. "The heavens themselves would've cracked open had such a thing transpired. That was the beauty of my jest. Loomis, he's just befuddled by the note and the wine, but Lorraine clearly comprehends the prank and is none too pleased. She starts scanning the room, looking for who's responsible, which isn't too difficult seeing as I'm sitting there dissolving into giggles. She parades herself over and starts lashing me with that sharp tongue of hers, telling me what a famous idiot I am. To my credit, I maintain my good humor and toss up my hands in surrender. I admit to her that I'm a jackass and offer to make amends."

"Here's where things get magical," Neil said flatly.

Patch pushed on. "Then I reach into my pocket and pull out this little thingamabob that I'd come by. Something I'd bought earlier in the day, just for the hell of it, from one of the street merchants who are always out peddling their trinkets. It was a little stone slate with a painting on it—a raggedy fellow playing a banjo. I press it into Lorraine's hand, saying, 'Here's a wee gift to ease the tension.' The thing is, I truly meant it as a peace offering. I'd had my laugh, but I didn't want any hard feelings." He looked to his brothers. "I'm not mean-spirited, now am I, lads? You can say I'm a bit daft, but you can't say I'm mean-spirited."

"Well, you *are* daft," Tim said. "I agree with you there."

Neil gave a straight answer. "No, Patch, there's not much meanness in you, but sometimes you're like a damned child poking at a hornet's nest."

"That may be accurate," Patch said. "So, back to Lorraine, she's standing there staring down at that bit of slate in her hand. It's a pretty enough painting, and I'm thinking she sees it for the honest gesture it was. Then, without a hint of warning, she tosses the thing on the table, right into a couple glasses of water that were sitting there. The glasses shatter, the water bursts out, and there I sit with my trousers drenched to the skin."

This drew laughter from his brothers. Even the kindly Kimla seemed to be holding back a smile.

Patch played at looking offended. "It's fine for you jackals to make merry. It wasn't you that was nearly drowned."

"Can you exaggerate any more wildly, Patch?" asked Tim.

"I can, but I won't," the elder Doonan answered. "So, as you might imagine, I'm perturbed now, and I say to Lorraine, 'What's wrong, did the picture remind you of all the poor sods you've filched tunes from?' 'Cause that's what she'd do, y'know— get some hardscrabble old hobos or dirt farmers to sing her the songs their grandfathers taught them, then swipe 'em and make her money. Well, that sends her through the roof beams. The woman takes to raging, informing me in no uncertain terms that she's not to be trifled with. Those were the very words—'I will not be trifled with.' Rather melodramatic, I thought, but then Lorraine could be the high queen of melo-drama when she got her steam up. Truth be told, this wasn't the first time she blew up so grandly."

"So we understand." I was thinking of her exchange with Byron Spires.

"Though perhaps it was the last time," Mr. O'Nelligan said reflectively.

"What was Loomis doing during all this?" I asked.

Tim smiled. "Fleeing the premises."

"Like a fox from the hounds," Patch added. "He wasn't about to stick around to see if Lorraine would turn on him next. Not with all the taunts and threats she was flinging at me."

"Threats?" Mr. O'Nelligan stroked his beard. "Is that how you interpreted her words?"

Patch laughed. "Whatever they were, they surely weren't prayers for my eternal soul. When I next ran into her a day or two later and tried to offer a kind word, she wouldn't even speak to me. Anyway, that's the tale."

"What?" Neil look distressed. "You'd leave out the best part?"

"I've told all that's important."

"Has it slipped your mind, then, Patch?" Tim smiled impishly and addressed my partner and me. "We still had to do another full set. Patch tried to beg off, but Mazzo wouldn't have it. So we take the stage with our brother's trousers still soggy as a swamp, looking to the whole world like he'd soiled himself."

Patch scowled. "Are we done with this nonsense?" He ground out his cigarette, drew out his flask, and took a long pull of the whiskey—not even bothering with the pretense of adding it to coffee. Patch had just removed the flask from his lips when something near the front door caught his attention. "Ah, here comes Byron. Is he playing tonight? I see he's got his new conquest with him. That perky little brunette." Sure enough, Byron Spires, with his vagabond good looks and unruly brown curls, was now crossing the room toward us, a female at his side. I adjusted my eyeglasses to better take in this "new conquest."

And nearly fell out of my chair. It was Audrey.

CHAPTER TEN

UDREY AND I SAW EACH other at the exact same moment. Midway across the room, she froze in place, her eyes wide and her mouth agape. Her look of shock quickly shifted to an expression I'd describe as excruciating discomfort. Or maybe mild horror. I'm guessing my own face must have registered a similar look. My brain stumbled over itself, trying to decide what words to push out for the occasion. I was spared a decision by Audrey herself, who spun promptly about and headed back for the front door.

Byron Spires, looking confounded and put-out, turned and followed, calling after her, "Hey, wait up! What's going on?"

Then they both vanished through the door. I sat there for several muddled seconds, waiting for my mind and body to agree on some course of action. Mr. O'Nelligan had had his back toward the entrance, and by the time he turned around, the newcomers were gone. So he hadn't seen Audrey. Telling him I'd be right back, I got to my feet and rushed across the room, nearly bowling over Mazzo at the doorway as I exited. Out on the sidewalk, I glanced down the lamplit street of tightly packed storefronts and saw two figures retreating around a corner. With absolutely no sense of what I planned to say or do, I gave chase. I found them at once, walking tightly together beneath the glow of a streetlamp. As I came pounding up behind them, they quickly turned around, a look of surprise and fear on their faces. Their elderly Chinese faces.

"Don't!" the old woman cried out in a strong accent. "We have no money! Don't hurt us!"

The man, well into his seventies, stepped in front of her, fists clenched, prepared to sacrifice himself against me in defense of his wife. I almost wanted to cry. I took a step back and began to stammer out apologies. After a moment, realizing that I was no threat, the couple turned their backs, linked arms, and continued on. I heard them speaking in Chinese as they walked away. No doubt something on the order of *What a pathetic crazy man . . .* I started back in the direction of the coffeehouse and, rounding the corner, again caught sight of someone heading off down the street. Now I opted for a brisk trot—rather than a psychotic dash—to pursue my quarry. I only had to get within a dozen yards to realize I'd gotten it wrong again. This time, instead of a huddled couple, it was a single man, albeit one of enormous girth. Deflated, I watched him waddle slowly away.

I stood there motionless for several minutes, letting darkness and despair wash over me. Why should I have been so shocked to see Audrey walk through the door with Byron Spires? After all, hadn't I had a strong suspicion that she was drawn to him? Wasn't that the main reason I wanted to decline this case—because it would place me in his realm and I might discover something I didn't want to? Had I been in such a state of denial that I never imagined that Audrey might pop up at the Mercutio on a Friday night in the company of Spires? She'd already admitted to me that she'd made the drive down here—the *hour and a half* drive—several times on her own. An unnerving thought suddenly presented itself: Had Audrey intended to make the ninety-minute trek back home tonight, or was she planning to bunk with her new best pal? That was more than I could bear to consider. Keeping the words "new conquest" at bay, I shook off my inertia and headed back toward the coffeehouse.

AS I APPROACHED the Mercutio, I was met with the sound of loud, agitated male voices. Drawing close, I discovered the source. Just outside the front door, in the amber light of a streetlamp, Patch Doonan was shouting and squaring off against another man.

"I've no fear of you, you big bastard!" The Irishman was half-crouched in a boxer's stance, fists thrust forward. "Come on and have it!"

His adversary was a large man with dark ebony skin, dressed in blue overalls and a red checkered shirt. In addition to his height advantage—about a half foot taller than Patch—the guy was wide-shouldered and physically imposing. Even given the fact that he was probably over forty, at least ten years older than Patch, he looked more than a match for him. I now noticed Ruby the waitress standing off to the side, clearly distressed.

"Patch! Manymile!" she called out. "Stop this now!"

"I'm *trying* to stop it," said the large man in a deep raspy drawl, "but this boy here won't see reason."

"I'll show you reason, you swarthy brute!" Doonan moved forward a step.

Manymile's big hands, unlike his adversary's, weren't curved into fists but instead were spread out open-palmed in a gesture of calming. "No need for this, Patch. You're drunk and mixed up."

With a tirade of obscenities, Patch shot forward and landed a blow on Manymile's jaw. Ruby screamed out something, and the larger man wrapped his arms around the smaller in a tight, unyielding bear hug. Pinned as he was, Patch thrashed about madly, his obscenities growing in violence and volume. At this point, Tim Doonan and Mazzo burst out of the coffee-house and stopped in their tracks, riveted by the scene before them.

"Come get your damned brother!" Manymile shouted to Tim. "He's drunk and crazy."

Tim and Mazzo moved forward, and Manymile shoved the struggling man into their arms. That didn't put an end to it. Even with Tim and Mazzo each gripping one arm, Patch continued to curse and kick and rail against them. Several more people had now emerged from the Mercutio, Kimla Thorpe and Mr. O'Nelligan among them. After observing the men for a moment, Kimla stepped resolutely forward.

"Stand back, Kimla!" Tim warned. "He'll harm you!"

"No he won't." The young woman placed a hand on either side of the restrained man's face, holding him in a firm grip and staring directly into his eyes. "That's enough now, Patch."

This seemed to throw him. "Back off, girl," he said feebly.

"You need to settle down." Her voice was calm and mesmerizing. "You're scaring people, and I know you don't want to do that. You need to go home with your brothers now."

"I was only—"

Kimla shushed him. "Go home."

The fight seemed to have suddenly gone out of Patch. He moaned and slumped between his brother and Mazzo. Kimla removed her hands from his face and stepped away.

Manymile stood rubbing his jaw. "You heard her, Tim. Take him home and pour some coffee down his gullet. A *whole lot* of coffee. That boy needs some sobering up."

"I'm not even that drunk," Patch muttered.

Manymile offered a slim smile. "Drunk enough to face off against a fella my size."

Patch looked up and eyed the larger man intently. For a moment, I thought he might charge him again. Instead, his voice cracking with liquor-fueled emotion, he sputtered out, "Jesus, I'm sorry I slugged you, Manymile."

"Okay, Patch."

"It's just that when I saw you kiss Ruby like that . . ."

"A little peck. That's all that was."

"I don't want you thinking it's 'cause you're colored, y'know?"

Manymile sighed. "Sure, Patch. Forget it."

"'Cause look at my own brother and Kimla here, and I love her like a sister."

"Yeah, okay."

"It's just that I fancy that Ruby so much. Now, where is she?"

Patch glanced around until he located the waitress, who

stood outside the circle of onlookers, keeping her distance. "Ah, Ruby girl!"

The long-haired beauty gave him a scornful glare and strode back into the coffeehouse.

"I've turned her against me," Patch said mournfully. "What an ass I am."

Manymile stepped forward and rested one of his huge hands on the young Irishman's shoulder. "You're talking 'bout the love of a woman, but I've got to say, Patch, sometimes it seems like you don't love but one thing. And that's whiskey. Now, if you'll 'scuse me, I've got me some songs to sing." With that, he marched into the Mercutio.

Head hung, Patch went off to lean against one of the farther storefronts. The Grand Mazzo made a flourishy announcement that there was still music to be had and led his patrons back inside. Mr. O'Nelligan and I now found ourselves alone on the sidewalk with Tim and Kimla.

"What was *that* all about?" I asked Tim.

"It's about my brother not being able to hold his liquor."

"How'd he get so drunk so fast? I was gone less than ten minutes."

"More than enough time to down a flask," Tim said wearily. "Besides, he'd been topping himself off since noon. That's just how it goes with Patch. Mix whiskey with a perceived cause for fighting, and you get the ugly mess you just witnessed. He's generally the easygoing sort, but, well, that's how he can get."

"What was the fight about?" I wanted to know. "A kiss?"

Kimla answered that one. "When Manymile arrived, Ruby went over and handed him the guitar pick he'd lost a couple of nights back. It was his favorite, and he gave her a little thank-you kiss for finding it for him. It was nothing, really."

"Enough for Patch to blow his top," I observed.

"Well, I don't think he saw the part about the pick," Tim said. "Though he surely noticed the kiss."

Mr. O'Nelligan now entered the discussion. "Does Patch have any claims on that young lady? Earlier, their connection appeared to be one of mischievous flirting on his part and firm rejection on hers."

Tim exchanged a glance with Kimla before answering hesitantly. "Ah, there may have been a bit of something more, well . . ."

"Substantial?" My partner had the right word for every occasion.

Before any answer could be given, the Mercutio's door swung open and Neil Doonan stepped out onto the sidewalk. For a few seconds, the bluesy plunk of guitar strings reached us from within, accompanied by a deep, resonant voice raised in song. Apparently, Manymile Simms had started work.

Neil was holding Tim's guitar, which he now pressed into his younger brother's hands. "Don't want to forget this, do you?"

"Where the hell were *you*?" Tim demanded. "We could have used you back when himself was going berserk." He nodded toward Patch, still lingering down the street.

"I'm done playing the nursemaid with that one," Neil said. "Ma's back in Ireland, so he'll just have to soothe his own damned self over here."

"Come on, Neil, you know how he can be," Tim implored.

"Oh, I do. I vowed to myself that the next time the drink and the brawling claimed him, I was steering clear. So I did." Neil now glanced uneasily at my partner and me, perhaps thinking that too much family business was being aired in front of strangers. "Well, what's done is done. Let's drag him on home."

Tim gave Kimla a parting kiss. "See you tomorrow, then."

He and Neil gathered up their brother, and the three Doonans headed down the street, disappearing into the Village night.

Mr. O'Nelligan turned to Kimla. "I must say, it seems odd that Patch was describing Lorraine Cobble with words like 'extreme' and 'melodramatic,' and then mere minutes later . . .'"

"He acts the same way," Kimla finished. "Or even worse. Yes, Patch can do that—flip from one side of the coin to the other as quick as anything. Of course, the alcohol helps."

"Like Stevenson's Jekyll and Hyde?" my partner suggested.

Kimla gave a thin smile. "Maybe just like Hyde and Hyde. Though one Hyde is kind of charming in his way, while the second one can turn all dreadful and nasty."

"The other Doonans seem of a different ilk," Mr. O'Nelligan noted.

"They are," Kimla agreed. "Neil is pretty solid, though maybe a little persnickety. As for Timothy . . ." Here, she lowered her eyes in a way both bashful and contemplative. "He's just a good, gentle-hearted person."

With that, she gave us a little nod and slipped back into the Mercutio.

"A sweet girl," I said.

Mr. O'Nelligan turned to me. "Now, pray tell, where did you vanish to back then?"

"I was trying to catch up with Spires but couldn't find him." That much, at least, was true. I wasn't prepared to offer up the fact that Audrey was with him.

My companion seemed to accept my explanation. "I won-der why he and his paramour made such a hasty exit."

Jesus—his paramour. "No idea," I lied. "Let's head home."

"What of Manymile Simms? Mazzo mentioned him as someone we might converse with regarding Lorraine Cobble."

"Maybe another time. I've had enough for one night." That was for damned sure.

AS WE DROVE out of the Village, Mr. O'Nelligan started in with his reflections on the investigation. "The late Miss Cob-ble seems to have left a trail of quarrels and bad feelings in her wake. Thus far we know of her confrontations with Byron Spires, Patch Doonan, and the singer known as Crimson."

Oh, right . . . Crimson. Besides Mazzo, we hadn't remem-bered to ask anyone else at the Mercutio if they knew the story.

My friend continued. "Then there was her duplicity with Minnie Bornstein."

"That one's ancient history," I said distractedly, my mind barely on the case.

"True, it was more than fifteen years ago, but it does fit into a pattern that kept up until her death. The pattern of conflict and deceit."

Deceit. Lorraine Cobble wasn't the only practitioner of that particular vice who frequented the Café Mercutio. Audrey, the woman I was supposed to marry, seemed to have staked her own claim in that department. The raw memory of her ex-pression when she saw me across the room now came rushing back.

Mr. O'Nelligan must have sensed something was wrong, and he asked, "Is anything troubling you, Lee?"

"Troubling me?" I was going to add something harsh and flippant but opted for a tidy denial. "No, I'm tired, that's all. If you don't mind, I'll just focus on the driving."

Then I flicked on the car radio and zeroed in on the path of my headlights as they cut through the darkness. Every time an image of Audrey and Spires crept in on me, I clamped down on it and concentrated on the music being offered. No damned folksingers, just Frank Sinatra, Pat Boone, and Perry Como—guys with smooth voices, neat haircuts, and no claim on the woman I loved.

I DREAMT ABOUT Audrey that night. Audrey and the Statue of Liberty. My fiancée and I were standing together high up on the crown, staring down into the harbor. There was a fierce storm raging, causing the waters to rise and fall as if we were on the open sea. Some of the waves rose so high that I was afraid we'd be washed over. If that wasn't bad enough, pterodactyls were flying overhead. A swarm of them. (Yes, dreams are like that.) It seemed a perilous situation to be in—angry waves below and flying dinosaurs above. In the midst of all this madness, Audrey turned to me and said something that she actually *had* once said—in real, waking life, I mean—when we'd been out strolling one evening.

"Let's agree to be a hundred years old together."

"Impossible," I responded in the dream, as I had in reality. "I'm older than you. When you're one hundred, I'll be one hundred and three."

"Then you'll just have to stop at one hundred, Lee, and wait for me to catch up."

In real life, I'd then made some little joke and we'd squeezed closer together and kept strolling. In the dream, it went differently. When Audrey suggested I needed to let her catch up, I cursed, climbed up on the edge of Lady Liberty's crown, and threatened to jump. Staring down into the sea mist below, I saw a number of ghostly figures writhing and beckoning. I suddenly wasn't so sure that this was the best course of action. While I stood there teetering, one of the pterodactyls swooped over my head and dove down toward the ghostly beckoners. Only it wasn't a pterodactyl anymore—it was Lorraine Cobble. Then, above me, the remaining pterodactyls began to explode, accompanied by Audrey's high-pitched, wild laughter.

As I say, dreams are like that.

PART 2

Tangled Roots

Folly is an endless maze;
Tangled roots perplex her ways;
How many have fallen there!
They stumble all night over bones of the dead;
And feel—they know not what but care;
And wish to lead others, when they should be led.
——*"The Voice of the Ancient Bard"*
Songs of Experience, *William Blake*

CHAPTER ELEVEN

NEARLY EVERY SATURDAY morning for the last five years, Audrey and I had gone to breakfast at the Bugle Boy Diner. Sometimes we would have been out together the night before; sometimes we might not have seen each other for several days. Either way, assuming we were both in town, it was our habit, our ritual, to break bread at our local diner.

I remember the first time. It was the same day that Audrey started working at the Thelmont Five-and-Dime. A couple named the Jeromes had opened that store nearly three decades before, and when Old Man Jerome died, his widow decided she needed help running the place. I wanted to get Audrey off to a good start, so I offered to meet her early and treat her to breakfast. We'd shared lunches and dinners before at the Bugle Boy, but that day was our first joint breakfast there. Midway through, we agreed that this was the meal that the Bugle Boy did best—that, in fact, *all* diners did best. In our months of steady dating, we'd begun to assemble a catalog of life's little truths, which, we realized, not everyone necessarily subscribed to. *We* did, though. That particular morning, over our pancakes, we'd ticked them off methodically to see how many we remembered.

"St. Bernards are one part dog and two parts tongue," I began.

"Pistachio ice cream is a mistake."

"President Eisenhower would be disturbing with hair."

"Babies look like marshmallows."

"Shovels should be shaped like spoons."

"Fred Mertz is a lousy landlord."

"Frankenstein is scarier than Dracula."

"But the Creature from the Black Lagoon is ickier," Audrey said emphatically.

We must have gone on with a dozen more truths before adding *Breakfast is the best meal in the world.*

"We should come here next Saturday," Audrey insisted. "Then the one after that, and the one after that, and again after that."

"That's a lot of Saturdays. How long should we keep coming?"

"Forever and a day, Lee. That's how long."

So we had, almost every Saturday for five years.

But not today. The morning after our unexpected encounter at the Mercutio was a different brand of Saturday. The night before, while I'd been on duty, she'd been on the sly, in the company of another man. To my mind, that put our breakfast ritual in definite jeopardy. What would we chat about over our muffins? What new cute little truth would we find to add to

marshmallow babies and icky fish-men? How about this one:
You can't trust anyone—not even your own fiancée.

I'd been up for more than an hour when the phone rang. I
considered letting it jangle itself into oblivion but eventually
gave in and answered it. Audrey.

The tenseness in her voice was palpable. "We should meet
this morning."

"I'm in no mood for breakfast."

"Not breakfast. We can just walk somewhere. We can talk."

"Talk? Talk about what?"

"Lee . . ."

I thought about slamming the phone down. Came close. Instead, I went with the hackneyed "We've nothing to talk about."

"Really, Lee?"

I suddenly felt stupid. Stupid and angry and broken. Of
course there was something to talk about. *Miles* of things to
talk about.

"Where are you, anyway?" I didn't try to keep the edge out
of my voice. "Still in the Village?"

"No, I'm at my Aunt Beth's in Yonkers. Since last night."

I'd forgotten she had a relative down there, probably only
about a half hour's drive north of Greenwich Village.

"That's where you stayed the night?"

"Yes. I'll be back in Thelmont in an hour. Can we meet
then?"

I grunted in the affirmative. We agreed to meet on the town
green and take it from there. I rang off, showered, and shoved
some burnt toast and undercooked eggs into my mouth. It definitely was no Bugle Boy breakfast.

* * *

I DROVE UP Thelmont's classic small-town main drag, glancing around for Audrey's Buick without success. The five-and-dime and the Bugle Boy were among the couple dozen modestly thriving businesses that lined the street. I'd lived in this town since I was seventeen, and Main Street was like a blueprint of my youth. I'd gotten my first professional shave at Owen's Barber Shop; I'd drawn my first paycheck at Selgino's Stationery; Eden Florists was where I'd gone to pick up flowers for Mom's funeral; I'd first met Audrey at the soda fountain of Rowland's Drug Store; and Huntington's Crystal Shop was where I'd bought my first Christmas present for her—a tiny grinning cupid. Sappy, I know, but it was a new romance back then . . .

I parked Baby Blue and walked over to the green. Glancing at my wristwatch, I saw that I was a few minutes early—or a couple of years late, depending on how you looked at it. If I hadn't put off marrying Audrey for so long, maybe I wouldn't be standing here now, trying to digest my own cooking and dreading our pending conversation. I settled onto a park bench—but only for the five seconds it took me to remember that it was the same one Audrey and I had sat on the night of our first date. Jarred by the memory of those early kisses, I popped back to my feet and went to lean against the large lone oak situated in the center of the green. It felt somehow like a kindred spirit.

I didn't have to wait long before Audrey appeared, walking toward me as hesitantly as I'd want her to. Once she was abreast of me, I stepped away from the tree and gave her what I hoped was a curt, masculine nod that registered supreme disapproval. I had decided that she was going to be the one to speak first. I had my dignity.

She complied, obviously nervous. "The traffic was a little thick. Hope you weren't waiting long."

I wasn't going to make this easy for her. Or me. I provided no information as to how long I'd waited.

In the face of my silence, she pressed on. "I need to explain why I ran out like that last night without even talking to you."

"*That's* what you need to explain?" I had maintained as much of my strong, silent male persona as I could—about twenty seconds' worth. My anger now came gushing out shrilly. "How about the fact that you were there at all? Or that you were there with that punk Spires? Seems like there's a boatload of explanations you owe me."

It took her a few moments to reply. "Yes, you're right. I need to tell you everything."

Suddenly, the previously benign word "everything" had acquired a weight and a disturbing power that I didn't want to see unleashed. I wasn't certain at all that I wanted to know *everything*. A black wave of nausea rose from breadbasket to brains, and I felt more than a little dizzy. I managed to squeeze out one word: "How?"

My monosyllabic query seemed to throw Audrey. She narrowed her eyes and parted her lips in an unspoken question.

I realized I needed to expand on my sentence. "*How* could you do this to me?"

My words seemed to hit Audrey like a belly punch, and she actually drew her hands to her stomach. Her face reddened as tears rose in her eyes. "Lee." She had become monosyllabic herself.

My thinking process had slowed to Neanderthal level. I didn't know whether to scream out in primitive torment or gather Audrey up in an embrace of comfort. I opted for simply standing there and waiting to see if she could summon more words.

She could, but not before gulping for air for several seconds. "Lee, I never ever meant to hurt you."

"Never ever . . ." I repeated the phrase mechanically. It seemed to be something out of a fairy tale—an ugly, hapless one with a lousy ending: *And they never ever were happy again.*

Audrey pulled a handkerchief from her purse and dragged it over her face. There was nothing ladylike or genteel about the gesture. Clearly, the floral-patterned cloth had ceased to be a hankie and was now more like the sop rag that a cornerman would use to wipe his boxer's bloodied face. Once she'd tucked the handkerchief away, I studied her features. The button nose, full lips, hazel eyes, and short, sassy brown hairdo were all there, but they somehow couldn't come together in the pretty, perky way they usually did. Right now, Audrey *did* have the look of someone who'd just been pummeled. Not outside but within, where it really hurt.

She cleared her throat. "I'll tell it from the beginning."

I didn't want to hear the tale chronologically. I wanted to hear the most dreadful part first. "Are you sleeping with Byron Spires?"

"No!" The firmness in her voice gave me hope, a hope that was further fortified when actual resentment crept into her tone. "Is that what you think of me?"

I tried to get out my own "No!" as quickly and firmly she'd gotten hers out.

Audrey drew herself up. "Just because I'm down in bohemia doesn't mean I've become a bohemian girl. Not in that way."

"In what way, then?"

She sighed. "A few days after you and I went to the Café

Mercutio, you were out of town working on a case, and I decided I wanted to go back. It seemed like such an interesting place."

"Meaning Byron Spires seemed like such an interesting guy."

"Yes," she said very softly, "but it wasn't just him. It was the whole scene."

"So you went down alone."

"Like I say, you were out of town, and I knew I could spend the night with Aunt Beth in Yonkers. It was a little adventure for me."

"An adventure," I parroted. "Of course, Spires remembered you from our earlier visit. I'm sure he was pleased to have you in his den again."

Audrey drew in a deep breath, as if filling her sails for a difficult voyage. "Yes, he was performing that night. I was sitting alone, so he joined me after his set, and we talked and had a little wine—not too much—and he told me about his travels and his music. It was . . . nice."

Nice. Again, a previously harmless word had suddenly become odious.

She continued. "He struck me as such a different kind of person than I'm used to. So are all the people down there, really. Of course, the Village itself is so very different from Thelmont. I mean, if you took the people who live in the Village and dropped them right here, it would seem like some sort of crazy carnival, wouldn't it?"

I was in no mood to speculate on cross-pollination. "So you kept going down without telling me."

"You weren't here. You'd flown out to California to help your sister."

"You and I spoke by phone a couple of times, though, and you sure didn't mention it then."

"We pretty much just talked about Marjorie's health, didn't we?"

"Sure, but you could have slipped in a passing reference to your new boyfriend."

Audrey shut her eyes and exhaled deeply. I was past trying to guess which particular emotions were gripping her now. I sure didn't have a clue as to what my own were. They were raw and ragged, that much I could tell you.

Audrey reopened her eyes and fixed them on my own. "Byron's not my boyfriend."

"Don't tell me he's your new fiancé." I said it in spite, but once the words had hit the air, I wondered, for a quick illogical moment, if I'd stumbled on the truth.

Audrey seemed to have regained some of her composure. "Of course he's not my fiancé. And he's not my boyfriend. I really don't know what he is. To be honest, I don't know what I am, either."

"What the hell's that mean?"

"It means I'm looking at myself these days, and I'm not sure what I'm seeing. I'm closing in on twenty-nine, Lee. Most of the girls I went to school with are married and have kids. A century ago, I'd have been known as Old Lady Valish and people would make up stories about me being some loopy old witch."

In better times, that would have dragged a laugh out of me. Presently, I was well inoculated against all mirth and merriment. At that very moment, as if responding to some onstage cue, three little children came bounding across the green in a giggling, gangly sprint. Somewhere there must have been a script that read, *Enter stage right: The Kids You Never Had.* We watched the little frolickers vanish into the day, then turned to face each other once more.

"I've barely been out of Thelmont," Audrey said earnestly. "You at least got to travel a few years back. You saw something of the country . . . journeyed out west."

"Are you blaming me for that?"

"No, I'm just—"

"Because that was before you and I were really together."

"I know, Lee. It's just that maybe I need some little escapades myself."

Escapades? That sounded worse than journeys or adventures.

Audrey continued. "For me, the Mercutio is like entering some wild realm. The people down there see life in a very different way than people do here. Not every guy there worries about cash and a career, and not every girl wants a husband and babies."

I was getting even more confused, if that was possible. "So which is it? You want to be a wife and a mother or you don't?"

"I want . . ." She tilted her head back slightly, her eyes fixing themselves on the clouds above. Was the answer somewhere up there in the ether?

"You want what?"

"I want . . ." she repeated hazily.

Realizing that nothing else was forthcoming, I returned to a more concrete line of questioning. "Have you kissed Spires?"

That yanked Audrey back down from the clouds. "Just once, last weekend," she said softly, but directly, "and only for about half a minute."

Only half a minute? Breaking through my shock, my mind

did some rapid-fire calculations: a lot of wanton, passionate kissing could be squeezed into thirty seconds.

"I was the one who pulled back," she continued.

"Did he force himself on you?"

"No, not at all."

I wasn't sure what answer I'd hoped for there. Probably, under the circumstances, no reply could be satisfactory.

"Since we've been together, I've always been faithful," I told her truthfully.

"This is the only time that, well . . ." She changed course midstream. "I left so abruptly last night because I was stunned and disoriented. For a moment, I wondered if you'd tracked me down there. Though afterward, I realized that since Mr. O'Nelligan was with you, you were probably on a case—maybe something to do with Lorraine Cobble's death. I'd gotten your message earlier that you were out on a job. Is that why you were there?"

"Yes, it was."

Audrey nodded thoughtfully. "When I was mulling it over later, it occurred to me how remarkable it all was."

"Remarkable?" That struck me as an odd choice of words.

"I mean that it almost felt like fate that your work should bring you down to the Café Mercutio just—"

I cut her off. "Just in time to catch you in the act."

"Listen, Lee, I went down to the Village last night because I'd already told Byron I'd meet him. I'd set that up before I knew you'd be home from California. Once I found out you were back, I was going to call him to cancel, but then I got your message. I figured that since you'd be working anyway, I might as well stick to my plans. I thought it would be a chance to, well . . . to make things clear to Byron."

"What about making things clear to *me?*"

"Lee, I do want to be your wife."

"Yeah?"

"Yeah. I know we keep putting things off, and that we've sort of cast you as the culprit in that, but, well, maybe *I'm* the culprit. Maybe it's always been me. Oh, I don't know . . ."

"You can't have a fiancé and a . . . a . . ." I settled on an O'Nelligan-ish word: "Dalliance."

"I know that. If I tell you I won't see Byron again, will you believe me?"

I took me a long time to answer. "To tell you the truth, I'm not sure."

I'm not certain what I expected Audrey's response to be—a renewal of tears or a steely protest or a huff of indignation. It was none of these. Instead, she smiled in a sad, contemplative way and sighed again.

"That's an honest answer, Lee." She reached over and squeezed my hand. "I appreciate that. I need to get over to the five-and-dime now. I'll be late for work."

Then she released me, turned, and headed off across the green. I stood there in the shadow of the large lonely oak—though, in reality, I had no idea exactly *where* I stood.

CHAPTER TWELVE

MR. O'NELLIGAN'S HOME always felt to me like some secret library. His living room was lined with about a billion books crammed onto shelves that reached to the ceiling. Allowing only for windows, doors, and a fireplace, this arrangement no doubt saved him a bundle on interior paint since very little wall space peeked out. There were a few amenities—a couple easy chairs, a sofa, one or two small tables, a phonograph—but the chief decoration came in the form of the books themselves, their spines creating a rainbow of clothbound color.

I'd come straight over from my encounter with Audrey, and my mood wasn't what you'd call bubbly. To add salt to the wound, I entered to the sound of Elvis Presley posing the musical question "How's the World Treating You?" Yes, Elvis the Pelvis—via the phonograph—was crooning on about hopeless tomorrows and shattered dreams. Just swell. It wasn't unusual for Mr. O'Nelligan to be listening to a Presley record. After first seeing the gyrating rock-and-roller on *The Ed Sullivan Show* back in the fall, my sexagenarian colleague had become an ardent fan. Somehow this fit his quirky personality. For a person whose enthusiasms ran from Tolstoy to Superboy, it wasn't surprising that Elvis held as much appeal for him as, say, Mozart or Beethoven.

My friend gestured me into one of his easy chairs, lifted the needle off the record, and settled into the other chair. "I find that starting off with my Tennessean troubadour helps ease me into the day. That and a poem or two." He reached over and patted a leather-bound volume resting on the adjacent end table.

"Yeats?" I guessed.

"No, this morning it's something different. You're familiar with the works of Blake?"

I was feeling perverse. "You mean Amanda Blake? The one who plays Kitty the saloon girl on *Gunsmoke*? I didn't know she wrote poetry."

Mr. O'Nelligan narrowed his eyes. "Do you imagine, Lee Plunkett, that I don't see through your teasing? I refer, of course, to William Blake, master poet and printmaker. The title of his grand work, *Songs of Innocence and of Experience*, might strike a chord for one in the detective trade, wouldn't you say? Speaking thereof, I see you've come to propel us toward an early start on today's tasks."

"No, the opposite." I removed my glasses for a moment to massage my eyes, feeling suddenly very fatigued. "I'm thinking of calling Sally Joan to tell her we've hit a brick wall and are withdrawing from the case."

"What?" Mr. O'Nelligan sat upright. "We're just getting our sea legs with this one."

"This isn't whale hunting with Ahab, you know. This is an investigation—and one that seems fairly futile."

"I disagree! Where you see a brick wall, I see an open vista. Yesterday's view revealed to us numerous colorful characters and intriguing tales."

"Again, that's all fine and dandy if we're talking about a novel or movie. Not nearly so dandy when it's a case that needs solving. To level with you, I'm not sure there's even anything to solve here."

"How can you be so convinced of that? I feel that we've just begun to scratch the surface of this mystery."

"That's because you're a romantic. The notion of some shadowy fiend throwing damsels off rooftops appeals to you."

Mr. O'Nelligan suddenly looked wounded, and his tone hardened. "Is that truly what you think, Lee Plunkett? That I derive some romantic satisfaction out of this tragedy? That I would view a woman's death as some poetic amusement? Do you find me that cavalier?"

His distress shamed me. "Of course not. I'm sorry. I know you take this all very seriously."

My friend gave a noncommittal nod, then reached over to the nearby end table and plucked up his mahogany pipe. He stuffed it, applied a match, and sat puffing silently for a minute or two. This was out of the norm, for he usually reserved his smoking for evening time, and not every evening at that. *Moderation in all things*—that was Mr. O'Nelligan's motto. It was clear that my insensitivity had disrupted his routine.

I tried to make further amends. "No one would ever doubt your good intentions. After all, you're O'Nelligan the Noble Knight. I should know—I'm your squire."

This earned a mild chuckle from my Irishman. "Squire, is it? Certainly it's the other way 'round. You lead and I, in a sense, merely bear your shield."

"We both know that's not true, but it's nice of you to lie."

Mr. O'Nelligan blew out a ribbon of smoke. "Before you make your final decision regarding the case, can we take a minute to review what we know about Lorraine Cobble?"

"Yeah, why not."

"So, what we have here is a rather driven woman. An individual of noted enthusiasm dedicated to her area of interest."

I made an effort to join in. "Though that enthusiasm doesn't necessarily extend to her fellow humans."

"So accounts suggest. Although Lorraine did seem to bear affection for her young cousin. Also, there's evidence that she reached out the hand of charity to such individuals as Mrs. Pattinshell and the ancient drummer boy. The latter, by the way, I believe we should make our next visit."

"Next visit? Don't forget, I'm talking about dropping this case."

"Oh, I've not forgotten," my friend said dismissively. "I'm merely being speculative."

"As for her kindness toward Mrs. Pattinshell, remember, Old Widow Spooky-Tunes had something that Lorraine wanted."

"The ghost songs . . ."

"Yeah, if such things be. So it wasn't exactly unbridled charity at play there. Maybe it's the same deal with the old veteran.

Maybe Lorraine kept him around to drum 'John Brown's Body' for her whenever she needed her mood sweetened."

"Perhaps. So, to continue, what we have is a woman whom everyone knows, whom everyone has opinions about . . ."

"Usually *unfavorable* opinions . . ."

"A woman whom no one recalls seeing in the days leading up to her death."

"That last part's not too surprising, is it? After all, she wasn't married, had no family nearby, and seemed to keep to herself when she wasn't pursuing her musical interests. Plus, she lived in Manhattan, and it's easy to get lost in the city."

"True, though one might argue that Greenwich Village is like a small town unto itself." Mr. O'Nelligan took a last draw of his pipe and set it aside. "Now, regarding Lorraine's demise, no one we've spoken to can propose a reason why she would take her own life. In fact, she's not perceived as a likely candidate for suicide."

"That happens a lot, doesn't it? Someone kills themself and afterward everyone says, 'Boy oh boy, I never would've expected it of them.'"

Mr. O'Nelligan nodded. "Certainly that happens. Conversely, it also often happens that, following a murder, people declare their astonishment that anyone would want to kill that particular person."

"Though, in the case of someone as prickly and provoking as Lorraine Cobble, maybe it doesn't come as such a shock that she'd be the object of foul play."

My colleague folded his hands across his stomach and smiled subtly. "As you say, Lee. Perhaps someone did indeed desire Lorraine's death."

"Hey, hold on now!" I suddenly realized that Mr. O'Nelligan had played the old switcheroo on me—now *I* was the one arguing for homicide. "I'm in no way implying—"

"Your proposal is a worthy one, lad."

I wagged a finger at him. "Don't try to trick me, you wicked old leprechaun! I know what you're doing."

"I'm merely echoing your own sentiments."

"I *have* no sentiments. All I have is facts. Or, in this case, the lack of them. You can speculate all you want to, but when it comes down to it, there's not a single thing here that screams murder."

"You're absolutely correct," Mr. O'Nelligan said. "Nothing screams. But perhaps, just perhaps, there is something that compellingly *whispers.*"

"Wait a minute! You've got an intuition, don't you? One of your annoying, unreasonable, infallible damned intuitions." I sank in my chair. "God, I hate those."

"Is intuition really that undesirable an attribute?"

"It is if you're a private eye being paid to deliver no-nonsense, rock-solid information."

My colleague gave a quizzical little pout. "Do you believe our client would disapprove of the intuitive approach? Was it not Sally Joan's own intuition that led her to employ you in this quest?"

I tossed up my hands. "Stop with the quests already!"

"Never," said Mr. O'Nelligan calmly. "For to quest is to seek adventure, and to seek adventure is to live life."

"Oh, good grief."

"Not just *any* adventure, mind you. Not, for example, simply a hedonistic one. But a *righteous* adventure, yes, that is what gives value to our being."

I groaned softly. "This is way too lofty for me, and way too principled."

"Ah, you misrepresent yourself, Lee Plunkett. You're a man of great integrity—as anyone close to you can testify. Why, just recently, your beloved Audrey was telling me—"

A nerve had been struck. "Yeah, well, Audrey has her own adventures to brag about. Not necessarily of the righteous variety."

"What are you saying?"

As if a plug had been yanked from a dam, it all came rushing out of me: Audrey's clandestine trips to the Village, her rendezvous with Spires, our unexpected encounter at the Mercutio, and her apparent identity crisis. I definitely hadn't intended to broach the subject at all, but once I'd started, I couldn't hold back. Maybe it was because Mr. O'Nelligan, with his stately gray beard and canyon-deep eyes, had the look of some wise father confessor. Or maybe it was because I'd been stockpiling hurt, confusion, and resentment since last night and was desperate to disperse it all. Either way, I immediately wished I'd kept my trap shut. I knew well that Mr. O'Nelligan thought highly of Audrey—had been her friend longer than he'd been mine— and I instantly cursed myself for presenting her as anything other than upright and virtuous.

Depleted by my venting, I crumpled in upon myself and waited for my companion's response. Would he disbelieve my story and lambaste me for casting aspersions upon a good woman? Or would he accept my account and pronounce Audrey a wanton strumpet who should be hounded from decent society? Or—more judiciously—would his reaction fall somewhere in between?

Mr. O'Nelligan fixed his eyes on mine, quietly *hmm*ed, and, after a few long moments, spoke. "I certainly understand your distress, Lee. May I offer here a tale from my days back in Kerry?"

Now, this might have been the first time he'd ever asked my permission to unleash one of his Celtic yarns. Normally, Mr. O'Nelligan would launch into a homespun parable at the drop of a hat—whether I wanted to hear it or not. Somewhat stunned by the courtesy, I mumbled a yes.

"My Eileen and I had been courting for some time," he began. "I'd not yet gotten down on bended knee, but I think, at that point, we both knew that day wouldn't be long in coming. To be sure, we were much taken with each other. One summer eve, we were attending a local dance and having an exceedingly fine time of it. The hall was bustling with friends and kinfolk, and the band, as I recall, was a spry one. I got in many a dance that night. You might not guess it, but I had a nimble step back in those days."

I had to smile. "I'm sure you were the Gaelic Fred Astaire."

"Well, that *is* going too far, but suffice it to say I was much sought after as a dancing partner. Eileen had loaned me out to the Widow McLinley, a rather full-bodied, robust woman who fairly unmoored me every time she gave a whirl. I was thus engaged when into the hall strides one Johnny Fitzgibbon, an old beau of Eileen's. Now, young Fitzgibbon had been off in Dublin for two or three years, and this was the first time the village had again set eyes on him. He'd left town a humble tanner's son and had returned as a fine-turned-out barrister's clerk. He entered the dance garbed in a tailored silk suit and beaver-skin derby, sporting an elegantly waxed mustache. Furthermore, some form of expensive cologne wafted off the fellow like a breeze from a rose garden. Certainly, there was nothing about him not to hate."

I couldn't resist a laugh. "Yeah, I can imagine. Especially seeing as he was a former rival of yours."

"As you say. So, like a bee to a blossom, Fitzgibbon made his way directly to my Eileen and swept her into a dance. Followed by a second. Whereas one dance was perhaps understandable, to my youthful sensibilities the second was excessive. Then, just when I was about to step forward and reclaim my lass, Fitzgibbon coaxed her into a third dance. A third! Having quit the Widow McLinley several minutes before, I now stood alone seething in a corner, oh so young and oh so wronged."

"You said it was only a dance, though."

"I said it was *three* dances! It was that third, don't you see, that unsettled me so. The number three has a certain power to it, as borne out in myth and history. In my distraught brain I was forming an argument to sway my stolen paramour: *Oh, beware, Eileen! Three is way too weighty a numeral to be trifled with! Just look to lore and legend—three Fates, three Magi, Macbeth's three witches . . . Why, the Holy Trinity itself! Trifle not, girl, with that portentous third dance!*"

"Sounds a little overblown, wouldn't you say?"

"In retrospect, yes, but at that heightened moment, the third dance felt to me like a final coffin nail being pounded home, sealing the lid on my fate. A fate that was not to include Eileen."

"Though that's not how it turned out, is it?" I said. "It wasn't Johnny Fitzgibbon who ended up marrying the girl—it was the dashing young O'Nelligan."

My friend leaned forward. "Exactly! But if, in the end, I was dashing, it was only because I cast aside the feeling of being *dashed*—which is how I felt that night in my miserable corner of the dance hall. While Eileen no doubt admired the fine cut of Fitzgibbon's clothes and the tang of his cologne, in due course none of that really mattered. Our bond was genuine and enduring, and no silky barrister's clerk could sever it. Eileen returned to me after the third dance, and we never parted for the rest of the evening, much to Fitzgibbon's disappointment—and the Widow McLinley's, I might add."

"Though what if there had been a fourth dance?" I asked. "Let's say an excruciatingly slow one?"

"Ah, but there wasn't, was there? And if I'd let myself dwell on the possibility of one, I might never have kept my heart open and, ultimately, acquired the mantle of husband and father." Mr. O'Nelligan rested his hands on his knees and smiled gently. "And now, in my silver years, I would not possess the succoring memories of that good woman who loved me so well and so long."

Mr. O'Nelligan went silent, no doubt to let the story settle in and work its magic with me. To be honest, I wasn't sure how his situation compared to my troubles with Audrey. After all, my Irishman was possessed of an exasperating saintly nature—at least compared to my own—and could be expected to take the high road. The roads I seemed to find myself on were consistently low, unpaved, and muddy as hell.

I rose from my chair. "I'll let you know later what I've decided."

Mr. O'Nelligan arched an eyebrow. "About Lorraine Cobble? Or about Audrey?"

"About Kitty the saloon girl." I headed for the door and called over my shoulder, "She's the only female I really understand."

CHAPTER THIRTEEN

THE GIANT SEEDPODS FROM space were hatching more frequently now, turning many decent American citizens into emotionless alien zombies.

I crammed another handful of popcorn into my mouth and waited to see if the invaders triumphed. At the moment, being emotionless didn't sound half bad. I'd had more than my share of emotions today, so the idea of succumbing to a deep slumber and waking up conveniently soulless actually held some appeal.

After leaving Mr. O'Nelligan's, I'd driven around aimlessly for a good hour or so as the twin hurricanes Audrey and Lorraine spun wildly around my beleaguered brain. I ended up grabbing a forgettable lunch at a forgettable greasy spoon on the outskirts of town before making my way over to the Bijou to catch the Saturday matinee, *Invasion of the Body Snatchers*. The sci-fi film had come out last year, but our local theater always seemed to lag months behind in getting new movies.

I'd heard somewhere that the body-snatching aliens were meant to represent the dilemma of modern angst. Or was it the rise of Communism? Or maybe the collapse of vaudeville. Damned if I knew. Never one for symbolism, all I could make out was that ugly, hog-sized, intergalactic seedpods were conquering Earth, and nobody liked them.

After taking sanctuary for an hour and a half in the darkened movie house, I stepped out into the annoying splendor of a sunny April afternoon. There were no pods in sight, but any solution to my problems still remained unhatched. I drove to my apartment—a bland cave that served as a slap in the face to interior decorators everywhere—and sprawled out on my slumping couch to read the weekend paper. Apparently, Singapore was about to gain self-rule, Egypt had reopened the Suez Canal, and Russia was doing some kind of nuclear testing in Siberia. Not one of those worldly events seemed to have any bearing on the state of my festering grumpiness.

Tossing the newspaper aside, I found myself staring at the opposite wall and the two wooden plaques that hung there. Each depicted a Revolutionary soldier leaning on his musket. Their expressions were so grim and unappealing that Audrey, wielding her pointed sense of irony, had christened them Martin and Lewis after the comedy duo. Studying those minutemen now, it occurred to me that the real-life Dean and Jerry were no longer a team—having split up this past summer. Once the most popular entertainers in America, the pair had grown sick of each other after a decade of success and called it quits. If money, fame, and accolades weren't enough to keep the top act in the country yoked together, was it any wonder that Audrey and I were straining at the bits?

Having spent a good chunk of the day avoiding my responsibilities, I decided it was time to tackle at least one of them. I shoved myself off the couch and fetched the telephone. A minute later, I began laying out the harsh truths of life to Sally Joan Cobble.

"Miss Cobble, after thinking it over, I've decided I'm not going to—"

She trampled over my opening. "Oh, Mr. Plunkett! I'm so glad you called! I've been trying to reach your office but couldn't get through."

Yeah, not being able to afford a secretary no doubt made for a glut of missed calls. It certainly kept my workload manageable.

"Miss Cobble, what I was starting to say—"

"The letter! I've found that letter. Or, rather, Mrs. Pattinshell has. Turns out it got mixed in with a box of magazines that I'd passed on to her a few days ago. She's out and about right now, but she left a note saying she'd found the letter and to stop by later and get it."

"Yes, well, that doesn't really—"

"Wait, there's also another letter Mrs. Pattinshell says you need to see. Apparently, this one's . . . now, what was the word she used?"

"It doesn't matter because—"

"*Menacing!* She said it was fairly menacing. Oh, I'm so glad I have you to deal with all this, Mr. Plunkett. You're like my white knight."

Wait a minute now—had my high-minded Irish colleague secretly fed Sally Joan that line? Dammit! When would the world get the message that Lee Plunkett was about as knightly as Howdy Doody?

"Can you come down today?" the girl asked. "Soon? I need to catch a bus at six. I'm heading back home to Pennsylvania tonight. I can give you both of the letters when you arrive. I'm sure they'll help in your investigation."

My investigation . . . Sally Joan had finally paused to catch a breath. Now was my chance to lay down the law, to deliver the news that, from here on out, I was no longer in her employ. *Sorry, Miss Cobble, your white knight has been unhorsed, and your cousin's death ceases to be his concern.* That's what I meant to say.

Instead, much to my dismay, what came out was "I'll pick up Mr. O'Nelligan and we'll head down shortly."

Sally Joan was, of course, gushingly grateful. I, of course, was flummoxed that—yet again—my own traitorous tongue had sold me down the river.

AS MY COLLEAGUE put it, we were returning to the quest with renewed vigor. Well, "vigor" is not really the word I would have held out for, but Mr. O'Nelligan seemed so pleased to still be on the case that I didn't argue the point. Upon learning that we'd be heading back to the Village, my partner made last-minute arrangements to meet an old theater crony there for a late dinner. We agreed to conduct the bulk of the work together first, then let Mr. O'Nelligan leave to meet his friend. Considering what I was paying him (nothing), it seemed only fair. We arrived at Lorraine Cobble's apartment late in the afternoon to find a note for us taped to the doorframe. It was from Sally Joan explaining that we'd find her below at Mrs. Pattinshell's. We trotted back down a flight, and in response to my knocking our young blond client flung open the door and shot a warning finger to her lips.

"*Shhh!* Mrs. Pattinshell's in one of her trances."

Oh joy. We entered haltingly. The lights were all off, the

heavy curtains drawn, and a taper candle on the lace-covered table provided the only meager illumination. Next to the candle, a stick of incense sent up a thin, pungent spiral of smoke that drifted before the gaunt face of Mrs. Pattinshell, who sat on the opposite side of the table, eyes closed and head tipped slightly back.

"She's just starting a song," Sally Joan whispered.

"Thank God," I whispered back. "I was afraid we'd miss the concert."

I shifted my stance and, in doing so, trod on something underfoot. A shrill, angry shriek made my heart bounce, and a low, agile creature sped across the floor and out of the room. The Siamese. The cat-shriek seemed to serve as a cue for Mrs. Pattinshell, who now parted her lips and launched into song. Her singing voice had a cracked, creaky quality to it that fit perfectly with the notion of *ghost chanter* . . . assuming you had a notion that such a profession even existed. Her song selection proved to be a fairly disturbing little ditty. The lyrics—which normally might have been harmless, even whimsical—took on a kind of pallor when delivered by the entranced woman:

"Go wander to the wishing well where all the children gather near.
Come listen as they drop their gift into deep water. Can you hear?
Splash it goes and deep it sinks. A lovely gift from childish hands.
Then all the wee ones race away, shifting like the desert sands."

The tune went on for another verse or two but never did explain what exactly it was those little darlings were flinging into that well. Via the mood set by Mrs. Pattinshell, I was thinking it was some unlucky wayfarer that those creepy kids had ambushed and tied up. I was happy when the song ended.

Mrs. Pattinshell opened her eyes and fixed them unpleasantly on my face. "You."

"Yep, it's me," I confirmed.

The slender woman stood, walked across the room, and flipped on a wall switch. The subsequent flood of electric light made me wince.

"No doubt you are still not convinced of my abilities, young man, even when you witness them firsthand." Then, turning to my partner, she added, "Though perhaps *you* are, sir, given your life experience and your Celtic heritage."

"I beg to reserve judgment," Mr. O'Nelligan said with an easy smile. "This was, after all, my first exposure to the phenomenon. What spirit provided you with that song? It's not an air I recognize."

"Nor do I," Mrs. Pattinshell answered. "My provider was a seamstress who perished in a hotel fire some eighty years ago."

"I see."

"Just outside Baltimore, I believe." She reached over and snuffed out the candle with her fingertips. "Died quickly, thank heavens."

I considered offering condolences but instead said, "So, there are letters for us to look at?"

"Yes! I was just about to give them to Sally Joan when the song came over me. I just never know when one will come bursting in." Mrs. Pattinshell reached into her skirt pocket and extracted two envelopes. "One of these is rather menacing, I feel."

I reached out my hand. "So we've heard."

The lovable Mrs. P ignored my outstretched paw and instead gave the letters to my partner. Mr. O'Nelligan held up the top envelope for me to see. The name Lorraine had been typed across it, but there was no address.

I turned to Sally Joan. "This is the one you first described to us?"

"That's right," she said. "The one about her morning meeting. Like I mentioned, it's dated the day before she died."

Mr. O'Nelligan removed the letter from its envelope, and we stared down at it together. The typed message didn't waste words.

3/23/57

I'll come by tomorrow at 10. A.M.

The women stood watching us as my colleague and I began lobbing observations and speculations back and forth.

"No signature," I said.

"Nor indication of where the rendezvous should take place," Mr. O'Nelligan added. "Although we might logically assume it was Lorraine's apartment."

"Yeah, and then there's the fact that there's no address on the envelope."

"Which suggests it was hand-delivered."

"That doesn't make sense, does it? Why would someone hand Lorraine a letter saying 'Let's meet' when they're staring face-to-face? Unless . . ." I took a guess. "Unless the person came to Lorraine's apartment, discovered she wasn't home, then wrote the letter and slipped it under her door."

"A spontaneous letter would only be possible if the visitor arrived with a typewriter tucked under his or her arm."

"Oh, right," I mumbled, feeling suddenly dense.

"Though there's also the possibility that the visitor had typed up the note earlier, just in case Lorraine happened not to be home."

"Or maybe they went to the apartment at a time when they knew Lorraine definitely *wouldn't* be home."

"Well reasoned, Lee," my friend said, making me feel a shade less dim. "The suggestion being that our unknown party strongly desired for the rendezvous to occur not in Lorraine's apartment but in a place of his or her own choosing."

"For whatever reason . . ."

"Of course, we might ask, why not simply arrange the meeting with a phone call?"

I shifted gears. "What about a third party? You know, maybe the letter writer arranged for someone else to deliver it to Lorraine."

"Possibly, but again, we must ask ourselves *why.*"

Sally Joan interrupted our volley with a bright little laugh. "This is pretty exciting! It's quite a thing to see a pair of detectives deducting away like this."

Mrs. Pattinshell didn't look nearly as impressed. "Well, it *is* what they're paid to do, after all."

"Sure, but still it's fun. It's all very—" The young woman stopped herself abruptly, and the smile fell from her face. No doubt she'd just remembered that the subject under discussion concerned her dead cousin.

I moved things on. "Let's see that other letter."

The second envelope had Lorraine's name and full address written in what looked to be an untidy, masculine hand. The stamp was canceled with a local postmark, though the date was smudged beyond readability. Mr. O'Nelligan pulled out the sheet within and unfolded it as Sally Joan stepped over to read along with us. What we had here was not just a terse note but an actual letter, short but complete:

"Dear" Lorraine,

So nice of you to screw over a fellow music lover in such an underhanded lousy way. Keeps me on my toes, that's for certain. Nothing wakes a guy up like having his song list stolen out from under him. Like being kicked in the head. So here's a big thank you for that, Lady Cobble. Please don't go thinking I'll forget your kind gesture. I'm not that sort. Call me Mr. Elephant. Long long memory, understand? Did you know elephants can hide in the shadows and pounce on someone unexpectedly? It's true.

Forever yours,

Cardinal

I looked over at Mrs. Pattinshell. "I suppose you're right—this comes off as more than a little menacing."

My nemesis squeezed out a gratified smirk. "Of course. Did you doubt me?"

I refused to fall into the trap of answering that.

"This is the first time I've seen this letter." Sally Joan gave a little shudder. "It's nasty, isn't it? So confusing. Lorraine certainly never mentioned it to me."

"Do either of you know who this Cardinal guy is?" I asked. Both women shook their heads.

"Isn't a cardinal some sort of Roman Catholic leader?" Sally Joan ventured. "Like a bishop? Lorraine wasn't Catholic, though. She wasn't anything, really."

Representing his faith, Mr. O'Nelligan offered a definition. "A cardinal is a high ecclesiastical official, in rank just below the pope himself."

"Such as Cardinal Spellman, the archbishop of New York," Mrs. Pattinshell added.

"Fair enough," I said. "Though I'm guessing *he's* not our Mr. Elephant."

Mr. O'Nelligan read aloud one line of the letter. "*Nothing wakes a guy up like having his song list stolen out from under him.* A stolen song list . . . Pray tell, where have we recently heard of such a thing, Lee?"

It flashed upon me. "From Minnie Bornstein! Crimson! The musician whose set Lorraine pinched and performed."

My colleague nodded. "Yes. Mrs. Bornstein admitted to being uncertain of the name. I'd venture that what she remembered as Crimson was, in fact, *Cardinal*—a crimson-feathered bird."

Sally Joan looked baffled. "Wait, what's this about Lorraine stealing a musician's set?"

Gently, but accurately, Mr. O'Nelligan repeated the anecdote as Minnie had told it to us. The young woman quickly swapped confounded for crestfallen.

"Does this surprise you?" I asked. "That your cousin would have done such a thing?"

"Yes!" Sally Joan answered impulsively. A second later, she followed with a softer, sadder, "No. Oh, I can't really say . . ."

Mr. O'Nelligan returned both letters to their envelopes and slipped them into his jacket pocket. "Well, there is certainly much to ponder here. Perhaps we can now go make the acquaintance of Mr. Boyle, the drummer boy of lore."

"That gentleman is old as Methuselah," Mrs. Pattinshell noted. "Nonetheless, one must admit that he still has his wits about him."

"Hold on!" Sally Joan's eyes had gone wide. "What about this new clue? I mean the second letter. It *is* a clue, isn't it? This man Cardinal obviously had threatened Lorraine, claiming he wouldn't forgive her for . . . well, for what he believed was an injustice. How do we know that *he* isn't the one who killed her? He's our best suspect, isn't he?"

"He may well be," my partner said calmly. "But at present, we know precious little about him."

"Then go down to the Café Mercutio! They may know something there."

"We shall certainly make the café our destination, Miss Cobble. This very evening. For the moment, however, Mr. Boyle is near at hand, and seeing as he had a connection with your cousin, it could be advantageous to meet him before we journey on."

"I guess you know what you're doing," our client responded, though her tone suggested that maybe she wasn't all that sure.

"I presume I may now reclaim my living space?" Mrs. Pattinshell drew herself up in a posture of royal inconvenience. "If that isn't too much to wish for."

I got it out before Mr. O'Nelligan could intervene. "Sure enough, ma'am. We wouldn't want to clutter up the room, just in case more of your spooks are planning a hootenanny."

I was immediately caught in a crossfire of withering looks— from my partner and Mrs. Pattinshell.

"You're quick to make light of things, aren't you?" the ghost chanter said testily. "Perhaps that stems from your unfamiliarity with Death. Don't fret, though . . . Death has a way of pressing itself upon even the most jocund of men."

Then her thin lips gave way to a terrible smile, curved like a Turkish saber.

CHAPTER FOURTEEN

SALLY JOAN ACCOMPANIED us back upstairs to Cornelius Boyle's apartment. Surprisingly, the person who opened the door there was none other than Tim Doonan.

"Greetings, lady and gentlemen!" Without a drunken brother in tow, the young Irishman had reverted to his more upbeat nature. "Well, Mr. O'Nelligan, I'm not sure how many unrelated Paddies we're allowed to cram into one apartment. There may be some city ordinance preventing it. Do come in anyway."

He ushered us into a small living room fitted out with a jumble of old, comfortable-looking furniture. The oldest thing in the room, by far, was seated in an armchair, scarecrow-thin and dressed in white, staring up at us with a quiet smile.

Tim gestured toward the ancient man. "I take it you gentlemen know the legendary Mr. Boyle, late of the Irish Brigade. Especially since you're standing in his abode."

"Actually, we don't," Mr. O'Nelligan said. "Except for a fleeting encounter in the hall yesterday."

Tim spoke to our host. "Look here, Cornelius, yet another Irishman for your amusement."

"All the better," the aged man said in a voice rough and a bit labored.

"This would be Mr. O'Nelligan," Tim explained, "and this here's Mr. . . . ah . . . Pickett, is it?"

"Plunkett," I corrected.

"Oh, of course. How could I forget? Like Joe Plunkett, the poor young poet the Brits executed back in the '16 uprising. Any relation?"

"Not that I know of," I said. "My Irish roots aren't too recent, and there's a lot of other things mixed in. I'm just an American mutt."

Tim chuckled softly. "Well, America is the land of mutts, no denying. More power to you."

Sally Joan had stepped over to Cornelius and now reached down to take his hand. "So good to see you again, Mr. Boyle."

The centenarian wrapped the young woman's hand with both of his own. "You, too, you lovely girl."

"Look at the man," Tim said with affection. "A hundred and five years on the planet and still quick with the flattery."

"What brings you here today, young sir?" Mr. O'Nelligan asked.

"Oh, not much. I like to stop by now and again for a little conversation. Sometimes I come with my brothers or Kimla, sometimes on my lonesome. Lorraine Cobble introduced us a while back. You see, Cornelius here was born in Galway like myself. Though, of course, he's got a few decades on me."

Mr. O'Nelligan turned toward the old man. "I did not detect a brogue, sir."

"You wouldn't," said Cornelius, still cradling Sally Joan's hand. "I left Ireland when I was five."

"I see. No doubt, ten decades will alter a man's tongue."

"No doubt," Cornelius echoed.

"I really should get a move on," Sally Joan announced. "I've got a bus to catch."

"I'll be departing, too," Tim said. "I leave you in good hands, Cornelius." He glanced at my partner and me. "I'm guessing you're here as part of your investigation?"

"Indeed we are," Mr. O'Nelligan answered.

Sally Joan gently released herself from Cornelius. "Oh, Tim, come over to Lorraine's for a minute, will you? She had a couple of Irish songbooks that I'm sure she'd have been happy for you to have."

She and Tim Doonan made their exit, leaving us alone with our prehistoric host. He gestured us toward the sofa, and we settled ourselves in.

"You're detectives," he said slowly but clearly. "The girl told me you wanted to talk to me."

I leaned forward and spoke extra loudly. "Yes, we would, Mr. Boyle."

"Make it Cornelius. No need to shout. I've got real good hearing for a man my age. That's what the doctors tell me. Good hearing to go with my good eyesight. I've pretty fine legs, too. I go for a walk several times a week, you know. Down four flights and back up again."

"Truly admirable," Mr. O'Nelligan said.

"Yeah, I moved in here near three years ago, even though my family thought the stairs would kill me. There was supposed to be a ground-floor apartment for me, but that fell through. Way I see it, climbing those stairs is what's keeping me alive. That and taking a nap precisely at four o'clock every afternoon. Consistency, that's my secret."

"So Lorraine Cobble's the one who brought you here?" I asked.

"Yes, she'd heard about me a while back and would come to visit. To learn some of my songs, you know. When I had to move from the place I was in, Lorraine helped set me up here. Nice of her. Of course, it made it easier for her to record those old songs from the war. *My* war, that is."

"We understand you were a drummer boy," Mr. O'Nelligan said.

"Second Corps, Caldwell's Division, Irish Brigade. I signed on as a drummer with the 88th New York when I was just nine years old. I was big for my age and claimed I was older. We were pretty much all Irishmen in the 88th. The whole brigade was. Anyway, Lorraine sure liked those old tunes. I'd sing her 'Tenting on the Old Camp Ground' and 'Aura Lee' and 'Just Before the Battle, Mother.' Would you fellows like to hear one?"

Just as I was about to state that we needed to stay focused on our investigation, Mr. O'Nelligan declared, "We would be much honored, sir."

"Here's one that got written after the war," Cornelius explained. "Long time after. It's called 'The Veteran's Last Song.'" Then in his creaky but surprisingly vigorous voice, the old man began (appropriately enough):

"I am standing on the summit of a century of years . . ."

He went on to sing of a generation that had known the sorrows of civil war, a generation of which he was one of the last men standing.

"We were boys when we enlisted and these wrinkled brows were clear
And our eyes were not dimmed in their vision.
The frost that never melts had not fallen on our hair
And our step had not lost its precision."

The song ended with a longing lament for friends dead and gone:

"We're going soon to meet them in the bivouac of the soul
As the shadows around us give warning.
Oh, I want to see my comrades when the angels call the roll.
All are ready for inspection in the morning."

The last words trailed off, and Cornelius gave a deep sigh, one befitting a century of living. "Lorraine particularly loved that song."

"I can see why," Mr. O'Nelligan said.

"She was a fine woman, Lorraine. The problem with living as long as I have is that you're forced to see so many die before you. When someone as young as her . . . well, it's just terrible."

"How long were you acquainted with her?"

"Almost four years . . . or ninety-four, depending how you look at it."

"Pardon, sir?"

The old man smiled slyly. "Think I've lost my marbles, don't you? No, no . . . I'll explain myself. It was back in 1863, early July, when my regiment found itself in Gettysburg."

Foolishly, I started to ask, "*The* Gettysburg?" but caught myself in time. There was only one Gettysburg.

"I wasn't but eleven," Cornelius continued, his voice seeming to grow stronger as he slid into the past. "Though I'd seen a thing or two of fighting by then. Of course, my weapon was a drum, not a rifle, but when those bullets get flying, they don't much care about age or intention. It was the second day of the battle, late morning. Our brigade chaplain climbed atop a boulder there to give us his blessing, and then they marched us out through the woods to a creek name of Plum Run. Just as I was about to cross, I heard something strange off to my right. Heard it even with the cannons booming up ahead. I turned, and there standing beside a tree on the edge of the creek was this woman with long blond hair, just staring off at nothing at all and singing. Yes, singing! There on the border of hell, in the midst of all these soldiers, she was singing to herself—some sweet, lonesome tune—like there was nobody around but her."

"What was she doing out there?" Mr. O'Nelligan asked. "On the edge of a battlefield?"

"That I don't know. Maybe she'd gone to gather water or wash some garments. All I know is that she was there in the flesh—though I might have taken her for my own private ghost if I hadn't seen other fellows turn to look at her. Though everyone else kept hurrying forward, I stood frozen in place, just staring at her and hearing that song. I couldn't make out the words, but her voice was so lovely that an odd kind of calmness came over me. For one quick moment, she turned and looked straight into my eyes. Then I was being bustled forward by the men behind me, and I lost sight of her."

"It sounds like something risen from a dream," my partner said in his flourishy way.

"Well, if it was a dream, I woke up from it real fast. I suddenly found myself in a big wheat field, full of yelling and smoke and bullets ripping through the wheat stalks. Truth is, we drummer boys were supposed to drop back before things got too hot, but somehow I got caught up in the moment and kept advancing. Finally, one of our sergeants grabbed hold of me, screamed in my face, and told me to get the hell to the rear. Just then, a stray shot drilled that man clean through, and he died right there at my feet."

"I've read a bit about the conflict at Gettysburg," Mr. O'Nelligan said. "The Irish Brigade sustained many casualties that day, did it not?"

Cornelius Boyle nodded. "One out of every three of our men went down in that wheat field. After the sergeant fell, a bullet tore through my drum, and that was enough to get me scurrying in a rearwards direction. When I made it back to the creek, I looked around for the singing lady, but she was nowhere to be seen. Nowhere at all. As it turned out, Gettysburg was the end of my career in blue. A few days later, a pack-horse kicked me in the side, breaking three ribs. They shipped me home, and I never did make it back into uniform."

A few silent moments passed before I spoke. "It's all a compelling story, Cornelius, but how does it tie in with Lorraine Cobble?"

Our host smiled thinly. "You think I'm just rambling, don't you? Well, I'm not. The first time I met Lorraine, that's who she reminded me of—that woman by the creek. They both were fine-looking with long fair hair, and when Lorraine opened her mouth to sing me a song, it brought me straight back to that calm moment before the battle. So you see, I had a particular fondness for her because of that."

"I know the police have already asked about the night she died," I said. "Whether you saw Lorraine or not. Detective Wilton told me everyone on this floor was away that evening. Were you staying with relatives?"

"I definitely was not," Cornelius answered firmly. "I was right here. The police didn't ask me a blamed thing. They never even spoke to me."

Mr. O'Nelligan cocked his head. "Truly, sir? And you being her neighbor?"

The old man snickered. "I suppose they figured a fellow my age was too rickety to bother with. Of course, if they had asked, I would have told them I hadn't seen her that evening. Though there *was* someone I saw out in the hall that night. Someone I was surprised to see there at such an hour."

My partner leaned forward. "Who was that?"

"Hector the delivery boy. Hector . . . ah . . . Escobar. Yes, that's it. Puerto Rican boy. His father owns a grocery a few blocks away. Hector comes by pretty often making deliveries to a few folks in the building, myself included. He'd already been by here a few hours earlier. That's why I was so surprised to see him again that late."

"What time was that?" I asked.

"Oh, it must have been at least nine thirty, maybe closer to ten. I heard someone in the hallway and stepped out to see who it was. Just out of curiosity. Down the hall I saw this skinny young guy standing near the upper stairs—the ones that lead to the roof. The light's not too bright out there, but I could tell it was Hector. I called out to him, but he didn't say anything right away."

"As if he were reluctant to respond?" Mr. O'Nelligan suggested.

"Maybe. So then I called out in Spanish because usually that's how we'd communicate. I spent a year in Mexico when I was young, and my Spanish is passable."

"I see," Mr. O'Nelligan said. "How did the conversation unfold?"

"Well, there wasn't much to it. I called out, *Hector, eres tu?*—Is that you?—and he answered, *Sí*. Then I asked what he was doing there at that hour, if he was delivering groceries. He said he was just stopping by to see if anyone needed anything."

My partner continued the questioning. "Stopping by after hours like that—was it something he was likely to do?"

"Not in my experience. I just figured maybe his pa was trying to drum up more business by sending him back around. I didn't much worry about it. Just told him I was all set for groceries and headed back inside."

"You say this was sometime between nine thirty and ten?" I confirmed.

"That's right. Maybe a touch later."

Mr. O'Nelligan and I exchanged a glance. Nine thirty to ten P.M. That would fit right into the official time range when Lorraine Cobble had died.

"Cornelius, did you approach Hector when you saw him?" my partner asked.

"No, I just called down the hallway to him."

"Might you show us the exact spot where he was standing?"

"Sure." With the aid of his gnarled cane, the old man rose slowly and led us out into the hallway.

As I'd already noticed, the wall lamps were dim and didn't do much to illuminate the narrow corridor. Cornelius' apartment was at one end near the main stairwell, then came another apartment, then Lorraine Cobble's. All three doors were on the same side. As we knew from our previous visit, Lorraine's was directly across from a flight of iron stairs that led to the rooftop. Our guide paused us there.

"This is where Hector was standing," he told us. "Between Lorraine's door and the roof steps."

Neither my colleague nor I said anything, just letting that fact settle over us.

"He was pretty much lurking in the shadows," Cornelius continued. "Kind of peculiar now that I think back on it— that boy skulking about that way. You might want to have a chat with him."

"Yeah, we just might," I said. "A lovely little chat."

CHAPTER FIFTEEN

ORNELIUS TOLD US HOW to find Escobar's Grocery, then vanished back into his apartment. Before leaving the building, Mr. O'Nelligan and I decided to try the other tenant on Lorraine's floor. If Detective Smack had blown it with Cornelius, maybe he'd done the same with Lorraine's next-door neighbor. In this case he hadn't. That individual—a vacuum cleaner salesman who'd only lived there a few months—informed us that he'd been out of town for nearly two weeks at the time of Lorraine Cobble's death. He'd barely even met her. Well, at least Smack had gotten that one right. We next checked to see if Sally Joan was still on the premises, but it seems she'd already left to catch her bus. When we descended to the street, we found Tim Doonan, clutching a couple of songbooks and doing his best to flag down a taxi. One whizzed by him without stopping.

He swore pleasantly and turned to us. "There always seem to be swarms of the buggers when you don't need one, but when you finally do, they're scarce as dodo birds. At least Sally Joan managed to catch one, running late as she was."

"I've a question, young sir," Mr. O'Nelligan said. "What is your assessment of Cornelius Boyle's senses?"

"You mean his wits?"

"Well, those and his sensory skills."

"Wits-wise, I hope I'm as sharp when I'm half his age. As for his physical abilities, they might not be quite as spiffy as he'd like to believe, but considering how long they've served him, they're still pretty damned good. After all, the man breathed the same air as Abe Lincoln, didn't he now? As Patch put it, 'If Cornelius were a tree, he'd have more rings than a brides' convention.'"

"An idiosyncratic comparison," Mr. O'Nelligan noted. (For *him* to label a thing idiosyncratic was really saying something.) "Speaking of your brother, you were starting to tell last night about his relationship with the waitress Ruby."

Tim stared at him. "Is it gossip you're after, Mr. O'Nelligan? You don't strike me as the type."

"We're conducting an investigation," my partner countered in an even tone. "It's helpful to know about those who peopled Miss Cobble's universe. One never knows what facts might prove useful."

Tim shrugged. "Not much to tell there. Patch and Ruby had themselves a bit of an interlude a couple months back. Briefly, you understand. Ruby has rather a penchant for that— brief interludes. Here in the Village it's not like it is back in old Erin, Mr. O'Nelligan. The young women can be somewhat more . . . casual, shall we say? Not to shock you . . ."

"I have spent time in the theater world," my colleague informed him. "I'm not easily shocked."

Tim smiled. "No, I suppose you wouldn't be, then."

The Unshockable O'Nelligan continued. "As to your relationship with Miss Kimla Thorpe . . ."

Tim raised his hand in another failed attempt to wave down a passing taxi. "Blast it. I'd better walk up to Bleecker Street. More likely to find a free cab there."

"We'll gladly stroll with you," my partner offered.

As the three of us walked together, Mr. O'Nelligan returned to his questioning. "Your relationship with Kimla. I presume that it's . . . more than an interlude?"

"Rather audacious, aren't you, sir? Well, I suppose private eyes need to be. Yes, Kimla and I are fond of each other. She's a darling girl, and I'm lucky to have found her." Then, seemingly as an afterthought, Tim added, "Of course, if I brought her back to Galway with me, we might have a rough go of it."

"You mean because of her race."

"As you know, Mr. O'Nelligan, there aren't many folks of her complexion in Mother Ireland. And you surely wouldn't find a checkerboard couple such as ourselves. Here in the Village, things that'd be uncommon elsewhere are taken in stride."

As if to illustrate this point, a man with a long, tattery beard, dressed in a Viking helmet and leather cape, crossed the street ahead of us and vanished around a corner.

"Moondog," Tim said, as if that explained everything.

Mr. O'Nelligan was not to be distracted. "Your young lady seems to have a stillness to her. A notable calm. It was admirable last night how she pacified your brother in all his agitation."

"Yes, Kimla knows how to soothe the savage Patch," Tim

agreed. "How to soothe me, as well. Not that I fly off the handle like my brother, but I can get churned up in my own way, and Kimla always steadies me. She's studied a bit of Buddhism, and it tells, I think."

I got in on the conversation. "Your other brother seems a pretty cool customer."

"Neil? Oh, sure. Neil can't be bothered to let himself get riled up. Too much expenditure of energy, y'know. Besides, as you've seen, Patch provides all the bluster that our family needs."

We soon reached Bleecker Street, and Tim again raised his hand and began scouring the traffic.

"We'll be stopping by at the Café Mercutio tonight," Mr. O'Nelligan told him. "Will you yourself be there?"

"I will. I'm meeting my brothers for dinner, then heading over there. Mazzo has a mix of music and poetry on Saturdays, and we're on the bill. A bunch of us are. It's always a bit of a challenge not to stumble over each other and end up covering the same songs. Of course, when we're there, the other singers pretty much stay clear of the Irish tunes."

The wronged Cardinal suddenly jumped to mind. "Have you ever heard of a musician Lorraine supposedly—"

That's all I got out. Just then, a yellow flash shot out from the traffic and slid over to our curb. The young Irishman jumped into the rear seat of the taxi and gave us a little wave of farewell.

"I'll see you gentlemen later, then. Happy snooping." He yanked closed the door, and the cab sped off.

Mr. O'Nelligan turned to me. "I prefer the term 'sleuthing' to 'snooping.' More dignity, wouldn't you say?"

"You're the one who reads dictionaries for fun," I answered.

"Not me. I don't care if they call it spelunking. Let's just get on with it."

"Such professional fervor! Lead on, Lee Plunkett. I am ever your liege man."

I had zero desire to know what that even meant.

A TEN-MINUTE WALK brought us to our destination. The green canopy bearing the words ESCOBAR'S GROCERY was squeezed in between signs for the neighboring businesses, a printer's and a cigar shop. This lineup made for a peculiar (yet strangely appealing) bouquet of ink, tobacco, and fresh produce. Beneath the canopy, several wooden stands presented a colorful array of fruit and vegetables. A pudgy, dusk-toned man in an apron stood there chatting with a woman cradling a bag of potatoes. By his age, accent, and apparel, I figured that this was the store's owner—and Hector's father—Mr. Escobar. When the woman departed, we stepped forward. The grocer turned to us with a good-natured smile, and I revealed our names and occupation. Immediately, the smile took a dive.

"*Investigadors?*" He stiffened. "Why do you come here?"

"We'd like to have a little talk with your son Hector," I said slowly. "He might be able to answer some questions for us."

His face reddened. "My son is trying to do good! There is no reason why you—"

He stopped abruptly, and I followed his gaze toward the doorway of the grocery. There stood a skinny young guy in a white shirt and black chinos, his hair whipped into a high pompadour. I wondered how long he'd been standing there. Apparently long enough . . . judging by the fact that he propelled himself out the door, shoved me aside, and took off down the street.

"Hector!" his father called after him, to no effect.

Now, as I've tried to make glaringly clear, I'm not the kind of PI they write hard-boiled novels about. Even if Humphrey Bogart hadn't died a few months back, I don't think he would have been anyone's first choice to play me in a film of my life. Maybe Stan Laurel. No, I was never one of that tough, tenacious breed that my dad had belonged to. So I'm not quite sure what motivated me at that moment to take off in hot pursuit of the fleet young Hector.

The teenager raced down a couple of blocks, then made a hard right turn. I sped up, my homburg flying off my head with the effort. Somehow I managed to keep pace with my quarry, but only barely. The only reason I was able to finally close the gap was that Hector turned down a narrow alley and wound up tripping over a trash can. When he emerged on the other side, I was within striking distance. To my own wonderment, I lunged—yes, lunged—and managed to grab him by the collar. We both fell to the pavement, locked together in an awkward wrestling match. We were on a back street now, not much more than an alley itself, and the few passersby all quickly made themselves scarce. All, that is, except for a quartet of young men who, in response to Hector's cries in Spanish, came running at us from down the street. In the lead was a huge, wide-chested guy in a brown bomber jacket.

From the ground, my captive looked up at them and cried, "*Toro! Ayúdame! Por favor, Toro!*"

My *español* pretty much begins and ends with the word *toro,* and since the lead youth was essentially built like a bull, I figured he was the Toro in question.

He stared down at us with a quizzical look. "Hector? Hector Escobar?"

The two of them engaged in a rapid Spanish exchange, which culminated in Toro grabbing me by my shirtfront and roughly hauling me off Hector. Now back on my feet—as was Hector—I took a moment to straighten my crooked eyeglasses. I tried hard to look unintimidated as the half circle of young hombres came a step closer, Toro in the forefront.

"So you guys are his friends?" I hoped I sounded fearless.

Toro, looming and glaring, said, "My sister once dated his cousin."

"Then that must make you blood brothers." I sure was choosing a lousy time to find bravado.

"No jokes," Toro cautioned me. "Why were you attacking him?"

"I wasn't. I just wanted to ask some questions, but he made a run for it." I pulled out my wallet and displayed my investigator's license. "Look, Toro, I don't have any problems with you and your gang. All I wanted was—"

"My gang?" The bull drew himself up even taller. "Do you think that every bunch of Puerto Ricans must be a gang? Do you think we're the Apaches or the Dragons?"

"We ain't," one of his pals spat out. "We're just us."

"I'm an electrician's apprentice," Toro said, pride evident in his voice. "I'm no gang bopper. I see you jumping one of my own, though, I got to step in. So, what do you want to ask Hector?"

"I'd prefer to talk to him alone."

"I'd prefer you talk to him with us standing here."

Since Toro was standing so well and so massively, I decided to comply. I turned to Hector. "First off, why did you run?"

The kid was intent on restoring his pummeled pompadour. "I heard you talking to Papa. Thought you were cops."

"What if we were?"

Hector avoided my eyes. "Don't like cops much."

"I got that. But why? You've had problems with the law?"

The kid smirked and shrugged. Toro, again reverting to Spanish, asked him something, and Hector gave what sounded like a guarded reply. That led to an extended, heated response from Toro, which, though I couldn't understand a word, had the noticeable tone of a lecture. Hector dropped his eyes to the ground and again shrugged—but this time sans the smirk.

I pressed on. "You know Cornelius Boyle? He's an old man—very old. A hundred and five. You deliver groceries to him."

"Yes, I know him," Hector admitted.

"Well, he told me a little story about you . . ." I related Cornelius' account of seeing the boy at that unusual hour and of their brief talk in the hallway.

"That wasn't me," Hector said flatly.

"Really now? Mr. Boyle says it was. This was the night that his neighbor Lorraine Cobble died. You knew Miss Cobble?"

"I brought her groceries sometimes. Not too much. People say she killed herself."

"Yes, that's what people say. On the same night Mr. Boyle saw you."

"I just told you!" A new fire filled Hector's eyes. "I wasn't there that night."

"You'd made a delivery there earlier in the day."

"Maybe I did."

"Then you came back after dark."

"No!" He turned quickly to Toro, and again there was a brisk exchange in Spanish.

Toro gave Hector a little nod, patted his shoulder, and stared down at me. "Hector's a good kid. He says he wasn't there that night. He's answered your questions, mister. Now he wants you to leave him alone."

"I'm sure he does, but I—"

"We *all* want you to leave him alone." Toro somehow managed to expand his chest to an even greater width, and I realized the interview was over.

Without further ado, Toro turned on his heel and led the others away, Hector included. I watched them disappear around a corner and swore to myself, softly but vigorously.

RETRACING MY STEPS, I only got halfway back to the grocery before I saw Mr. O'Nelligan approaching, gingerly bearing my hat.

Upon reuniting me with my homburg, he asked, "Did the youth elude you?"

"Not at all." I described my interlude with Hector, Toro, and company in as accurate—and face-saving—a way as possible.

My partner nodded. "While you were admirably risking life and limb, I took the opportunity to have a few words with the elder Escobar. He told me that his son had been involved recently with some rather iniquitous individuals."

"In-*what*-itous? Why can't you ever say things plain?"

He gave me an exaggerated smile. "Excuse me, Lee. Should I have said nasty? Naughty? *Bad?* Are those words plain enough for you?"

"As a matter of fact, yes. So Hector was hanging out with bad guys . . ."

Mr. O'Nelligan sighed. "It seems that there was an armed robbery in Gramercy for which two of Hector's friends were arrested."

"Hector was part of that?"

"He insists he wasn't. Apparently, the police more or less agree—although they did believe his connection to the robbers was perhaps too cozy. Consequently, Hector is on the police's radar, so to speak, which troubles his father a great deal. He says that lately the young man has been rather, shall we say, jittery where the police are concerned. Mistaking us for them might well account for his flight."

"Do innocent people usually run from the police?"

"They might if they feel they are being unfairly targeted. Be aware, there exists some real prejudice against Puerto Ricans, a prejudice that might even be harbored by members of the police force."

"Okay, that's one theory," I said. "Another is that Hector, who was seen on the premises the night Lorraine Cobble died, was involved in her death . . . and that's why he ran from us."

"And still another theory is that the antique Mr. Boyle was mistaken about seeing Hector that night. Or . . ." Here my partner paused and stared off, silent for a long moment.

"Or? Or what?" I prompted.

Mr. O'Nelligan answered quietly. "Or Cornelius Boyle deliberately lied."

CHAPTER SIXTEEN

FTER RUNNING A ROAD race with a kid half my age and barely avoiding a street brawl, I wasn't up for any more detective work till I'd put something in my belly. That something proved to be a vendor-cart wiener, murdered with mustard, sauerkraut, and an unidentified purple condiment. Mr. O'Nelligan, frowning at this delicacy, firmly begged off my offer to treat him to one. He reminded me that he had a dinner appointment later (which, I'm guessing, would include no gloppy hot dogs). After I'd wolfed down my all-American repast, we fetched Baby Blue and drove over to the Mercutio.

As we'd done the day before, we entered at twilight. The coffeehouse itself seemed to dwell in its own perpetual candle-lit dusk—at the moment, a very hushed one. No singing greeted us this time, and the Grand Mazzo wasn't on hand to provide a welcome in his hepcat lingo. In fact, the only other person in the room besides us and the waitress (not Ruby this time) was Manymile Simms, who sat at a corner table tuning a twelve-string guitar.

Mr. O'Nelligan approached him. "I believe you're the gentleman called Manymile. May we join you, sir?"

The big man looked up and answered in a smoky rasp, "I am and you can."

Seating ourselves, we declined the waitress' passing offer of beverages.

"You two are the detectives," Manymile stated matter-of-factly. "The ones been scrounging around asking 'bout Lorraine."

"No denying," I said.

"Mazzo mentioned you'd been on the prowl."

"Where's Mazzo now, by the way?"

"In his office raising up a poem or two. He's wanting to read some of his stuff tonight, only he's got to write it first. Says he likes to deliver it so fresh that the ink still stinks." Manymile chuckled. "Funny man, that Mazzo."

"We knew he was a patron of the arts," Mr. O'Nelligan said. "We didn't realize he was a poet himself."

"Mister, everybody's a poet in this city, in one damn way or another. Mazzo, I guess he's a bunch of things. Writer, ringmaster, radical . . ."

I nodded. "Yeah, we heard about him taking on McCarthy's people some time ago."

"Sure, down here we've all got our tales." Manymile's fingers now danced over the scarred old guitar, plucking the strings swiftly and expertly.

"Impressive," I said.

"Thank you, my man." He set the instrument to the side

and gave it a little pat. "Me and Philomena here been together a long time. Had me my share of women and a wife or two, but this lady here, she's been the most faithful. Manymile and Philomena—just like Romeo and Juliet, only nobody'd dare try to pry us apart." He let go a laugh.

"Your name is a unique one," Mr. O'Nelligan noted. "How did you acquire it?"

"Well, I done so much traveling and playing that some juke-joint owner slapped the moniker on me. Seemed fitting, so I kept it. I've been to all the forty-eight states but one, and that's Kansas. Kansas! Ain't that a kick? The state right smack in the middle of the country, and it's the only one I never happened to step foot in. Life can be a curious thing."

"It can indeed," my partner said. "On another note, I must say, sir, that you showed admirable restraint last night when Patch Doonan was trying to incite you into fisticuffs."

Manymile waved one of his huge mitts dismissively. "Just a misunderstanding, that's all that was. I gave Ruby a friendly little peck, and Patch got all stupid about it. That boy needs to put some distance between himself and the whiskey, that much I know. I ain't talking from some high and mighty place, neither. Truth is, booze laid me low in my own life."

"How so?" my partner asked, rather boldly I thought.

"In a whole pile of ways," Manymile said. "Hate to tell you how young I was when I started in to drinking. Picked up the bottle around the same time I picked up the guitar—and lost some good opportunities because of it. You know, I was once a lead boy for Blind Lemon Jefferson, the finest bluesman ever there was."

"Lead boy?"

"Yeah, since Lemon didn't have no eyesight, he'd hire on kids to lead him around. I was one, and he taught me a few neat tricks on the guitar. As it turned out, the job only lasted 'bout a month. Even at that young age, the liquor was having its way with me. After I misled Lemon into one too many doorjambs, he had to fire me. If I'd stayed on with him, Lord knows what I might've learned from that man. Still, there's no sense lamenting what's come and gone."

Mr. O'Nelligan nodded sympathetically. "I take it that, in time, you put yourself on a straighter path."

"I did, but it took some prison walls to do it," Manymile said. "One night in Baton Rouge, I got fueled up on some Louisiana moonshine and punched a fella so hard I broke his jaw. Normally, the law wouldn't be too concerned about one colored man whupping another, but it turns out that fella was Senator Kingfish Long's chauffeur. I wound up doing three years at Angola. Couple good things come of that, though—I took to studying on the Bible, and I got serious 'bout my playing. Once they let me out I decided either I steered myself clear of hard drink and fighting, or my life wasn't going to be worth much. I bought me Philomena, started to scrounge up some gigs, and never looked back."

"An inspiring tale," Mr. O'Nelligan said.

"That's why I hate to see someone like Patch Doonan boozing and angering up like he does. Not saying he's quite the wastrel I was, though he'd best take care or he will be. Anyhow, you fellas ain't here to hear all my trials and tribulations. You're here to do what you do—sniff about like hound dogs vexing a rabbit."

"That's one way of looking at it," I said.

" 'Course, the question is, is there even a rabbit to vex? Word is, you're thinking someone threw poor Lorraine off that roof. Seems a hard thing to prove."

"I certainly agree," I said for Mr. O'Nelligan's benefit.

"Not saying such things don't happen," Manymile continued. "For sure, in my own trade there's plenty of murder ballads that testify to that."

"What's a murder ballad?" I asked.

"Pretty much what it sounds like," Manymile said patiently. "A song that tells about one person killing another. There's a heap of 'em—'Stagger Lee,' 'Tom Dooley,' 'The Fatal Flower Garden' . . . Then there's hundreds of old English murder ballads, but they ain't in my repertoire." He glanced over my shoulder. "What are some of the names, Kimla?"

I turned and now noticed that a number of people had entered the room, Kimla Thorpe among them. She stood just behind my chair.

"Well, there's 'The Cruel Mother' and 'The Twa Sisters,' " she said. " 'The Bramble Briar' and 'Eggs and Marrowbone.' Oh, there's a lot of them, but I don't sing many myself."

"Me neither," Manymile said. "I prefer blues to murder songs. A man sings the blues and he don't need to put harm on nobody else."

"So, how would you define the blues, sir?" Mr. O'Nelligan asked. "I know that it's a uniquely American art form."

" 'Specially for Americans of our particular shade." Manymile lit himself a cigarette and leaned back in his chair. "When the blue devils—meaning melancholy and lonesomeness—got their grips in you, mister, then that's the blues. When you got no home, no money, no lover, you get to thinking dark thoughts, and you got the blues. Here's the thing, though—if you grab them dark thoughts and put 'em into your music, it's like taking a spoonful of medicine. Helps you feel better. Did I put that right, sister?"

Kimla, still standing near us, patted the large man's shoulder. "You always put things right, Manymile."

The bluesman laughed. "Keep up with the flattery. Now that the gray's creeping into my hair, a young gal's sweet talk especially makes my day."

Mr. O'Nelligan indicated an empty chair. "Please join us, Miss Thorpe."

Kimla glanced around. "I was just waiting for Tim to arrive."

"We'd be grateful for your company while you do so," my partner added.

Kimla slipped in next to us. "Are you on the bill tonight, Manymile?"

"I surely am," the big man answered. "For two or three songs at least. You, girl?"

"The same."

"Mazzo gets a bargain out of us on these poem nights, don't he? Signs up a bunch of us to play for a few bucks each, scattered in with the poetry. Not that I'm complaining. A dollar's a dollar."

I thought it was time to get back on track. "Tell us about Lorraine, Mr. Simms. How much of a connection did you have with her?"

"If you've been making your inquiries, then you know Lorraine wasn't one to do a whole lot of connecting. Unless, of course, it had to do with her song hunting and such. We first ran into each other in Massachusetts a couple years back. She heard me playing up in Cambridge and told me to come here and that she'd find me some gigs. She hooked me up with Mazzo and some other folks, and I was grateful for that, but it ain't like we'd go paint the town red together."

"So you weren't friends," I said.

"I like to think I'm everybody's friend, but Lorraine wasn't someone who craved the company of others. Kind of contrary that way, wouldn't you say, Kimla?"

The young woman answered softly. "I suppose you're right. She's deceased, so I don't like to speak unkindly."

"It's not unkind, just true." Manymile puffed out several rings of smoke. "Well, maybe now she's in the company of angels. Hosts of singing angels. That'd be nice for Lorraine, wouldn't it?"

"It would." Kimla, in her low-key way, seemed to brighten at the thought. "Angels singing songs that no living soul ever heard. I wish that for her."

The room was filling now, and the noise level rose accordingly. My partner leaned in toward Kimla.

"Are you a religious person, Miss Thorpe? Your young man mentioned that you study Buddhism."

"I've studied it a little. Dabbled really. Many people down here do."

"Buddha, bongos, and wild ways!" Patch Doonan was suddenly standing over us; he looked sober. "That's what makes these bohemians down here tick. How goes your sleuthing, friends?"

"The work progresses, young sir," Mr. O'Nelligan said. "It's as the old Buddhist writings have declared: Three things cannot be hidden—the sun, the moon, and the truth."

Patch grinned. "Hear that, Kimla? My countryman here can give you a run for your money with the Oriental ponderings."

Kimla looked appreciatively at my colleague. "You're obviously familiar with the *Dhamma*."

"Familiar but not fluent in," Mr. O'Nelligan said. "I do try to be aware of the world's sacred texts."

Patch smirked. "The only sacred text that concerns me is the beer list at McSorley's."

"Dear God, Patch." Neil Doonan appeared at his brother's elbow. "Must you add blasphemy to your other sins?"

"McSorley's Old Ale House is not a sin," Patch protested. "It's a place of deep reflection and wondrous moments. At least if you're a man."

"It's a men-only establishment," Neil put in for our benefit.

"That's right," Patch said. "Though, not a month ago, I saw none other than the late Lorraine march in there like Joan of Arc and drag a man outside. It was that wretched Loomis Lent she came for. Grabbed him by the collar and hauled him out the door before the barkeep could protest her presence."

"What did Miss Cobble want of Mr. Lent?" my partner asked.

"I wouldn't know," Patch said. "Apparently she'd seen him enter the bar, desired his company—for whatever unfathomable reason—and made sure she acquired it."

The third of the Doonan Brothers now came up behind Kimla and rested his hands on her slender shoulders. Kimla looked up and gave him a sweet smile.

"What's the order of battle tonight?" Tim asked the table in general.

"Mazzo told me I'm up first," Manymile answered. "Then some poetry, then some more music. Not sure 'bout the exact lineup."

Over the growing clatter and chatter of incoming patrons,

a high-pitched voice cried out energetically from near the doorway, "Detectives! Oh, detectives!"

As I turned toward the entrance, my eyes were snared by a gaudy display of stripes—wide, brash swatches of pink, orange, lavender, and green. It took me a few seconds to realize that I was looking at Minnie Bornstein, squeezed into a dress so vivid that yesterday's polka dots seemed downright drab. The plump music-shop owner beckoned with an animated wave. Mr. O'Nelligan and I excused ourselves from the table and went to join her.

Minnie downshifted from shout to urgent half-whisper. "Gosh! Dammit! Sorry, guys. Did I blow your cover?"

"We have no cover to blow, madam," Mr. O'Nelligan told her. "We are guileless and transparent in our endeavors."

"You betcha," I more-or-less echoed.

"I was hoping to find you two here," Minnie said, adjusting her horn-rimmed glasses. "Or just leave a note for you in case you dropped by. I found out a couple things concerning Lorraine that you might want to know."

My partner pursed his lips. "Have you now?"

"Yeah, last night after you left, I was telling my Abe all about our conversation. I mentioned that I told you about Lorraine stealing Crimson's set and all that. Now, Abe's got a mind like a bear trap—once he hears something, he never lets it go—but me, well, I can get a bit scattered in the memory department. Anyway, Abe says, 'Don't you remember, Minnie? You told me that story a while ago—it wasn't any Crimson, it was a fellow named—"

"Cardinal," I finished.

Minnie Bornstein looked deflated. "You know already? Aw, here I was thinking I'd help crack your case for you."

Mr. O'Nelligan promised her that any information was helpful and went on to show her Cardinal's letter to Lorraine.

"Any thoughts on this correspondence?" he asked.

Minnie read the letter over and handed it back. "Only that it confirms the story I heard. This guy sounds pissed off big-time, doesn't he? Think he's the culprit?"

"We're not sure if there's really a culprit at all," I said. "As for Cardinal, we don't know anything about him. Not even his last name."

"Meriam! It's Meriam!" Minnie beamed in triumph. "Abe remembered that, too. That's more info for you. Say, maybe I'm not such a washout after all."

O'Nelligan, the king of consolation, assured her that she wasn't, then asked, "Do you happen to know Mr. Meriam's first name? I presume Cardinal is a sobriquet."

"Nope, sorry. Ask some of the musicians here. Someone might have the lowdown on him."

"You said you'd found out a couple of things," I reminded her. "Is there something else?"

"Yes! Today I heard an interesting thing from a customer of mine, this guy Tucker who stops in occasionally to buy sheet music. He's a waiter but also an aspiring accordionist."

"Down here, isn't every waiter an aspiring something-or-other?" I asked.

"You're not kidding! Anyway, I mentioned to him about your visit—after all, I don't get gumshoes stopping in every day—and Tucker remarked that he'd seen Lorraine the very morning she died."

That got my interest. "Really? No one else seems to have seen her that day."

"He says she was having breakfast at the restaurant where

he works, Horton's Grill. He was in sort of a hurry today, so he wasn't able to tell me much, but he's working the evening shift there now. Here, I wrote the address down in case you wanted to pop in later and talk to him." Minnie fished a scrap of paper out of her purse and handed it to me.

Mr. O'Nelligan leaned in to read the address. "Ah! That's a mere two blocks from where I'm meeting my friend tonight."

"I hope you'll learn something useful," Minnie said. "Now, I've got to run. It's Passover in a couple days, and we're having a small mob over for Seder. I've got to clean house and clear a path to the dining room. Abe says I don't know a broom from a bowling ball, and I wouldn't deny it! Good-bye and good luck, fellas."

Minnie spun her sizable self around and headed for the exit. Halfway out the door, she stopped abruptly and hurried back to us.

"You two be careful, okay?" she said earnestly. "I'm sure you know your job and all, but do be careful. Sometimes I get feelings . . . like my Bavarian grandmother did . . . odd feelings. I got one just now."

"What sort of feeling?" I hated to ask.

"I'm not exactly certain. Something about . . . about one of you being in harm's way. Oh, maybe I'm just being foolish." Minnie Bornstein smiled wanly and patted each of us on the chest. "Just be careful."

Then she blew out of the room like a bright, bustling storm.

CHAPTER SEVENTEEN

FTER MINNIE LEFT THE coffeehouse, Mr. O'Nelligan and I returned to our table. The Doonans had taken our seats, but a couple more chairs were promptly dragged over for us.

"That was Minnie Bornstein, wasn't it?" Neil Doonan wondered. "The lady who owns the music store."

Patch laughed. "Jesus, do you need to ask? Who else would be brave enough to jam her girth into such a smock?"

"The room's crowded," Neil grumbled lightly. "I didn't have a clear view of her."

"She dresses like Fourth of July fireworks!" Patch argued. "You could spot her in a sandstorm, for God's sake."

"Oh, sod off," suggested Neil.

I intruded on this brotherly warmth. "Cardinal Meriam—does that name mean anything to any of you?"

Turns out it did.

"Banjo player," Manymile said quickly. "Skinny white guy with bright red hair."

"Hence the name Cardinal," Patch added. "Hair as red as the bloody bird. Hails from Canada, doesn't he, Manymile?"

"That's right. From Ontario, I believe. Good finger picker, that Cardinal."

"A sturdy voice as well," Tim Doonan said. "Kimla, what was that song he did about the shipwreck?"

" 'The Loss of the *Antelope*,' " his girlfriend answered.

"Sure, that's it. I really like that one. A good shipwreck ballad always does me in."

"So Cardinal lives here in the Village now?" I asked.

"No, he was just passing through," Manymile said. "He was only around for a month or so during the winter."

"He performed here?"

"Not at the Mercutio," Tim said, "but at a few other places around town. We caught him a couple times, Kimla and the lads and I."

"He had some style," Neil added. "Mazzo would have booked him eventually."

"Aye, if he hadn't left town in such a flurry." Patch added, "Not to speak ill of the defunct, but it was Lorraine who's to blame for that."

Mr. O'Nelligan leaned forward. "Are you referring to the incident in which Miss Cobble stole Cardinal's set of songs?"

Patch grinned. "Heard of that business, have you? That was Lorraine at her most conniving. It happened at a place on Bleecker called the Golden Hut."

"You were there that night?" I asked.

"Alas, I was not," Patch said. "Kimla here was, though, weren't you, lass?"

"Yes, I was on the bill," Kimla answered in her quiet way. "With Lorraine and Cardinal. Well . . . as it turned out, only Lorraine. Because Cardinal refused to go on after Lorraine performed almost the whole set he'd planned to do."

"So Cardinal was visibly dismayed?" my partner asked.

Kimla sighed. "Oh Lord, yes. I was sitting at the next table and saw him simmering the whole time. Song after song, he'd be mumbling to himself, 'That's one of mine, too.' When Lorraine finally left the stage, Cardinal went up to her and whispered something in her ear. I couldn't tell what he said, but they ended up swearing at each other and storming out a few minutes apart. I had to perform right after all that, which wasn't pleasant. I think I flubbed half the lyrics of my first song."

"Why would Lorraine have done something like that?" I asked. "Seems pretty underhanded."

Manymile gave a little grunt. "Bad behavior on Lorraine's part, no question 'bout it. I think, in a way, she thought she had a natural claim on any song that ever there was. Didn't matter what anyone else's intentions were. After that night, Cardinal made damn sure all the musicians hereabouts heard the story. Testified up and down the street as to how Lorraine Cobble done him wrong."

"Does anyone know Cardinal's actual first name?" I asked.

A tableful of heads shook in response.

"Were any of you well acquainted with him?" Mr. O'Nelligan asked.

Again all heads shook.

"He wasn't here very long," Patch said. "Just another roving gypsy who tumbles into town, makes a little ripple, then tumbles out again. I had a drink or two with him once, but that was it."

Manymile scratched his chin. "Sort of a touchy young guy, wasn't he? Took himself real serious."

"That he did," Patch confirmed.

"Didn't he get arrested once while he was here?" Tim asked.

"Yeah, that's right," Manymile agreed. "Wasn't much of anything, though. Some rich guy claimed Cardinal leaned on his car and broke the antenna."

"Desperado stuff," Patch said. "Anyway, after the incident with Lorraine, I remember Cardinal declaring that he was done forever with the city and all its shenanigans."

"So he went back to Canada," I guessed.

"Farther still," Patch said. "All the way to bloody Australia. Or so I heard."

"I heard it was New Zealand," Neil put in.

Patch shrugged. "Either way, he set a couple of oceans and a grand sprawl of land twixt us and him. Vanished into the cosmos, he did."

"Did he leave before or after Lorraine died?" I asked.

"Not really sure," Patch said. "I hadn't seen him for a while before her death, but that doesn't necessarily mean he'd already left for Australia. Anyone else here see him around then?"

No one at the table had.

I let this all sink in. "No one's heard from him since he left town?"

"Neither hide nor hair," Manymile said. "Least no one I know ever mentioned it." He reached over and picked up his guitar. "Well, Philomena and I best get to work. I see Mazzo just emerged from his dungeon."

The Grand Mazzo strode over to our table, waving a fistful of typewriter paper. "The opus is finished!"

Manymile rose to his full impressive height. "Good for you, maestro. I'll loosen up the crowd, and you can floor 'em with your fancy rhymes."

"Blank verse!" Mazzo declared. "Always blank verse. Should I introduce you, man?"

The big bluesman smiled. "Nah, if they don't recognize me by now, they never will."

Manymile slapped Mazzo's shoulder and marched over to the small stage. With a robust strum of Philomena, he jumped into a song about a Mississippi Delta sharecropper pining for a girl called Honeylips: *The sweetest thing that I ever done had.* His full raspy drawl filled the room like a great wave.

Mazzo dropped into the vacated chair and spoke loudly over the music. "How's the investigation going, gentlemen? Anything new and dazzling?"

I recapped the Cardinal discussion for him.

"Cardinal? Yeah, I heard about that cat," Mazzo said. "Banjo plucker. Yesterday you were asking about someone named Crimson, so I didn't make the connection. Lot of wandering minstrels sliding through these days. Hard to keep track of 'em all."

Manymile finished his Honeylips homage and then announced, "I'd like to dedicate this next number to the gentlemen yonder."

He gestured toward Mr. O'Nelligan and me, then launched into a tune called "Hellhound on My Trail."

My colleague turned to me. "Ah! It seems we're being serenaded. I'm quite humbled."

When Manymile had finished his short set, Mazzo jumped up and replaced him onstage.

Mazzo gave his ringmaster mustache a whirl. "Friends, I'd like to inform you of a mighty injustice that was perpetrated yesterday. Customs officers of our own fair land seized five hundred copies of the poetic epic 'Howl' penned by the beatific young Allen Ginsberg. Seized them because they consider that work obscene and objectionable. Well, I object to their objection! Here's a poem I just wrote, inspired by yesterday's events."

Consulting his pages, Mazzo rambled out a poem that, as I far as I could tell, had nothing to do with customs officials but everything to do with a swimmer's well-toned naked body undulating in the ocean. It took me several stanzas to realize that the description was not of a female but of a young man— specifically a cowboy, though how he'd traded the prairie for the seashore I'd no idea. In any case, the portrayal was fairly graphic.

Patch Doonan leaned over to my partner. "Don't be too stunned now, Mr. O'Nelligan. The Village can be a scandalous place."

"I'm not stunned," my friend said. "After all, do we not hail from the land of Oscar Wilde? He was the grand emperor of scandal."

Patch chuckled. "He was, he was. My, aren't you cosmopolitan for a Kerryman."

Mr. O'Nelligan never got to respond to that, since a loud tide of applause and finger-snapping now washed over the room. His ode completed, Mazzo bowed dramatically and called out, "Next up, the undeniable Miss Ruby Dovavska!"

Though I hadn't noticed Ruby in the room before, she now stepped out of the crowd to commandeer the stage. Still garbed all in black, the waitress of yesterday promptly became the poetess of tonight. With a toss of her long midnight hair, she explained that the upcoming poem had been composed after a sleepless night of absinthe drinking.

"I call this 'Billboards and Blood,'" she said in a tone that suggested she didn't much care *what* it was called.

Poetry, even at its most concrete, usually left me perplexed. Ruby's verses shot over me like a squadron of jet planes. For the most part, I couldn't tell what the hell was happening. Each line started with the phrase "The billboards of lunacy proclaim . . ." and then went on to further confound me. For example:

> *"The billboards of lunacy proclaim that Burbank mates with demons.*
> *The billboards of lunacy proclaim that Sacco ate Vanzetti.*
> *The billboards of lunacy proclaim that malt shops breed new Hitlers.*
> *The billboards of lunacy proclaim that Death's a frantic puppet . . ."*

I whispered to Mr. O'Nelligan, "You're the poetry connoisseur. Do you get any of this?"

"Well, it's certainly not Yeats," he whispered back.

"Guess not. Tell me, do you think it's true?"

"Do I think *what's* true?"

"That Death's a frantic puppet?" I tried to sound concerned. "Because that would really unnerve me."

My friend held a firm finger to his lips.

Ruby's second offering was called "Epidermis Enchantress." Her description of the title character was so lurid that, in comparison, Mazzo's nude cowpoke now seemed like a Puritan. It suddenly occurred to me that since Audrey had recently been partaking of the local nightlife, this sort of fare might have become commonplace to her. A prudish little shudder passed through me as I imagined my fiancée swaying dreamily to the carnal rhythms of beat poetry.

Patch Doonan reached over and poked my shoulder. "Sweet Ruby knows how to titillate, doesn't she now?"

"Sure."

"At a loss for words, eh? By the way, in case you're interested, there's Loomis Lent standing over there in the corner. He's the little ne'er-do-well I've told you about."

Patch pointed across the crowded room to a short man half-heartedly watching Ruby's reading. Lent was five feet six at best, probably in his late thirties, with a longish nose, untidy blond hair, and a smudgy mustache. His nondescript clothes looked like they'd been slept in. In fact, everything about the guy seemed rumpled.

"Perhaps we should have a word with him," Mr. O'Nelligan said.

"If it pleases you, but keep a hand on your wallets." Patch glanced at Kimla. "Now, don't go bounding madly to his defense, girl. Who knows what manner of mischief that rat's inclined to?"

"Stow it, Patch." Tim stared warningly at his brother. "I've told you not to harass Kimla."

The young woman patted Tim's arm. "It's all right. I'm not feeling harassed."

Patch flashed a toothy grin. "See, Timbo? The lasses always find me charming."

"I wouldn't go as far as that," Kimla said with a sly little smile.

Patch laughed loudly. "Oh, you wee provoker!"

"Hush now and listen to the damned poem!" Neil Doonan demanded, though I think he was barely listening himself.

That might have changed once Ruby began screaming out a long string of profanities. At that point, I figure, everyone was listening. I certainly was as she ended with a fiery declaration:

"Kill! Kill! We live just to kill!"

CHAPTER EIGHTEEN

S THE WORD "KILL" ECHOED across the hushed room, Ruby yielded the stage to another poet. Patch led us over to where Loomis Lent stood slumped against a wall directly beneath a sideshow poster featuring Yazzy the Astounding Rodent Lad. The gaudy illustration showed an individual with jutting teeth and an impossibly extended nose. In view of Patch's uncharitable references to Loomis, the poster seemed ironic.

Ignoring my partner and me, Loomis fixed Patch with a harsh stare. "What do you want, Doonan?"

Patch grinned tauntingly. "Why the tone of spite, Loomis? I'm only attempting to expand your social circle. These gentlemen here would like to make your acquaintance."

Loomis eyed us with suspicion. "Who are they?"

"I'll let them handle their own introductions. Just don't be an utter shite, will you now, Lent? That's a good fellow."

"Go to hell!"

"All in good time." Patch turned and winked at me. "Remember what I said about your wallets."

Once Doonan had left us, Loomis tensed and pressed himself deeper into his corner. "What do you people want from me?"

"Just a moment of your time, sir." Mr. O'Nelligan said.

As my colleague laid out our pedigree and purpose, Loomis listened intently, his eyes widening.

"This is superb!" He seemed weirdly thrilled. "Really superb! Yeah, private eyes . . . that's just what's needed."

"Glad to hear it," I said.

Loomis glanced furtively around, as if fearing eavesdroppers, then signaled us to follow him. Moments later, the three of us were standing outside in the amber circle of a streetlamp's glow. Loomis ran a twitchy hand across his face in what might have been an effort to smooth his mustache. Instead the gesture left his upper lip looking like an overused toothbrush.

"I told everyone that Lorraine didn't bump herself off," he said, agitation propelling his words. "Does anybody ever believe Loomis? No they do not! Though maybe they will now, huh? Now that you guys are kicking over stones. What's under them, that's what I want to know. Maybe bones and secrets, yeah? Poor Lorraine!"

I halted his rant. "We're not jumping to any conclusions, one way or another. We're just—"

"This dirty, filthy city!" Loomis raced on. "The Village is part of it. Don't let the so-called hepcats here fool you that they're knee-deep in paradise. Hell no, there's plenty of putridity all around. You guys know what putridity is?"

Mr. O'Nelligan did, of course. "Decay. Decomposition. Corruption."

Loomis nodded emphatically. "That's it! The earth's de- praved with putridity and stinking of violence—the Bible says something like that."

"Well, yes, *something* like that," my partner conceded.

"And now Lorraine's dead," Loomis said in a tone of finality. Somehow I was missing his point here.

Mr. O'Nelligan got back to business. "Mr. Lent, your name has come up occasionally in reference to Miss Cobble."

"Sure, why shouldn't it? We were musketeers."

"Musketeers?"

"Yeah, like in *The Three Musketeers,* only there were two of us. It's that book, you know. By some French guy."

"I'm well aware of the works of Monsieur Dumas," my part- ner sniffed. "Père *and* fils. So you're claiming that your rela- tionship was a close one?"

"Yeah, yeah. Like I say, musketeers. That's what I called us."

"Right, but did *she* call you that?" I asked. "Or was Lor- raine not that gushing about your friendship?"

"Lorraine never gushed about anyone or anything." Loomis sounded defensive now. "I mean, for example, she and I were out having a drink together this past Boxing Day, when who should walk into the lounge but Zelda Fitzgerald. Yeah, F. Scott's wife! We had a martini with her even, but Lorraine didn't act impressed at all, and this was Zelda Fitzgerald we're talking about."

Mr. O'Nelligan eyed him carefully. "This past winter, you say?"

"Yeah, that's right."

"Sir, Zelda Fitzgerald died a good number of years ago. Back in 1948, I believe."

"No, this was her."

"I think not."

"Or maybe F. Scott's other wife."

"There was only one Mrs. Fitzgerald," my partner stated.

Wisely, Loomis let it go—maybe sensing it was dangerous to play chicken with Mr. O'Nelligan where literary data was concerned.

"Anyway, how did my name come up?" he wanted to know.

Briefly, I recounted the story about Patch Doonan sending the bottle of wine over to Loomis and Lorraine, and her subsequent outburst.

Loomis responded with a scowl. "Yeah, Doonan's a goddamned idiot. Always trying to stir things up and get my goat. Stupid mick." Then, seeming to remember my colleague's brogue, he added, "I enjoy the Irish for the most part. Especially when they're sober."

You really haven't experienced a withering look unless you've received one from Mr. O'Nelligan—as Loomis learned at that moment. Properly withered, he dropped his eyes and gave his mustache another rumpling swipe.

My partner continued evenly. "Would you say Lorraine's reaction to Patch was threatening in any way?"

"If it was, he deserved it," Loomis muttered. "Damned Doonan."

"Was there menace in her tone that night?" Mr. O'Nelligan asked.

Loomis smiled feebly. "There was always a little menace in her tone. That's what was so outstanding about Lorraine. She never let anyone get the better of her."

In my mind's eye, I saw a sinister phantom hurling a woman off a rooftop. If Mr. O'Nelligan was right, someone had indeed gotten the better of Lorraine Cobble.

"There was another anecdote that concerned you," my colleague said. "Regarding Lorraine dragging you out of McSorley's one evening."

"Yeah, that was real gutsy of her!" Loomis seemed fond of the memory. "Everybody knows McSorley's has a strict no-females policy. Lorraine, she didn't give a damn. "

"So what did she want you for?" I asked.

"Want me for?" Loomis wrinkled his brow. "What do you mean? I've told you already—she and I were like musketeers. All for one and one for all."

"Yeah, we get that," I said. "What was the urgency that night at McSorley's? Why'd she drag you away from all the other nice boys?"

Loomis' face reddened. "I don't like to be belittled, brother. I hold my own in this town. I know how to navigate, understand? I navigate through all the crap and putridity. Not like some of these poets and perverts around here."

"I wasn't trying to—"

"I hold my own! Lorraine, she always appreciated Loomis Lent. She knew she could count on me for the truth."

"For the truth of what?"

"The truth of people's souls! Their lousy, poisoned souls!"

I wanted to ask Loomis who the heck fed him his lines, but he kept barreling on.

"Lorraine was a special person! It was like she was made of music, you know? Like she was some slow sad song that nobody understood."

"Except perhaps you?" Mr. O'Nelligan suggested.

"I dunno, maybe . . ." Loomis scrutinized his shoes for several seconds, then reared back his unkempt head. "She needs to be avenged! The cops were completely useless. You get that

sonuvabitch who killed Lorraine and nail his head to the wall.
Will you do that for me? For Lorraine?"

"Well, head nailing isn't traditionally in our line," Mr.
O'Nelligan said. "We will, however, certainly endeavor to find
the truth."

Though not the lousy-poisoned-souls variety, I longed to add.

My partner moved on. "Mr. Lent, do you have any theories
as to who would want to harm your friend?"

"Nah, that's your profession, not mine. You're the ones who
get paid to figure things out."

"By the way," I said. "What's *your* profession?"

Loomis squared his shoulders in a posture of pride. "I'm a
speculator. Like, for example, I can help you guys speculate on
the Dodgers' chances of triumphing Tuesday. It's opening day
and the Bums take on Philly. Campanella's due for a good season. There's all that talk of moving the team out of Brooklyn,
but that's just bull. Pure bull! Campy and the boys are here to
stay, and Tuesday looks golden. Want to make a little side profit
while you're doing your investigating?"

"No, that's all right," I said. "We'll just survive on our
meager earnings."

"Suit yourselves. If you change your mind, just come tug
on my sleeve. I'll be inside for a little bit more." Loomis started
toward the door but did a double take and turned back to us.
"Hey, I just remembered what Lorraine wanted that night."

"The night at McSorley's?" I asked.

"Yeah, yeah. She was pretty heated up and wanted to ask
me about a particular musician who was around back then. A
guy named Cardinal."

Cardinal again. "What did she want to know?"

"She'd just gotten a letter from him. A nasty one."

"When was this?"

"I dunno. February? Maybe March. Anyway, she wanted to see if I'd heard anything about the guy. Because, you know, I'm the kind of person who hears things."

"Had you?"

Loomis shrugged. "Not much. Only that he was Canadian and played banjo—but she knew that already—and that he was a magician."

"What do you mean?"

"Just what I said—a magician. Yanking rabbits out of hats, making girls disappear . . . that sort of stuff. He was a quick-change artist, too. Before he took up the music, he'd had himself a magic act—Cardinal the Conjurer. I think he did it for a year or two."

"How did you know this, Mr. Lent?" my partner asked.

The prideful look returned. "Like I told you, I'm the kind that hears things."

"A useful gift, no doubt. How did Miss Cobble take the imparted information?"

"You mean that Cardinal had been a magician? Neither one way or another, I guess. It's not like Lorraine was afraid he'd saw her in half or anything. Anyway, that's what I've got for you. Like I say, if you're up for speculating, don't be shy. I'm taking odds on Sugar Hart over Pineapple Stevenson in the welterweight bout."

"We'll decline both Mr. Sugar and Mr. Pineapple," my partner countered. "Still, thank you for the offer."

"Whatever suits you. Just avenge Lorraine, okay? Get the gruesome creep who killed her. He was a goddamned blue darter, y'know? Aiming right at my poor Lorraine."

With that, Loomis Lent zipped back into the Mercutio.

"What a skittish little guy," I said. "I can see why Patch isn't head-over-heels over him."

My partner turned to me. "Our Mr. Lent just made a rather curious statement, did he not?"

"Which one? If you ask me, most of his statements seemed pretty off-kilter."

"I mean his suggestion that Lorraine was killed by a 'blue darter.' An odd supposition, indeed. It may well be a reference to the blue poison dart frog, so named because of its bright azure skin and toxic secretions. The Emberá huntsmen of Colombia are known to smear dart frog venom on their blowgun darts, though usually of the golden variety. The creature is of the family *Dendrobatidae*. Genus *Dendrobates*, I believe . . . though I might have that piece wrong."

"You've got it *all* wrong!" I laughed, happy as a clam—or a dart frog. " 'Blue darter' is a baseball term. It means a low, fast line drive that's impossible to catch. In his quirky way, Lent was just saying that Lorraine's death came in fast and furious."

"Oh . . . then . . . uh, well . . ." Mr. O'Nelligan stumbled along. "Apparently . . . there are gaps in my knowledge."

"Apparently!" Maybe I came off as a little too pleased—it wasn't often I got to one-up my scholarly sidekick. "Anyway, do you think Loomis and Lorraine were as cozy as he makes out?"

My partner adjusted his tie—and his composure. "Who knows? My people have an old proverb—'It's better to be quarreling than lonesome.' Perhaps the relationship between those two could be thus defined. In general, though, I'd say Mr. Lent's allegiance to the truth is suspect. Imagine claiming he recently had drinks with Zelda Fitzgerald! What will he say next—that he shared brunch with Christina Rossetti?"

"Yeah, that would be ridiculous." I was guessing that Christina was another long-dead lady. "So we can add Loomis and his ramblings to all the other vague characters spinning around Lorraine Cobble—Cardinal Meriam, Hector Escobar, the mystery scribe who wrote that first note . . ."

"Our situation brings to mind a parable from antiquity. Are you familiar with Plato's Cave?"

I took a stab at it. "Is that where Mickey Mouse keeps his pet dog?"

Mr. O'Nelligan groaned. "I badly need to believe that that was one of your pithy little jokes. Certainly you know the difference between Plato and Pluto."

"Certainly!" I hoped I sounded adamant.

"Listen now. The great thinker Plato proposed the following analogy. Imagine, if you will, a group of prisoners chained within a cave for their whole lives. They face a blank wall and are shackled in such a way that they cannot look over their shoulders. Behind them are various people and objects, on the other side of which blazes a large fire. Since the prisoners have never been able to turn around, they perceive naught but the shadows of those people and objects projected on the wall. So they see these shades not as reflections of a reality beyond, but as reality itself."

"So you and I, we're seeing only the shadows of . . . of what?"

"Of Lorraine Cobble's life and death. We see one flickering shadow of her that's been offered by her cousin, another by Minnie Bornstein, another by Loomis Lent, and so forth. In Plato's parable, one prisoner eventually goes free and learns the reality outside the cave. That is our goal here, Lee Plunkett—to stride forth from the cavern of illusions and learn the truth of this woman's final moments."

"My task is to pocket a fee for services rendered."

"Only if you exit the cave." Mr. O'Nelligan drew out his pocket watch and eyed it. "It's time for me to go meet my friend for dinner."

"Right. He's an old theater crony of yours, isn't he? Will he show up in a flowing toga, fresh from playing Julius Caesar?"

"Knowing Marguerite, I imagine she'll show up in something tight and sparkly."

"*Marguerite?* It's a lady friend? A sparkly lady friend?"

Mr. O'Nelligan held up a hand. "Now, don't let your imagination run amuck, Lee. My bond with her is that of comrades who have faced the spotlights together."

"Sounds real fraternal," I said with a smile.

"I'll stop first at Horton's Grill to have a word with Tucker the waiter. Let's see if he can provide any illumination regarding Lorraine's last morning of life. After my dinner with Marguerite, I'll return here to rejoin you."

Noting an oncoming taxi, Mr. O'Nelligan promptly stepped out to the curb and flagged it down. Just as he was crouching to enter the cab, he turned quickly back to me.

"Be on your guard, Lee."

As the taxi sped off, I wondered if my friend's parting advice had been inspired by Minnie Bornstein's warning. Instead of heading straight back into the Mercutio, I decided to take in more of the evening air before resuming work. I began to walk in no particular direction, glancing into darkened shop windows and observing my fellow nocturnal wanderers. The night was warm and inviting, and I took some comfort in not thinking about women plummeting off roofs. After fifteen minutes of aimless strolling, I started to retrace my tracks. Just short of the Mercutio, I came upon an entwined couple leaning against a wall, the girl's long auburn hair acting as something of a veil between them and me. I could hear the sounds of their energetic kissing and sped up to spare myself an embarrassing encounter. Without warning, the male half of the pair chose that moment to disengage and take a couple of sideways steps. This resulted in our awkwardly colliding.

"Hey, sorry there, man," the young lover said.

I might have accepted the apology had it come from someone else. Anyone other than Byron Spires.

CHAPTER NINETEEN

"I KNOW YOU," SPIRES SAID.
I adjusted my glasses in a gesture that I hoped conveyed scornful scrutiny—rather than just lousy eyesight. "Yeah, and I know *you*. We need to talk."

Spires turned to his honey du jour. "Hey, Coco, go wait for me inside. I'll be right along. Here, take this with you."

He grabbed up a guitar case that had been leaning against the wall and passed it to the young woman. Was Spires afraid that if the instrument was at hand I might be tempted to smash it over his curly cranium? Not a bad idea, but before I could fully consider it, the girl and guitar were headed off for the Mercutio.

Spires smiled without warmth. "We've met once before, man."

"I'm not a man—I'm a detective." Yet another instance where my mouth managed to outrace my brain.

That response caught him up. "Uh, yeah, well . . . You told me last month you were a private eye, remember? The night you—"

"The night I was down here with my fiancée?" I felt the blood racing to my face. "With Audrey? You recall Audrey, don't you, Byron? Or have you forgotten her since you've acquired your latest little friend?" I nodded down the street in the direction the girl had vanished. "Does Audrey know about her? You *have* properly introduced them, haven't you, Byron? That's just good etiquette."

Spires took a large step away from me. No doubt to keep my surging craziness at bay.

I rushed on. "How many sweethearts do you have squirreled away, Byron? Cratefuls? Truckfuls? Must be nice. Myself, I only have the one. Audrey. Or, at least, I *did* have her till you came along."

"Listen, friend, there's no need to—"

"*Friend?* Gee, Byron, I don't think friends steal fiancées. I've read up on it, and I'm pretty sure I'm right about that. Ninety-nine percent positive, I'd say."

At this point, my words were leaping into the air with mad abandon. Some disembodied part of me stood on the sidelines, watching curiously to see what insane thing would come out next. Just as I was gathering steam, Spires did an about-face and hurried toward the Mercutio.

He called over his shoulder, "I don't mix with kooks."

With that, all my fondness for Spires drained away. I sprinted after him and caught up just as he was reaching for the Mercutio's door. Then, surprising myself with my actions, I grabbed his shoulder, spun him around, and pinned him to the outer wall.

"You're not going anywhere!" I had no idea what I planned to do next—if I was even capable of anything else—but Spires sure looked distressed.

"You're nuts, man!"

"Maybe I *am* nuts. Losing your girl can do that to a fella."

Just then the door opened and Loomis Lent stepped out onto the sidewalk.

Spires turned to him. "Christ, Loomis, help me! This guy's gone around the bend."

The interruption didn't stop my little tirade. "Shut up, Spires. I know what you did to her."

"*To* her? What makes you think—"

"I know what you did."

Spires made another appeal. "Lent! Get this guy off me, will ya?"

The rumpled bookie just stood there looking concerned and confused.

"Keep walking, Loomis," I said, doing my best James Cagney. "I'm on top of this."

After a long moment, Loomis Lent turned and shuffled away down the street. Apparently, he had no immediate plans of rushing to anyone's aid. Once it was only myself and Spires again, my wrath seemed to flag. I'd never thrown a blow in anger, and I didn't know that I really had it in me now. I took a step back and exhaled deeply.

"Now get lost, you bum," my Cagney self said.

Ideally, Spires would then have whimpered a thanks for sparing his life and raced off into the fugitive night. Instead, he studied me for a few quizzical seconds, snickered, and straightened his collar.

"I didn't do anything at all to Audrey," he said, defiance in his voice. "You think I'm some wolf who led her astray? No, she was more than glad to hang out with me. Anyway, there's something you should know. Audrey called me up a few hours ago."

I tensed. "Yeah?"

"Yeah. Want to know what she told me?"

"Let's not make this a game. Just spill it."

"She said she no longer wanted to keep company with me." Spires smirked. "That's actually how she put it—keep company—like it was the turn of the century and we'd been out to a tea party."

"Audrey's an old-fashioned girl," I said protectively.

"I guess. Anyway, what I'm saying, man, is I've moved on."

"Yeah, I get that impression." I was thinking of his new girl-friend.

Spires read my mind. "Coco's a sweet little thing, isn't she? Just goes to prove what they say about fish in the sea. You just need to know how to reel them in."

"Like you reeled Audrey in?"

"Hey, this is 1957, not 1907. Girls don't need a lot of bait these days. Just a nice shiny hook."

"I'm coming real close to slugging you."

"I'm only trying to speak the truth here. I do that with my music, and I do it with my life. Verity, man. I'm all about the verity."

I needed to get off the topic of girl-fishing. The practice seemed a far cry from *The Old Man and the Sea,* and I'm sure Mr. O'Nelligan would be appalled. I remembered my trade and decided to ply it again.

"I'm investigating the death of Lorraine Cobble."

"That's what they say."

"When I was down here last month I got to see firsthand what a warm connection you two shared."

"Oh yeah, our little dustup over 'The Wild, Weeping Heather.'"

"She claimed you stole that song from her."

"She's one to talk. Did you happen to hear the little saga of Lorraine and Cardinal Meriam?"

"I did."

"Then you know who the real song thief was." Spires ran a hand through his thick brown curls. "Look, it's a drag Lorraine killed herself, I'm not saying it isn't. But trying to conjure up some big bad murderer is just fairy tale stuff. Lorraine Cobble had a bitter little heart, and I guess she just got tired of listening to its lonely beating." His eyes brightened. "Hey! That's not a bad line, is it? I gotta remember it when I'm writing my next lyrics."

At that moment, perhaps for the first time, I truly *did* want there to be a big bad murderer; and desperately, oh so desperately, I wanted it to be Byron Spires. I couldn't think of a more satisfying conclusion to this case.

"Did you spend much time with Lorraine?" I asked tersely.

He gave the answer I'd heard a dozen times already. "No, Lorraine didn't do a whole lot of socializing. Now, if we're done here, I should go join Coco—so she doesn't think you executed me out here."

Spires sauntered past me and entered the coffeehouse. Deserted by my nemesis, I stood there for several minutes, digesting the remaining morsels of my anger. I didn't know what I'd really gained just then by playing the crazy tough guy. Whatever discord existed between Audrey and me probably wasn't going to get resolved by confronting Spires. The fact that she'd told him it was over between them—whatever *it* was—had to be a good sign. Yeah, let Coco take her chances with the cur. One of the questions I'd flung at Spires now came back to me—*did* Audrey know about Spires' auburn-haired canoodling partner? Probably not, since I couldn't see Audrey consenting to join the roster of anyone's personal harem.

When I reentered the Mercutio, the Doonan Brothers had taken the stage and were belting out a ballad of Irish rebellion. I saw Spires and his girl sitting off at their own small table. I passed them without engaging. In my murky mood, I considered ordering a full bottle of wine and a deep glass, but reminded myself that I was on the clock. And a piss-poor drinker. While maneuvering through the crowd, I heard someone call my name. Turning, I spied the Grand Mazzo beckoning me from the entrance to the back rooms. I made my way over to him.

"Been looking for you for the last few minutes," Mazzo said. "Your cohort O'Nelligan's on the line." He led me into his office and handed me the phone.

I waited till he'd left the room to speak. "Hi. I'm here."

My partner's familiar brogue greeted me. "I was beginning to think you'd abandoned ship, Lee. Where have you been off to?"

"I'll tell you later. What's up?"

"I'm at Marguerite's about to dine, but I wanted to convey to you what I've just learned. On the way here, I stopped in at Horton's and spoke briefly with Tucker the waiter. He confirms that he served Lorraine Cobble breakfast on the morning of her final day."

"Did he mention what time?"

"He couldn't say for certain, but he thinks it was no earlier than nine and well before eleven."

If I'd been a cartoon, a little lightbulb would have flashed over my head. "The letter from the unknown person indicated a ten A.M. meeting. That fits with what the waiter says."

"Exactly."

"So, was Lorraine with anybody?"

"Yes . . . someone we most likely know."

"Go on."

"A young woman. Tucker had never seen the lass before, but he described her as attractive with extremely long black hair, her nose a tad slanted, and a small scar under one eye. Sound familiar?"

It did. "Ruby."

"Yes. Ruby Dovavska, the provocative poet. I'm not sure if she'll still be on the premises by the time I rejoin you, so I was thinking you might fly solo on this. Are you up for speaking with her on your own?"

"Of course I am. You know, I *can* talk to a woman without you holding my hand."

"Delighted to hear it," my partner said. "Good luck. I'll see you fairly soon."

After he rang off, I returned to the main room and began scanning the crowd, trying to locate Ruby. Unsuccessful, I finally buttonholed Mazzo and asked if he'd seen her.

"She just went back to her apartment. It's about a fifteen-minute walk." He flashed a suggestive smile. "Maybe less if you're in hot pursuit."

I didn't like the smile or the insinuation. My pursuit's centigrade was none of his damned business.

CHAPTER TWENTY

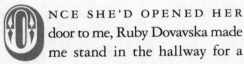NCE SHE'D OPENED HER door to me, Ruby Dovavska made me stand in the hallway for a good half minute—which can be an extremely long interval under certain circumstances. Such as, for example, when a striking young woman with a jagged little smile is scrutinizing you from head to toe.

After a tiny eternity, Ruby gestured me in. I was met by the lingering odor of what I assumed was old incense, though it seemed oddly sweet.

She locked the door behind us. "There's more than a few questionable types in this neighborhood. Being a private eye, you must be used to all sorts of creeps."

I tried to sound cool and confident. "I know my way around unsavory lowlifes." When I heard my words hit the air, I wanted to cringe.

Ruby tilted her head. "You don't say?"

"I don't." *What the hell?*

I found myself wishing she would just turn her back on me so I wouldn't have to stare at that lovely, disorienting face. After all, it wasn't like I needed to study it more to confirm that Ruby was the female Tucker the waiter had seen with Lorraine. All the components were there: long black hair, slightly off-kilter nose, faint half-moon scar high on her left cheek. On another woman, those features might have added up to something less than attractive. On Ruby, they were fairly riveting. The waiter hadn't mentioned her eyes, but up this close, they, too, were compelling. Then there were her lips . . . full and carnivorous specimens which parted now to say:

"I'm going to get you a drink. A nasty one."

"Uh, that's okay, I'm—"

"Don't worry, nasty can be a good thing."

She stepped into the apartment's small kitchen, giving me a chance to glance around the living room. The walls were covered with an assortment of Oriental tapestries, and the sparse furnishings consisted of two battered armchairs, several towers of books piled in corners, and a stack of canvases leaning against one wall. The topmost painting depicted a voluptuous woman garbed in nothing but a stovepipe hat. Bending over, I flipped through the seven or eight other paintings. One and all, they featured naked people, men and women, sporting the same headgear. I was no judge of what constituted good or bad art, but this was certainly *bizarre* art. Straightening up, I now noticed a stovepipe hat—no doubt *the* stovepipe hat—perched atop one of the book stacks. The one thing I didn't see anywhere was an easel. I wondered if Ruby kept it in her bedroom.

"Perusing my nudes, were you?" She had suddenly reappeared, holding two glasses.

"No . . . Yes . . . That is . . ."

"I know they're not great, but they're mine. I did a show-ing at a gallery last month. Believe it or not, I sold three paint-ings." She extended one of the glasses. "Here."

I took the drink and downed half the copper-hued liquid in one swig. It was burning and strong, and I didn't bother to ask what it was. Ruby finished her own drink in one pass. She set the glass on a book stack and stretched her arms high over her head, fingers interlocked, in what might have been a yoga move. Whatever kind of move it was, it served to hike her black shirt well above her navel, compelling me to kill the rest of my drink in one wild gulp. Thankfully, Ruby's arms de-scended without incident.

She looked intensely at me. "I could do you."

"Excuse me?" I think I took a step backward.

She pinched the fingers of her right hand together and made a sweeping movement in the air, back and forth. I was mesmerized and unnerved. What, for the love of God, did she have in mind?

Sensing my confusion, Ruby laughed softly and dropped her hand. "Painting. I could paint you."

"Oh . . ." Any ease I might have fleetingly felt was dispelled by a glance at the stovepipe in the corner. "You mean . . ."

"I've done a prizefighter," she said, "a concert violinist, a burlesque queen, and a doctor . . . a specialist. Ear, nose, and throat."

"Oh?"

"I've done a few authors, a couple of socialites, and even a minister." She reflected for a moment. "Well, a former, disgraced minister. I've done them all. Never a private eye, though."

"Thanks, but . . ."

She came a step closer. "If you want, you can keep your spectacles on."

I swallowed hard, feeling both stirred and stupid. Here I was, a seasoned PI (well, if not seasoned, then at least not a total rookie), unsettled by this young bohemian dabbler. Whether with paintbrush, pen, or the proximity of her curvy body, she seemed hell-bent on generating commotion—an unhurried, detached commotion, but commotion nonetheless. Audrey's face suddenly popped into my brain. My fiancée wore a scowl mixed with disappointment at seeing me in my present situation. I felt a spark of indignation. Who was *she* to be judging me after her recent outings with Byron Spires? It would serve Audrey right if I were to disrobe this very second and reach for that tall black hat—

Then I remembered her call to Spires, the one breaking things off. *No more keeping company.* When the chips were down, Audrey had done the right thing.

Now so did I. "You'll have to find yourself another model, Miss Dovavska."

"Are you sure? You don't want to be in the company of boxers and fan dancers?" Ruby gave a playful frown.

"Plus maybe an Irish troubadour or two?" The words leapt out of me.

The frown lifted itself into an amused little smile. "You're referring to Patch Doonan, maybe?"

"Maybe."

She gave a dismissive flip of the hand. "I know you saw Patch facing off against Manymile last night . . ."

"Battling for your hand, by the looks of it."

"Oh, come on. Manymile's just a friend. As for Patch . . ."

"Yes?"

"Patch was a couple of nights' distraction."

"That's very tender of you."

"Look, he's an okay guy, good for a laugh, but it's not like I'm going to take him back to Chappaqua to meet my folks." Ruby took my empty glass. "Not that my parents would want to see *me,* either."

Something like sadness passed across her face. Retrieving her own glass, she vanished back into the kitchen. I followed her in.

"There's a reason I came here," I said.

"Yeah, I figured as much." She dropped the two glasses in the sink—deliberately dropped them. I gave a little jolt as at least one of them shattered. Ruby placed her hands on either side of the basin and examined the broken fragments, her long hair draped on either side of her face.

"Kind of beautiful," she said in a strange, distant voice.

I waited for her to expand on that thought, but she didn't.

Eventually, Ruby turned back to me and folded her arms across her chest. "Well? You have some detective business to conduct?"

I cleared my throat. "I know you wrote a letter to Lorraine Cobble asking her to meet you for breakfast on the day she died."

"That's false."

"You were seen. At Horton's Grill."

"Sure, I was there, but I never wrote any letter. Also, it wasn't even breakfast. Lorraine was the one eating. I just had tea."

"Still, you arranged to meet there."

"False again. I happened to be passing by when Lorraine tapped on the window and waved me to come inside."

"Why?"

"Because she liked me, I suppose. Some people like me."
Ruby headed back into the living room, with me in tow.

"Did you get together often?" I asked.

"Never, really."

"Though that morning she wanted to chat?"

"Seemed like it."

"What about?"

"Reckon I can't recall, Sheriff," Ruby said flippantly, plopping herself into one of the armchairs. "Wait a minute—actually, I can. We talked about Quetzalcoatl."

"Who's that? Another musician?"

She laughed at me. "Not exactly. Quetzalcoatl is the feathered serpent god of the Aztecs. Lorraine was reading a book about Mexican folklore and was telling me about him."

"That's all you discussed? Nothing else?"

Ruby leaned her head back, seeming to give my question some thought. "She talked about Manymile Simms a little . . . how she thought the blues were going to make a real comeback. Then she talked about being a kid."

"A kid?" Somehow I couldn't picture Lorraine Cobble as a pigtailed, rosy-cheeked child.

"Lorraine told me about the first time she visited the Village, when she was eleven. She'd gone to Washington Square Park, and there was a mandolin player from Portugal there who sang her a song from Wales. She said that really struck her as amazing—that here was this Portuguese man playing a Welsh tune on an Italian instrument in New York. That this was how music worked . . .'"

Ruby went quiet for a moment, then looked straight up at me. "Mostly Lorraine just seemed to want to talk. About nothing, about anything. She wasn't usually so loquacious, but that

morning she just seemed like she wanted to converse with another human being. I just happened to be the one she found. I
wonder if . . ."

She became silent again.

"You wonder if what?"

When Ruby finally answered, she seemed to have changed
topics. "My grandfather got up one day and ironed every shirt
and pair of pants he owned. Even ironed his neckties. Everyone says he barely ever touched an iron prior to that. He went
to bed that night and never woke up. It was as if he knew. So
I wonder if it was like that with Lorraine—that she somehow
sensed it was her last day on earth and wanted to connect with
someone to tell them stories from her life."

"My partner would probably buy into that."

"Not you, though?"

"I don't believe in premonitions," I said. "Did Lorraine
mention if she had plans to meet anyone else that day?"

"She didn't say."

"Do you remember what time you were with her that
morning?"

Ruby thought about that. "I'd say I sat down sometime
before ten. We were together for maybe forty minutes. I know
I definitely left by ten thirty because I had a doctor's appointment to get to." She smiled at me and added, "Gynecologist."

I suppressed a blush. "Did she seem like she might be expecting someone else to show up at the restaurant?"

"Not at all. We left at the same time. I've no idea where
she was headed, and like I say, I was going to—"

"The doctor's, right. So that was the last time you ever saw
her?"

"Yes, it was." A look of mild wonder played across her face. "Have you heard from anyone else who was with her that day?"

"Not besides the waiter. You're the only one."

Ruby gazed off and, after a moment, began speaking softly, seemingly to herself. "Maybe that night on the roof Lorraine looked up and saw Quetzalcoatl flying across the moon. Maybe she was so entranced that she jumped into the air and landed on his back. Then they flew off through the stars together and never returned."

I thought of informing her that the only true part of that story was the bit where Lorraine never returned. I didn't. At that moment, Ruby looked so tranquil and reflective that I was reluctant to intrude on her fantasy. Instead, I thanked her for the drink and for answering my questions. She shifted in her chair and stared up at me, as if waking from a dream and noticing me for the first time.

I gave a little nod and let myself out.

CHAPTER TWENTY-ONE

I WAS IN SIGHT OF THE CAFÉ Mercutio when a shadow slid out from around a corner and seized my arm. I pulled free and stumbled backward, my hands curling themselves into fists. Since I never carried a gun, I was hoping against hope that my own mitts would prove effective weapons.

"At ease now, Lee Plunkett!" a particular brogue commanded. "You wouldn't want to thrash your own assistant, now would you?"

Mr. O'Nelligan stepped out beneath a streetlamp.

I dropped my fists. "What the hell are you doing skulking around like that?"

"It's not skulking. Well, maybe it is a bit, but it's not for your benefit."

"For whose, then?"

"For the Doonans. I was just in the coffeehouse and saw

them making stirrings to leave. I thought I'd wait out here to intercept them in case you didn't return in time and I needed to confront them on my own. Mazzo informed me you'd gone to see Miss Dovavska and I should expect you from this direction."

"Wait a minute, why do the Doonans need confronting?"

"I learned something interesting during my dinner with Marguerite—a very pleasing repast, by the way. Do you remember Patch Doonan mentioning that he'd spent some time as a local thespian?"

"Couldn't you just say 'actor'?"

He didn't answer that. "Well, it seems that Marguerite and Patch happened to share the stage a few months back in a modest production of J. M. Synge's *Deirdre of the Sorrows*. Certainly that work is not up to the caliber of Synge's *Playboy of the Western World*, but since *Deirdre* was written on his deathbed, one can't expect—"

"Whoa!" I held up a hand. "Please tell me that a lecture on Irish drama isn't the 'something interesting' you promised."

"It isn't. Though it *would* be to your betterment if you immersed yourself more in the arts."

"I'll take that under advisement. Now, what about Patch?"

"In Ireland, this past winter, a certain incident occurred," Mr. O'Nelligan said. "One I'd already heard of prior to tonight. On New Year's Day in County Fermanagh, there was a failed IRA attack on the Brookeborough police barracks. Most of the insurgents escaped, but two were killed. Afterward, an effort was made in some quarters to make heroes of the dead men. As it so happens, the three Doonan brothers were back in Ireland visiting their family at the time."

"Okay, but what does that—"

"Listen now. By mid-January, the Doonans had returned to New York, and Patch and the rest of the cast had begun rehearsals for *Deidre*. One of the stagehands was another Irishman, from Fermanagh as it turns out. Apparently, he mentioned to a few of the actors, Marguerite included, that the Doonans had an uncle, one Michael Doonan, who supposedly took part in the barracks attack. Furthermore, there was a rumor afoot that Patch was somehow involved."

"Huh. What did Patch have to say about that?"

"Apparently, the stagehand only mentioned it to Marguerite and three or four others before someone told him to stop spreading unproven gossip. As far as Marguerite knows, Patch was never aware that tales were being told about him."

"Well, I grant you, that's certainly interesting," I said. "So how does it play into our investigation?"

"I'm not sure if it does or doesn't. Here's another little piece—Loomis Lent had a minor role in that production. Though Marguerite doesn't know if he was party to the rumors about Patch."

"Again, interesting, but is it important?"

"Again, I don't know, but these are people who were associated with Lorraine Cobble, and anything of an unusual nature should be explored."

"I suppose we can go talk to this stagehand if we want to pursue things."

Mr. O'Nelligan shook his head. "Unfortunately not. The man moved back to Fermanagh at the end of February."

Down the street, a couple of people emerged from the Mercutio, but no one I recognized.

My partner glanced at them, then back to me. "While we wait for the Doonans, tell me of your own adventures."

"Adventures . . ." I sighed. "Sure." I told him first about my encounter with Byron Spires, not sparing the niceties of my Cagney impersonation, Little Miss Coco, Spires' fishing analogy, or Audrey's phone call severing their friendship. That last elicited a smile and nod from my partner. He obviously was pleased that Audrey had slammed that door shut. I next went on to detail my time with Ruby, discreetly leaving out any mention of stovepipe hats. Mr. O'Nelligan mulled over what I'd just shared. "Hmm, if Miss Dovavska did keep company with Lorraine at ten that morning—yet did *not* write the letter requesting a ten o'clock rendezvous—then that clouds things. What became of Lorraine's meeting with our unknown letter writer?"

"Maybe she just decides to blow them off. Maybe she chooses to decline the offer and instead go for breakfast by herself. Then she sees Ruby and invites her to join her. The letter writer gets stood up."

"Perhaps appearing at Lorraine's later that night, embittered at being shunned."

"I guess that's one direction to go with this."

My colleague drew a slow hand down his gray whiskers. "I'm intrigued by Ruby's theory that Lorraine sensed her end was nigh. What if it's true?"

I tried for a nonfanciful take on that. "You mean Lorraine might have learned someone meant to harm her?"

"I wasn't thinking in such tangible terms."

"You're not thinking spooky voodoo omens, are you?"

Mr. O'Nelligan cast a chilly eye on me. "Are you truly expecting me to answer in the affirmative?"

I didn't need to reply to that since, just then, the Mercutio's door opened again and four figures stepped out onto the sidewalk. The Doonans and Kimla. They were heading our way, their voices filling the air. Well, mostly Patch's voice.

Upon reaching us, they halted and the eldest Doonan called out, "Well now! It's our deductive duo again."

"May we have a word with you, Patch?"

"What's your pleasure, Squire O'Nelligan?"

"Perhaps you'd prefer to converse privately with us?"

Patch offered an uneasy grin. "Uh-oh, I don't like the sound of that."

"What is it, sir?" Neil stepped next to his brother. "Anything you say to one of us, you can say to all."

"Wise sentiments those," Patch readily agreed.

Tim came a step closer as well. The brothers were closing ranks. Kimla, standing just to the side, didn't look like she was going anywhere either.

"Very well," said Mr. O'Nelligan. "If that's how it is."

"It is," Tim said, by way of punctuation.

My partner began, "Patch Doonan, a tale has been circulating concerning you . . ."

Without mentioning his source, he repeated the account of the attack on the police barracks and the subsequent suspicions. The Doonans listened raptly.

When Mr. O'Nelligan had finished, it was an agitated Tim who spoke first. "That's rubbish! You can't fling loose allegations around like that."

"Aye, rubbish," Neil echoed, though more evenly. "There's no truth at all in it."

Tim kept on. "It's true we're for a united Ireland and that we've some relations in the north who've been involved in a thing or two. That doesn't mean Patch or any of us had anything to do with Brookeborough."

"You have an uncle who might have," I put in.

Tim turned to me. "Uncle Mike? Forget it. He's a breezy enough fellow, but more than half daft. Not even the most desperate republicans would tap him for an operation. Sure, and wouldn't it be just like Mike to try to make himself the big man by lying that he'd been in on that business?"

"Indeed it would," Neil added. "Especially with people making martyrs of Sean South and young O'Hanlon. I wouldn't put it past Michael to throw Patch's name into the bargain. He's always favored Patch, since they both play the idiot."

"There you go," Tim said. "In his twisted way, Mike would see it as a kindness to include his favorite nephew in the lie."

Mr. O'Nelligan had been listening intently, assessing the merits of what was being proposed. He now weighed in. "That would be a dangerous piece of bragging, would it not? After all, the men who actually conducted the raid and lost comrades wouldn't look kindly on false claims of participation. On the other side, we have the authorities, who would certainly want to come down hard on anyone involved in the attack."

Tim had an answer for that. "Likely as not, Uncle Mike's just passed the lie around to a few drinking mates, not thinking it would travel far. Besides, you'd have to know the man . . ."

"That's right," Neil said. "Mike's an utter gobshite."

Oddly enough, the one present Doonan who'd remained silent throughout the discussion was the one most central to it—and the one who generally kept his tongue running nonstop.

Mr. O'Nelligan now addressed the curiously hushed Patch. "What's *your* perspective on all this?"

Patch didn't answer at first, choosing instead to stare off down the currently deserted street. When he did at last speak, his voice was tight and strained, as if he were trying to hold back a wave of anger:

"You want to know what my bloody perspective is? Glad to convey it. I'm thinking people who don't know what they're bloody talking about should keep their gobs shut. Whatever I've done or haven't done, no bloody idle gossips have a right to speak my name."

"Yet they have," I said. "We're just trying to help figure out what—"

"Bollocks!" The wave broke. "Don't be pretending to assist anyone but your own snaky selves! You're paid snoops, the pair of you. You say you're down here about Lorraine Cobble, but maybe it's the British bloody crown you're working for."

Tim tried to intervene. "Be still, Patch! You've no cause to say that."

Patch now turned to face Mr. O'Nelligan. "Wouldn't it be just like the Brits to use one of our own against us."

"Ease up. Now," Neil said. "He's a countryman of ours."

Patch kept his eye on my partner. "So what? Our history is rife with traitors!"

My partner stood his ground, betraying no reaction. I wondered how Doonan's words were affecting him. After all, in his youth Mr. O'Nelligan had been an armed rebel, fighting the English for Irish sovereignty.

Patch plowed on. "So what've you to say, O'Nelligan? Where do you fall on Irish independence? Are you a nationalist or has John Bull swayed you with a few greasy shillings?"

Tim grabbed his brother's arm. "Enough, Patch! You're raging like a proper madman. Just say now that the Brookeborough rumor was nothing but fiction, and be done with it."

Patch shook Tim loose. "Leave me be! I don't need to speak out like a damned trained parrot. I'm finished here."

Then he turned away and began heading down a dimly lit side street.

"Patch, wait up!" Tim called out. "Stay with us."

Patch shouted over his shoulder, "A pleasant bloody night to all!"

Tim moved as if to follow, but Neil placed a hand on his chest. "Let him go," the middle brother said. "There's no reasoning with him now."

"Where do you think he's headed?" I asked.

Tim answered wearily. "To some hole-in-the-wall where the whiskey's cheap and the company's too drunk to talk."

Kimla came up and took the young man's hand. "Let's be going, Tim. You know he'll show up in the morning like he always does—drained and repentant."

Tim gave a pained little chuckle. "You're right, of course." He kissed Kimla on the cheek and put his arm around her shoulder.

Neil turned to Mr. O'Nelligan. "Sorry for our brother's accusations. He can be a grand lunatic when the mood's on him."

"His words slid off me like rain from a steep roof," my partner said. It sounded like the kind of adage you'd see stitched on a pillow in a great-aunt's home, and I wasn't convinced it was true.

I thought of squeezing in another question or two, but no one looked in the mood. With halfhearted waves, Neil, Tim, and Kimla moved off together down the street. We watched quietly as they dwindled into small shadowy forms, then vanished.

Mr. O'Nelligan broke the silence. "Interesting. Tim and Neil Doonan were left to protest their brother's innocence while he remained mute on the matter."

"Yeah, you wouldn't exactly call Patch's little outburst a profession of innocence. Do you think he's mixed up with that attack?"

"I don't know," my partner answered. "Our inquiries certainly roused him to an agitated state. There's an old acquaintance of mine who lives hereabouts, O'Hallmhurain by name, who is often privy to certain goings-on back in Ireland. When I get the chance, I'll give him a call to see what he might provide."

"As meaty as this little subplot may be, we've still no reason to believe it ties in at all with the Cobble case."

"Correct. Just as we don't know if Cardinal's letter or Loomis' gambling or Manymile's prison record has anything to do with it. These are all colors on our palette. It remains to be seen which of them figure in the final portrait."

The mention of portraits made me a little queasy, reminding me as it did of Ruby's recent invitation to nudity. For a terrible moment, I imagined I'd succumbed, resulting in a piece of artwork with a title like *Private Eye as Public Disgrace.*

"Lee?" Mr. O'Nelligan summoned me back from that horror. "Are you all right? You look a touch ashen."

"I always look pale when the old brain gears are turning."

"Truly?" my partner sounded unswayed. "I didn't know that about you, Lee."

"Yeah, well, I'm a complicated cat, daddy-o."

Mr. O'Nelligan grimaced wonderfully.

*   *   *

THE DRIVE HOME to Thelmont was uneventful. After a final review of the day's events, we contented ourselves with the Saturday evening radio fare. For Mr. O'Nelligan's pleasure, we found an uninterrupted half hour of Elvis Presley tunes. Then, for me, there was a rip-roaring episode of *Gunsmoke*. It was a whodunit of sorts, in which Marshal Dillon had to decide which of three cowboys was guilty of murdering a Pawnee brave. I hoped we'd be as successful in our endeavor as Dillon was. Preferably we wouldn't have to dodge six-gun bullets to do it.

Once home, I embraced my pillow like a long-lost pal. Sleep came swiftly. Tonight's dream had some of the elements of the previous one but was lacking others. For example, there was no Statue of Liberty. No pterodactyls either (and, thankfully, no Quetzalcoatls in their place). Audrey wasn't there, though Lorraine Cobble was. As in yesterday's dream, I found myself standing at a considerable height. Not quite so high as Lady Liberty's head, but high enough. This time I was atop the giant arch in Washington Square Park. Lorraine was up there beside me, her long golden hair whipping about in the strong wind. Her hand was almost touching mine, but not quite.

She asked me a question. "Did you know that the Washington Arch was modeled on the Arc de Triomphe in Paris?"

I answered yes, because I did. I'd learned that little tidbit somewhere along the line. I stared down and took in the great concrete sprawl of the park below. It was alive with movement. Around the central fountain, which was spouting bright silver water, hundreds, maybe thousands, of people were roaming about in a spiral. Most of them carried guitars that they strummed with wide sweeps of their arms. Strangely, though, this legion of strings made no sound. All I could hear was the wind whirling around me.

Eventually, Lorraine asked me another question. "Did you know that I really, really wanted to live?"

Her voice sounded so brittle and sad then that I turned to look at her. Only she had changed. She was a young girl now, perhaps eleven, with her hair in long braids. She wasn't looking back at me but at what lay below—which now was nothing. The people had all vanished, as had the fountain and the park itself. There was nothing there at all, not even last night's churning, ghost-filled sea. Just an abyss, black and endless. Instinctively, I grabbed for the girl and held her tightly to my side.

"Be very, very careful," I told her.

"You, too," she said back, her voice soft and trembling. "You be careful, too, Mr. Plunkett."

CHAPTER TWENTY-TWO

I CALLED AUDREY FIRST THING in the morning. "What would you think of breaking tradition this once and doing the Bugle Boy Sunday instead of Saturday?"

The silence at the other end of the line made me think a rejection was being prepared. Then she spoke, sounding a little subdued but pleased. "Breakfast? This morning? Sure. I don't think anyone will chastise us for switching things up."

She was wrong. Forty minutes later, Beatrice, our seventy-seven-year-old waitress, was raking us over the coals in her crusty, merry way.

"So where were you two yesterday?" she demanded. "I almost sent out an all-points bulletin. You get to be a certain age, you expect a little consistency in your life. You don't want your customers jumbling things up, for mercy's sake."

We offered a contrite apology, leaving out the reason for

yesterday's absence. Fortunately, Beatrice didn't probe further, content to take our order and trudge off to badger more of her beloved customers.

Once we were alone, I was the one to start things off. "I saw Byron Spires last night."

Audrey gulped softly. "Yes?"

"It was in the course of the investigation. I wasn't there to track him down."

"Um-hm."

"I wasn't looking for him, but—I won't lie to you—when I ran into him I wanted to punch the living daylights out of the guy."

In less complicated times, Audrey probably would have interjected some playful barb here. Maybe something about the unlikelihood of me being able to beat a single sunbeam out of a guy, never mind a full complement of daylights.

She didn't do that now.

"I stayed my hand." That sounded remarkably noble, so I said it again. "I stayed my hand—after giving him a piece of my mind, that is."

For a moment, I heard my father's voice, blunt and growly, lecturing me: *Are you kidding, Lee? Bum tries to steal your girl, and all you do is give him a scolding? What are you, a schoolmarm?*

I shoved Dad back to the beyond. This was *my* problem, *my* life.

"Spires told me you called him yesterday," I said.

Audrey held my gaze. "Did he tell you why?"

"He did."

Then we didn't say anything for a while, but Audrey did reach over and scoop up my hand in both of hers.

She spoke again first. "You and me, Lee—I'm in it for the long haul."

For some reason, that struck me as an extraordinarily tender thing to say. When I opened my mouth to respond, I found that some damned frog must have snuck in there. How else to explain the fact that my throat was suddenly hoarse and I could barely get a word out? Seeing my affliction, Audrey squeezed my hand tighter.

Beatrice appeared at the perfect moment, juggling coffee cups, plates of waffles, and bowls of cereal and complaining spryly about the demands this job made on her poor old bones. We barely waited for her to exit before delving into our breakfast. I was suddenly feeling famished, as if I'd just run a hundred-meter sprint. Maybe Audrey was feeling the same. We weren't kidding ourselves that this race was by any means really done. No doubt, down the line, there was still a lot of hashing out for us to do, a lot of bruised feelings for us to shift through. For now, though, this was just fine. Here we were, as the gods of Thelmont intended, breaking bread together at the Bugle Boy Diner (albeit a day late) with our coffee steaming, Beatrice grousing, and the warm April sun spilling through the windows. Life was okay. Good, even.

AFTER BREAKFAST, I told Audrey that I needed to go to my office to attend to some paperwork. She suggested riding over there with me, just to stay together for a little while longer. Though she'd already missed morning church to join me at the diner, Audrey assured me she could catch a later service at no danger to her soul. Since the church was only a modest

walk from my office, it seemed like an orderly plan. I was happy
to have her beside me once again as I steered Baby Blue across
town. As I've previously mentioned, my Nash always looked at
its jazziest with Miss Audrey Valish in the front seat. It was
one of those curiosities that probably belonged in our Catalog
of Life's Little Truths.

Entering my office, Audrey moaned softly, as was her habit
whenever finding herself in my cramped, drab workspace. For
the hundredth time, she surveyed the beat-up furniture, murky
green walls, and one curtainless window and cringed a little.

"You know, Lee, a coat of paint and a set of drapes wouldn't
be a crime."

"To Yowler Yarr they would."

"Remember how we've said Fred Mertz is the worst landlord? Well, your Mr. Yarr deserves serious consideration."

"One reason he keeps my rent low is because I preserve the
space like Dad had it. Yowler and Buster were old chums, and
this space is sort of a monument to that chummery."

"Chummery's not a word."

"Tell that to Yowler."

Audrey stared up the Theodore Roosevelt portrait, the
room's only decorative touch. "Couldn't you even replace Teddy
here? He always looks so perturbed."

"You would be, too, if you had to wrestle rhinos in darkest
Africa."

"He did that?"

"*Dad* thought he did."

It was good to be bantering in the old comfortable way. It
gave me hope for our future.

Audrey volunteered to rummage through the mail from

the last couple of days, a task she knew I wouldn't fight her for. I turned my own attention to organizing the notes I'd been compiling from the current investigation. Though I couldn't boast my father's toughness or my Celtic colleague's keen mind, I was hell on wheels with the note-taking. I began writing up a diagram of sorts featuring the individuals we'd encountered, plus the various threads that had presented themselves. For example:

LC jumps/thrown from roof in evening.

→ Cornelius sees Hector Escobar near stairwell → Hector denies this.

Letter #1 (by unknown writer) requests meeting at 10 a.m. day of death.

→ Ruby meets with LC at 10 a.m. that day, not planned (?)

LC steals Cardinal Meriam's song set → Letter #2 (Cardinal, threatening).

→ Compare with: LC stealing Minnie Bornstein's Navaho trip (1945).

→ Compare with: Spires stealing LC's Scottish song.

Etcetera. I put it all down very neatly and concisely—without knowing what in God's green acre anything really meant. As I was completing my diagram, Mr. O'Nelligan stepped into the office.

"Ah! Behold the twain!"

By that, I assumed he meant Audrey and me. I could see

his pleasure in finding this particular twain keeping company again.

Audrey gave our Irishman a warm hug and told him, "It's a good thing you showed up. Poor Lee has been sitting here groaning and gnashing his teeth trying to crack the case."

"That's a big stinking lie," I begged to differ.

Audrey smiled wickedly. "He's flummoxed. Please solve it for him."

"Not I alone. *Coniunctis Viribus!*" my partner proclaimed.

Audrey scrunched up her button nose. "That sounds like some kind of rash."

"It's Latin for *With Powers United*," my partner explained. "Not through any individual effort but by exploring side by side will Lee and I unravel this mystery."

"You make us sound like the Hardy Boys," I said.

"The Hardy Boys?" Mr. O'Nelligan seemed genuinely at a loss. "Are they rival investigators?"

I grinned. "Aha! Finally, I've stumped the Great O'Nelligan with a literary reference. Yes, the Hardys *are* fellow PIs—though their beards aren't as gray and distinguished as your own." Then, to sweeten the pot, I added, "They leap into their cases as fast as blue darters."

"Touché," my partner muttered.

The three of us spent the next several minutes tossing more good-natured banter back and forth. With Mr. O'Nelligan in the mix, it was feeling even more like the glorious pre-Spires days of yore. Eventually, Audrey checked the time and announced that she needed to be on her way. I told her I'd walk her outside.

Mr. O'Nelligan parted with her poetically, as he was want

to do. "To draw from Yeats, dear Audrey: Go forth . . . and seize whatever prey the heart longs for."

She assured him she'd do just that, and we headed down the staircase. Outside, we paused on the sidewalk for our good-byes. Audrey took one of my hands and squeezed it tightly.

"Will you be around later, Lee?" she asked, a certain tentativeness returning to her voice.

"Not sure yet," I said. "We haven't talked over what our next step is. Maybe another trip to Greenwich Village."

She nodded and smiled gently. "Well, if you want to go snowshoeing . . ."

It was a running joke with us. We'd tried donning snowshoes several winters back and had ended up spending most of the experience on our snow-numbed butts. Now, no matter what the season, we'd reference that fondly remembered failure.

"I need to restring my pair," I joked. "Once they're fixed, just try to hold me back."

We laughed together. Not boisterously, but comfortably. If the ghost of Byron Spires wasn't fully dispelled, it at least was receding into the shadows. We shared a kiss, long enough for the moment, and got in a final squeeze of the hands.

"Off now toward the steeple," I said.

"I'll put in a prayer for you. A long, drawn-out one." She was only half-kidding, I think.

AS I REENTERED the office, Mr. O'Nelligan was lowering the telephone receiver.

"Did someone call?" I asked.

My partner, seated now behind my desk, didn't reply for

several seconds. When he did, there was a certain far-off quality to his tone.

"That was Mrs. Pattinshell," he said.

"Our dear old spook-crooner?"

"What she had to convey was brief—yet intriguing."

"Did the ghosts send her a snappy new tune?"

"In a word, yes. Mrs. Pattinshell wanted to sing it to me over the phone, but I told her it would be best if we came down and heard it in person. I've arranged for us to meet at her apartment at five P.M. today. You see, the point of origin of this particular song is rather startling."

"Well? Who'd she claim sent it?"

"Lorraine Cobble," my partner said quietly. "She says it's the spirit of the murdered Lorraine."

CHAPTER TWENTY-THREE

FOR THE THIRD TIME IN as many days, we found ourselves in Mrs. Pattinshell's darkened, Gothic parlor. Again, she was seated behind the round table with its covering of black lace. And again, candle smoke and incense wafted across the room. My partner and I sat opposite our hostess. As with our previous visits, the resident Siamese had shown its displeasure by bursting out of the room like a low, shrieking rocket.

"Lorraine told me that she wants you to hear this song," Mrs. Pattinshell said.

"Us specifically?" Mr. O'Nelligan asked. "Lee and I?"

"Yes. The song just came to me this morning. Lorraine feels you need to hear it and learn what truth it affords." She flashed me a look of minimal expectation. "If you are at all capable of doing so."

I smiled warmly at her. "We're all ears."

Noticeably unwarmed, the gaunt woman looked away and settled herself in her high-backed chair. "I'll attempt to retrieve the song now."

I pulled out my notepad to jot down the lyrics. Mrs. Pattinshell now closed her eyes and tilted her head back, just as she'd done yesterday. Then her lips parted, and her creaky singing voice pushed out the song. Lorraine's song. It was a slow, haunting ballad, the melody of which seemed to wander all over the place.

"O, learn ye now my woeful end, so high above the town.
Yes, high I stood and saw him come to hurl my poor life down.
His feathers they were red as blood, his name it was red, too.
He said he'd have his vengeance soon, and what he said proved true."

I glanced over at Mr. O'Nelligan. Was he interpreting this in the way I was? The song continued, the singer's voice growing more agitated with the final verse.

"Seek him not within this place, he of the blood-red form.
For he is fled across the waves where none can brave the storm.
Yes, he is fled to face God's wrath, so leave him to his fate.
And leave me to my paradise, and close the churchyard gate."

Having come to the end, Mrs. Pattinshell opened her eyes and straightened herself in her chair. "So there you have it."

"You say it comes from Lorraine?" The skepticism had to be obvious in my voice.

She stared at me. "*Lorraine* says it comes from Lorraine. I've nothing more to add. I've fulfilled her request to pass on the song, and now it's up to you to do with it as you choose."

Mr. O'Nelligan studied the woman for a moment. "As you say, madam. Tell me, did Miss Cobble give a reason why she wished us to hear this ballad?"

"I've already told you," our hostess said sharply. "To learn whatever truth it might offer. Now, I really must get on with the remainder of my day."

She rose and led us to the door, not bothering to turn on the lights or say good-bye or, for that matter, extend her hand to Mr. O'Nelligan for a parting kiss. Instead, she just gestured us into the hallway and stood there, as if barring us from reentering. As we headed off, I glanced back and saw her still framed in the doorway, gazing after us. Behind her, incense smoke drifted in the candlelight like the breath of a ghost.

WE HAD DECIDED beforehand to stop in on our favorite 105-year-old before leaving the building. After we'd left Mrs. Pattinshell's, it was late enough in the day that Cornelius Boyle would already have gotten in his precise four o'clock nap. We climbed up to the fifth floor and knocked at his residence.

The door swung open and I caught my breath. Standing before us was a figure who, by all rights, should not have been there. Looking no more than nine or ten, he was dressed in a worn blue Civil War jacket and cap, with a marching drum strapped over his neck. Staring up at us with big deep eyes, he raised his wooden sticks and beat a rapid tattoo on the drumhead. My brain did a quick contortion, trying to make sense of what I was seeing. An uncanny explanation rushed in on me: *Cornelius has died, and this is his ghost. In death, he's returned to his boyhood.* I stood gaping.

For all his Irish mysticism, it was Mr. O'Nelligan who

responded in the more rational fashion. "Well hello, young lad. Thank you for the musical greeting."

The boy smiled and gave another thump on the drum.

From elsewhere in the room, a stocky, dark-haired woman in her midthirties came forward to stand beside the little drummer. "Who is it, Paulie?"

"There's two men, Mama." Another drumbeat.

A third party now appeared—the one we'd been expecting to find.

"It's all right, Tess. I know these gents." Cornelius, leaning on his gnarled cane, waved us into the room. "This is my granddaughter Tess and her boy Paulie."

"Great-grandson," Paulie announced. "That's what I am."

"Right you are." Cornelius reached over and patted the kid's head. "Paulie here likes to dress up in my old uniform. 'Course, the drum's not the same one I had back then."

"I presumed not," Mr. O'Nelligan said. "Since that one was drilled through at Gettysburg."

The old veteran smiled. "Ah, you remember."

"We studied about Gettysburg in school," Paulie chimed in.

"As well you should have," my partner said. "It's a significant part of your nation's history."

Paulie nodded energetically. "Especially since popcorn was there."

Confusion showed on Mr. O'Nelligan's face. "Well, yes, I suppose . . . Popcorn can be traced back to ancient Peru, I believe, so perhaps . . ."

"No, no, no." Cornelius chuckled. "*I'm* Popcorn. Grandpop Cornelius. Get it? Popcorn."

"That's right, he is," Paulie said definitively.

"Duly noted, young man." Mr. O'Nelligan turned to Cornelius. "We would just like to confirm something with you, sir, if we may."

The old man touched his granddaughter's sleeve. "Give us a minute, will you?"

Tess draped an arm around Paulie's shoulder. "Come on, buddy, you can help me fix Popcorn's dinner."

Mother and son marched out of the room.

Cornelius took a step closer to us. "I wouldn't want to upset them if we're talking about Lorraine's death."

"Of course," I said. "We just wanted to double-check something you told us. About the night she died."

My partner took up the questioning. "You informed us, Cornelius, that sometime between nine thirty and ten that evening, you saw young Hector Escobar standing down the hallway."

"Yeah, I saw him."

"He was positioned near the stairs which lead to the roof."

"That's right."

"You called out to him. You spoke together briefly in Spanish."

"Yes we did. I told you all that yesterday, didn't I?"

"You did, sir," Mr. O'Nelligan said. "The thing is, Lee here has spoken with Hector, and the youth denies having been here at the time you've indicated."

I jumped in. "We're wondering if you might have been mistaken about seeing him then."

"Mistaken?"

"The hall was pretty dark, after all. We're wondering if—"

"I said I saw him, didn't I?" Cornelius sounded edgy now. "A skinny young Puerto Rican kid who answered to the name Hector. Do you think I made that up?"

"We're not saying that," I said.

"Another thing, he called me by my name. He called me Mr. Boyle. Yeah, it was Hector." The elderly man scowled. "You go talk to that kid again. He's hiding something. I saw what I saw. I'm old as dirt, but I'm not daft."

"An observant person would never suggest such a thing," Mr. O'Nelligan said soothingly. "Thank you once again for entertaining our inquiries."

Cornelius gave us a curt nod. "Well, that's all I can tell you."

Paulie now reentered the room, treating us to another erratic drumroll. We took that as our cue to exit.

ON MR. O'NELLIGAN'S insistence, we made another trip to the rooftop. As we'd done on Friday, we walked around the edge with its low bordering wall, pausing at the spot where Lorraine Cobble had stood before her plunge.

"What are you looking for?" I asked my partner. "We didn't notice anything last time evidence-wise."

"I'm not seeking physical evidence," Mr. O'Nelligan said.

"What, then?"

He took a while to answer. "This is the exact spot where a woman stepped from one state of existence to another."

"Stepped or—according to you—was thrown."

"What I mean is that right here is where the veil parted for Lorraine Cobble. One minute she was a human being with desires, flaws, aversions, affections. The next she was . . ."

"A specter?" That's where I thought he was going with this. "A bodiless phantom?"

His eyes met mine. "In one sense or another, yes. Whether we believe in spirits or simply the echoes of a lost life, an energy was released here. The grand spark that coursed through Lorraine's body, motivating her thoughts and actions, flew elsewhere the moment she struck the earth below. I'm just observing the magnitude of that fact."

"I don't know if I believe in grand sparks," I said. "Or in elsewheres."

"There's no shame in that," my friend said quietly. "In not knowing."

"While we're on the general topic, there's the matter of Lorraine's alleged ghost song."

"You don't accept its legitimacy?"

"Do you?"

"I found it . . . worthy of attention. *His feathers they were red as blood . . .*"

I pulled out my notebook and flipped to the lyrics. "*His name it was red, too.* Who does that bring to mind?"

"Cardinal, obviously."

"So do you think Lorraine is telling us that Cardinal Meriam killed her? Because I sure don't. Our ghost chanter obviously made the song up."

"For what purpose?"

"Just to convince us of her eerie abilities," I guessed. "Or maybe she sincerely thought she received it from Lorraine, but it was her own psyche feeding her information. Either way, she'd read the letter from Cardinal just like we did, and she knew the threatening tone of it. The song goes, *He said he'd have his vengeance soon.* Mrs. Pattinshell obviously got that notion from the letter."

"Perhaps. If I recall, the song then directs the listener to leave the killer to God's judgment. To not pursue him. What was that line about the waves?"

I read it to him. *"For he is fled across the waves where none can brave the storm."*

"Yes, that seems to be a reference to the fact that Cardinal abandoned North America for Australia or New Zealand."

"Right. So clearly Mrs. Pattinshell incorporated that info into the song as well."

"Explain, though, how would she know that Cardinal had in fact 'fled across the waves'? Remember, Lee, she told us yesterday that she'd never even heard of Cardinal. Thus, how would she have knowledge of his traveling over the sea?"

"She could have been lying yesterday."

"In order to implicate Cardinal today? Possible, of course. Confounding, but possible." Mr. O'Nelligan smiled lightly. "There are no easy answers here, are there?"

"You want me to believe that a dead woman identified her murderer, tossing in a nice melody to boot?"

"I only want you to believe what your heart and head decree."

I sighed. "If you must know, my heart and head are like some two-bit vaudeville team that never quite got its act together."

My partner's laugh would have been louder, I think, if we hadn't been standing at a place of death.

CHAPTER TWENTY-FOUR

OT HAVING EATEN since breakfast, I talked Mr. O'Nelligan into grabbing some supper nearby. We stumbled upon a little restaurant with a sign boasting "The Best Stew in America!"

"Can't pass *that* up," I reasoned.

The food we were served was certainly top-notch and no doubt American. These days, every time I ate stew, an image of my father intruded. There he was as described by his pal Muleface, clutching his heart over a steaming bowl of the stuff and slumping forward. You'd think I might have avoided that particular meal because of this, but no—being a private eye, I lived dangerously. Besides, just before he died, Dad told ol' Mule that it was the best damned beef stew he'd ever had. As I took in the present warm, tasty spoonful, I wondered how Buster's last stew would have measured up against this one. Between bites, we planned our next moves.

"A return trip to Café Mercutio might be useful," Mr. O'Nelligan suggested. "In addition to a stop at Escobar's Grocery. Though perhaps this time *I* should be the one to talk with Hector."

"Maybe you should," I agreed. "Seeing as my previous exchange with the kid involved tackling."

My partner nodded. "That was my thinking. Your rough-and-tumble methodology might not be appropriate here."

I laughed. "Rough-and-tumble? Yeah, that's me to a tee. A two-fisted terror."

Mr. O'Nelligan pointed his soup spoon at me. "You underestimate yourself, lad. When properly roused, even the mildest creature will bare its fangs."

I thought of last night and my bushwhacking of Byron Spires. "Well, maybe . . ."

"Anyway, let's see if Hector still holds to his story," my partner said.

"Or if he wilts under the power of the patented O'Nelligan glare."

"Aha! Let no one say that Lee Plunkett cannot turn a phrase."

"Coming from you, that's quite the compliment."

"Correct," my friend said with a smile. "It surely is."

The decision was made that my partner would walk over to the grocery while I drove to the coffeehouse. Mr. O'Nelligan would then catch a cab, and we'd reunite at the Mercutio.

"Our path is thus determined," my friend said with his usual flourish.

"By the way, did you reach that acquaintance you said might have some info on the barracks attack? You know, the guy with the excessive name?"

"O'Hallmhurain? I tried calling him, but never got through. I'll give it another go later."

I pulled out my notebook. "Do you still have the letters with you?"

He drew the pair of envelopes from his coat pocket and handed them over. I took a couple minutes comparing Cardinal's letter to Mrs. Pattinshell's song. Yes, the two certainly made interesting companion pieces, but I wasn't prepared to admit more than that. I then gave the shorter typewritten note another look-over. It was as terse as I remembered it:

3/23/57
I'll come by tomorrow at 10. A.M.

"Not much to it, is there?" Mr. O'Nelligan said.

I was about to agree when something caught my eye. I hunched closer over the paper and adjusted my glasses. "Huh. Maybe this is something . . ."

"Yes?"

"Or maybe it's not. Look here." I turned the note sideways so we could both see it. "I hadn't noticed before, but do you see after the '10,' there's a period?"

My colleague leaned in. "Why, yes . . ."

"Normally, if you were indicating a time, you wouldn't put a period between the number and the A.M., would you?"

"No, lad, you would not."

"Maybe it just means there was a slip of a typewriter key. Or . . ."

"Or maybe something more significant." My friend's face broke into a smile. "Lee Plunkett! Ye observant seeker of truth. Well done, lad."

It's possible I blushed. I probably should have acknowledged right then my debt to Miss Beddleton, my fourth-grade teacher. The truth is, had that dedicated educator not been so crush-inspiringly pretty, I would never have bothered to master the niceties of grammar. Under the scrutiny of her bright blue eyes, I'd learned to distinguish a colon from a semicolon, and how to spot a wayward period.

I attempted to follow through. "So, if it's supposed to be an actual period, that means the sentence ends as 'Meet you at 10.'"

"If that's the case, then the requested rendezvous may not have been for the morning after all."

"It may have been for ten in the evening."

"Quite correct," Mr. O'Nelligan said. "Which is within the time interval when Lorraine died. Therefore, whoever typed that note may have been the last person to see her alive. For the very reason that—"

"You're going to claim that the person who wrote that note hurled her off the roof, right?"

"I don't claim anything. I merely suggest possibilities."

"Let's backpedal a second. If the A.M. isn't indicating time of day, then it must stand for something else. Something like . . ."

Like what? I leaned back and began tapping my spoon in the empty bowl. The answer fluttered just out of reach like some elusive butterfly.

"Initials." Mr. O'Nelligan snatched the butterfly. "A. M. might well be the writer's initials."

"You think that's it?"

"I wouldn't bet my soul on it necessarily, but I'd say it's a fine possibility."

"A. M. . . . Who could . . . ? Wait!" I snatched up Cardi-

nal's letter and waved it at my partner. "*M* for Meriam! Cardinal Meriam could have written *both* of these notes. Remember,
we haven't learned his real first name. It could be Andrew or
Arthur, for all we know."

"Very true."

"You know, it occurs to me that Smack Wilton might actually be of some use to us. Since Cardinal had been arrested
in town, the police would have his name on file. His full name.
I'll call the station. Smack probably wouldn't be working late
on a Sunday, but at least I could find out when he'll next be in
and leave a message."

Mr. O'Nelligan stared off and drummed his fingers on the
table. "Yes, Cardinal could be the one who composed the note.
Of course, to fulfill the theory that the note writer killed Lorraine, Cardinal would obviously need to be in the Village—
and not in Australia. It's possible, certainly, that he left New
York right after Lorraine's death or that he never left at all. After
all, no one we spoke to could confirm if Cardinal had ever really
departed. It's also possible, I suppose, that he traveled overseas
briefly, then returned to these environs."

I was trying to keep this all straight. "Okay. So, let's say
Cardinal Meriam is A. M. and he wrote the note asking to
meet Lorraine at ten in the evening . . ."

"Of course, ten could still refer to the morning."

"Don't confuse the issue! You're the one who wants to place
Cardinal on that rooftop with evil intent."

"I'm not sure I said that exactly."

"Anyway, like you pointed out, he'd obviously need to not
be in Australia in order to commit the crime. Unless Cardinal
the Conjurer is such a slick magician and quick-change artist
that he can be in two places at once."

"So you accept now that there was indeed a crime?"

"For the sake of argument. Anyhow, what I'm trying to say here is—" I stopped midsentence, suddenly aware that I didn't know *what* I was trying to say.

Seeing my confusion, Mr. O'Nelligan offered a kind smile. "Yes, it's a complex case with many a twist and turn. It just occurred to me that in order for Mrs. Pattinshell's ghost song to be accurate, Cardinal must have departed *after* Lorraine's death. Because the song says that the man with the blood-red form is now off across the waves."

"Precisely," I said, not feeling precise about anything at the moment.

My brain was spared further overexertion by a loud crash from across the room. A distressed waiter stood surveying three shattered bowls of food that had slipped from his tray. Somebody wasn't getting their best-ever stew tonight.

Mr. O'Nelligan used the disruption to check his pocket watch. "I should be off in pursuit of young Master Hector."

We paid up and parted. On my way to retrieve Baby Blue, I located a telephone booth and called up the police station. As luck would have it, Smack Wilton happened to be on duty.

He sounded fairly pleased to hear from me. "Hey, it's Buster's punk! Crapped out on that Cobble business yet?"

"Alas, no."

Even as I said it, I realized Smack wasn't the sort of guy you'd want to use "alas" with. Clearly, I'd been spending too much time with a certain O'Nelligan.

"Yeah, well, it's your funeral, kid." Smack's tone managed to blend a grumble with a grin. "So, what can I do you for?"

I put out my request for Cardinal's full name and anything else the records might provide. The police detective grunted several times as I was talking, whether in support or disapproval I couldn't tell.

"Think you'd be able to fill me in on that?" I asked.

"Hey, what am I, a contestant on *Twenty-One*?" Smack barked. "I fill in your answers so you can score points?"

"I was just hoping that—"

He spat out a laugh. "Don't sweat it. I'm just kicking your goat there."

I wanted to ask if goat-kicking was a desirable thing but held back.

"Sure, I'll track down your guy for you," Smack said. "Thing is, my shift's ending now and I'm heading home. Since these bastards got me scheduled for tomorrow morning again, I can dig through the files then. Okay, kid?"

"Sure. Thanks."

"Hey, we got Wilton and Plunkett collaborating again, just like when your pop and I raised hell back in the old days. Pretty swell, huh?"

The swellest. I thanked Smack again, rang off, and resumed my walk.

As I was approaching my car, a tall, stooped man came limping toward me, a bulging sack slung over one shoulder. His unkempt hair, uneven shave, and overlayered clothes made me guess that the street was his home.

Without pausing, he fixed bloodshot eyes on me and hissed, "The world's a shadow!"

Somehow, the way things were going, that actually made sense.

CHAPTER TWENTY-FIVE

ET AGAIN, WITH SUNSET rolling in, I entered the Café Mercutio. Stepping through the door had become a familiar little ritual. Candlelight, sawdust, and circus posters. The same as last night, I found an almost empty room. At one table, Kimla Thorpe sat alone drinking coffee and reading a newspaper. At another, two bearded young men were arguing politics in low urgent voices. To-night, Ruby Dovavska was again the attending waitress.

She favored me with her thin sardonic smile. "Back so soon? Reconsidering posing for me, maybe?"

"Not at all." I nodded toward the whiskered debaters. "Why don't you recruit those guys? You could get two for one."

"It wouldn't be the first time," Ruby said.

I blushed. "Where's your boss?"

"He probably won't be in till late. Sunday nights are pretty slow here. No music."

An elderly woman in a trench coat and beret entered, and Ruby went to take her order.

I approached Kimla. "Anything of interest in the papers?"

She glanced up from her reading. "Only the usual confusion, crime, and sadness."

"What about Little Orphan Annie? She's in there, too, isn't she? Annie always sees the bright side of life."

Kimla smiled gently. "You're right, she does."

"Remember now, that kid's even an orphan. Say, did Patch ever show up last night?"

"I'm not sure. I left Tim and Neil soon after you saw us. Knowing Patch, he probably staggered home at some god-awful hour, cursing or weeping or possibly both."

"Have any of the regular musicians been by today?"

"Only Manymile, and only for a second. He stopped by just to say that he'd gotten a series of gigs in the Midwest and was hitting the road." Kimla took a sip of coffee. "Any updates on your investigation, Mr. Plunkett?"

I nearly blurted out about Lorraine Cobble's ghost song but thought better of it. After all, Mr. O'Nelligan and I hadn't yet discussed if we wanted to make that piece of the puzzle common knowledge. Suddenly, one of the intense beards shouted out, "Trotsky, without question!" In response, his friend slapped the table, and across the room the lady in the beret laughed heartily.

The front door now opened, and in walked a young couple, one half of whom—of course—just had to be Byron Spires. Unsurprisingly, he had a lovely young woman on his arm, and, what do you know, it was a brand-new model. Just as Audrey had given way to Coco, Coco had yielded the field to a thin waif with blond bangs. Upon noticing me, Spires halted, spun his girl about, and headed back out the door. I followed.

I caught up with them just down the street and maneuvered to block their way. Spires sighed deeply and turned to his date. "Go back inside and grab us a table, will ya, Nicki? I'll be right there."

Nicki didn't seem too pleased with being yo-yoed around, but she complied. Spires and I were mirroring our dance from the night before. He folded his arms across his chest and stared at me. This time he had no guitar and, by the look of it, no patience.

"Okay, so what the hell do you want?" he asked.

It struck me just then that I didn't really know the answer to that. What was my intention here, anyway? To shove him against the wall again? To apologize for last night's ambush? To further interrogate him about Lorraine? Or maybe to ask him what the blazes his secret was for enticing women . . . "So we meet again," I said for want of anything better.

Spires maintained his stare. "Look, man, I'm just trying to exist. I don't want no agitation, and I don't want no enemies. Just trying to live and love like any beast on two legs. Like I told you last night, your girl digs you, not me. So we've got no quarrel, you and I, right? You want to drop by here sometime and hear my music, fine. Otherwise, you go your own way and I'll go mine. Nobody likes being hunted, friend. I'm gonna go live my life now. Happy trails."

With that, Spires turned and headed for the Mercutio.

He never got there.

The gunshot echoed through the twilight like an angry shout. I saw Spires stagger and clutch his chest, and I caught a glimpse of someone standing just beyond us down the street. It was a man in a slouched hat and long black coat. Something bright flashed in his hand, and another shot rang out.

That's when the hammer struck the side of my head—at least that's what it felt like. Next came more sounds: shoes slapping concrete, agitated voices, a shrill whistle, and a low drawn-out moan. It took me a while to realize that the moan was coming from me and that I was lying sprawled on my back on the sidewalk, my face turned to one side. Something warm and wet was sliding down my right temple. My glasses had somehow remained on, and I could make out Byron Spires a few yards from me. He, too, lay crumpled on the sidewalk, the two bearded debaters leaning over him. He seemed very still.

Then a hand was resting on my cheek. Somehow I knew it was a feminine one. Carefully, my head was shifted so that I was now staring upward. What I saw was two sweet, beautiful faces, a single bright halo drifting high above them. I assumed they were angels, one light-skinned, one dark, who had come to guide me away. I felt deeply grateful. For a fleeting second, they took the form of Ruby and Kimla, their concerned faces silhouetted against the ring of a streetlamp. Then they became angels again, wonderfully radiant, and under their loving protection I slipped into blackness.

PART 3

Riddle Song

What is higher than a tree?
What is deeper than the sea?

What is sharper than a thorn?
What is louder than a horn?

    Heaven is higher than a tree.
    Hell is deeper than the sea.

    Hunger is sharper than a thorn.
    And guilt is louder than a horn.

        —Traditional British ballad

CHAPTER TWENTY-SIX

WHEN I WOKE IN THE UN-familiar bedroom, for a minute or two I thought I'd just had one of my crazy dreams—maybe was still having one. Then I felt the throbbing in my head and brought my hand up to touch the bandage there. Oh, hell. Right, the gunshots, the ambulance, the hospital. The fast-speaking doctor telling me I was lucky, damned lucky, that the bullet had only kissed my temple. Kissed it, that's what the doc had said. I remember thinking, *I've had better kisses.*

I pushed myself out of bed and stood on wobbly legs. Morning sunshine slanted in through white lace curtains. There was a ton of white lace in the room, come to think of it. A woman's room. But what woman? Had my rattled brain led me into some sort of spicy intrigue? No. Clearly, I wasn't thinking straight. Then I remembered: Marguerite, Mr. O'Nelligan's Marguerite—this was her apartment. I'd been brought here last night after leaving the hospital. My clothes had been neatly folded and placed on a chair, but definitely not by my own hand. I could never fold anything that precisely, but Mr. O'Nelligan undoubtedly could. I got dressed and went in search of him.

The aroma of coffee led me to a small kitchen, where my friend greeted me eagerly. "Lazarus has risen!"

"Barely. Yeah, apparently I'm alive."

"I've brewed you some coffee. Shall I whip you up an omelet? Or some French toast?"

"No, just the coffee." I seated myself at the kitchen table. "Where's your lady friend? I don't remember seeing her last night."

"Because you didn't." Mr. O'Nelligan poured me a cup. "Marguerite was heading out of town for the evening, but she passed on her keys to me. Once I'd explained your situation."

"Too bad, I wanted to meet her. You said she was sparkly." I took a deep drink of black coffee and immediately felt less fuzzy. "Speaking of my situation, what the hell is it?"

"Do you remember what transpired?"

"Sort of. Some guy shot at me. Me and Spires." The image of the young singer's crumpled body returned to me. "Jesus, what happened to Spires?"

"He's alive, but apparently his injury was severe. A bullet in the chest. I believe he was operated on last night."

"When did you get there? Right after we were shot?"

"By the time I arrived at the Mercutio, you'd already been transported to the hospital. I hastened there directly. I must admit, it was a terrible interval for me—waiting to see how badly you . . ." My partner glanced away and blinked several times. "Thank God, you were intact."

I touched my head. "Sure, you could call it that. Just a graze—isn't that what they say? In the Westerns, it always sounds so rugged. *I'm okay, Dusty, it's just a graze.* Truth is, it barely seems like I've been shot. Feels more like I tried to butt a brick wall. So, what about the guy who did it? Did they catch him?"

"As it happened, a young patrolman was only two blocks from the Mercutio when he heard the shots. He raced to the scene in time to give chase but never caught up with your attempted assassin."

"Assassin . . . Lincoln had an assassin. Gandhi had an assassin. I don't think I'm important enough to merit one."

"Someone might have thought differently. Though, of course, we don't know if you were the intended target or Byron Spires."

"Must be Spires, right? I suppose some irate boyfriend might have resented him romancing his girl." I could have added *I speak from experience.* "After all, he's the one who took the full brunt of things."

"True, but it's equally possible that you, Lee, were the intended victim, and young Spires was struck down by accident. It's also possible that our investigation into Lorraine Cobble's death might be the reason for the attack."

"You think that's really it?"

"I couldn't say for certain, but someone may have found our explorations threatening."

I pondered that a moment and suddenly felt more than a little woozy. It was one thing to think I'd been an innocent bystander caught in the wrong place at the wrong time. It was another to imagine someone wanted to turn me, specifically, into a cadaver. If that was the case, then Spires was the unfortunate bystander. I suddenly felt remorse—an emotion I sure didn't want to have where Byron Spires was concerned.

"I may have put Spires in harm's way," I said, mostly to myself.

"In harm's way . . ." Mr. O'Nelligan repeated the words slowly. "That's the phrase Minnie Bornstein used, remember? When she shared her concern that one of us two might run into trouble. It seems her premonition has proven accurate."

I gave a little shudder. A dim memory from the hospital floated to my brain. "Some police detectives talked with me last night, didn't they? Everything's a little cloudy."

"That's not surprising," my partner said. "After all, you suffered what nearly amounts to a concussion. Yes, the detectives did speak briefly with you."

"Smack wasn't one of them, was he?"

"No. I inquired about Detective Wilton and was told he was off duty. You were asked last night if you'd gotten a look at the gunman. You reported that he wore a black coat, but provided nothing beyond that."

Something occurred to me. "I didn't happen to say he had red hair, did I?"

"No, why? *Was* his hair red?"

"I don't know, since he was wearing a hat, but I'm thinking of Cardinal Meriam. Maybe he's here in town and got wind that investigators were poking around. Maybe he's the one who pushed Lorraine off the roof."

"What makes you suggest that?"

Whatever my answer was—and I'm not sure I had one— was put off by the sound of a door buzzer.

"Expecting someone?" I asked.

"I am." My friend vanished deeper into the apartment, and I heard him buzz in whoever was down below.

I set my cup aside, stood, and gently touched my head again. Still there. I heard a door open in another room, followed by muffled greetings. Mr. O'Nelligan reentered the kitchen with his guest.

Audrey had her arms around me so fast I barely registered that it was her. She kept me enwrapped for almost a minute. I could feel her body tremble against mine and knew she was sobbing silently.

Finally, she stepped back and wiped her eyes. "I was out late last night at the drive-in with my folks. Mr. O'Nelligan didn't reach me till this morning."

"I thought it best not to distress you in the middle of the night," our friend explained. "Especially since the patient had already been put to bed."

Audrey drew in a deep breath. "Oh God, Lee. When he called and said you'd been shot in the head—"

"Geez!" I stared sharply at my partner. "You didn't really put it like that, did you?"

Mr. O'Nelligan looked aghast. "I certainly did not! My presentation was commendably subtle."

"He's right. Sorry," Audrey said. "Still, no matter how carefully worded, it still amounted to you being shot in the head."

I deepened my voice. "It was just a graze, Dusty."

"What?"

"Never mind. I'm okay, Audrey. I was lucky."

"Lucky?" She gave me a quizzical look. "Do you realize, Lee, that in the year and a half since you took over your father's business, that skull of yours has managed to get rammed, punched, or shot at least three times that I can recall?"

I thought about it and realized she was right. "Even Dad would have been impressed with that record."

My fiancée scowled. "Only *you* would brag about getting your brains addled."

"It's nice when a woman is proud of her man."

Audrey smiled begrudgingly. "What a piece of work you are, Mr. Plunkett."

There was something I needed to bring up. "You know about Byron Spires?"

Her smile faded. "Yes, it's dreadful. I've been praying for him. I hope he pulls through."

"So do I." However much the singer rankled me, I certainly didn't want him laid out in a morgue. Especially if he took a bullet intended for me.

Audrey made me review what had happened last night. She listened intently, squeezing her eyes shut when I came to the moment when the shots were fired. I did my best to minimize the situation, but I knew I wasn't fooling her. When I finished the account, Audrey reached over, gripped my hand, and said nothing.

I suddenly remembered Mr. O'Nelligan's mission. "How'd it go yesterday with Hector Escobar?"

"I never saw him," my colleague said. "By the time I arrived at the grocery, he'd already left. I can try again today."

"If you want, but it's Cardinal I'm wondering about now. I need to call Smack and see what he found out. Where's the telephone?"

Mr. O'Nelligan led me into the adjacent living room, and

Audrey followed. I pulled out Smack's number, grabbed up the phone, and started dialing. I was feeling motivated and mad.

"Lee, don't just go leaping back into things," Audrey said. "You need to rest up. You've been shot, for heaven's sake."

"Shot, but not shut up." My Cagney was going full steam, and his dialogue was atrocious. "I've got a little red bird I need to pluck."

Mr. O'Nelligan softly groaned.

Smack Wilton was in at the station. "Heard you had a little mishap," he said. "Coulda been worse, though, kid. At least you didn't take one in the chest like your buddy Spitz."

"Spitz?"

"Mortimer B. Spitz." It sounded like he was reading it off some notes. "The guy who got shot with you. Goes by the moniker Spires, but I guess that's just his show business name."

Before last night, I would have been delighted to learn that the dashing Byron Spires was, in reality, Mortimer Spitz. Under the present circumstances, I wasn't deriving much satisfaction from the fact.

"Any word on his condition?"

"I hear it's touch and go," Smack said.

"Did they find the man who shot us?"

"Nothing solid yet, but the guys on the case tell me they may have some witnesses who saw him when he was galloping off."

"What about Cardinal Meriam? Anything on him?"

"Not a lot. Canadian. Arrested for vandalism last winter. Charges dropped. Present whereabouts unknown. That's all I found."

"What's his real first name?"

"Spencer. Y'know, like Spencer Tracy."

Nothing with an *A*. "How about his middle name?"

I heard Smack ruffling through papers. "Lawrence."

After thanking Smack for his trouble, I hung up and shared what I'd learned with Mr. O'Nelligan.

"Spencer Lawrence Meriam." My partner rolled the words around on his tongue. "No A. M. there."

"So there goes that theory," I said. "Seems Cardinal wasn't the one who wrote that note. Not to say he couldn't still be our rooftop rogue."

"What are you two trying to figure out?" Audrey asked.

Briefly, I explained about the note and its unknown author.

Audrey listened carefully, then nodded. "I get it, Lee. Well, I can think of someone right off the bat."

"Someone who could be A. M.?"

"Uh-huh. Maybe you overlooked him because you've only heard his name in its short form."

"Short form?"

"Yes, like 'Lee' is short for 'Leander.'"

I cringed a little; I hated to hear my full name.

"Likewise, 'Tony' is short for 'Anthony.'" Audrey paused for effect. "A. M. could stand for Anthony Mazzo, couldn't it?"

Mr. O'Nelligan and I turned to look at each other, neither saying anything.

Audrey laughed. "I'll take that as a yes."

CHAPTER TWENTY-SEVEN

BACK TO THE MERCUTIO. All three of us. This followed an impassioned debate in which I adamantly refused to let Audrey join us in confronting the man who might have killed Lorraine Cobble. The other half of this debate consisted of Audrey, with equal adamance, refusing to let me an inch out of her sight after I'd nearly gotten my fool head blown off. When I looked to Mr. O'Nelligan for support, he merely shrugged, unwilling to get caught in the crossfire. I ended up caving in, but only under the condition that I could be sure of her safety. I called Smack Wilton back, explained that we might be facing off with a dangerous man, and asked if he could meet us at the Mercutio. Not sounding overly convinced or concerned, he told me he was presently spoken for but would arrange for a uniformed officer to show up.

Audrey drove us across town. She located a space to park

right behind Baby Blue, whose windshield, in my absence, had been decorated with several parking tickets. Outside the coffeehouse, we found Smack's promised cop, a stocky, cynical-looking fellow.

"We don't need you to go in with us," I explained, "but we'd be grateful if you stayed within shouting distance."

The cop nodded curtly and stationed himself a few yards away. It wasn't yet noon, and the Mercutio's door was locked, but after some persistent knocking, Tony Mazzo opened up and ushered us in. There was no one else in the place.

Mazzo looked surprised to see me. "I'm so glad to find you ambulatory, man! After last night. Vicious, just vicious. Poor Byron. You're doing okay, though?"

I removed my homburg, revealing my bandaged head. "In a manner of speaking. We need to talk with you."

Mazzo gestured us to a table. I made sure to take a seat between him and Audrey. Whatever his response to our accusations might be, I didn't want the tall, blocky ex-soldier within arm's length of my fiancée.

I pulled the typed note out of my jacket and smoothed it out in front of him. "Did you write this?"

Mazzo's jaw clenched as he stared down at the piece of paper. "Why would you think that?"

"A. M.—Anthony Mazzo." I glanced over at Audrey and caught a tiny smile on her lips.

"You know, I don't have a monopoly on those initials." Mazzo fidgeted with his handlebar mustache. "Could be anyone. Like . . ." He glanced around, trying to conjure up a name. Any name.

"Like Ace Morgan, perhaps?" Mr. O'Nelligan offered. "His initials are also A. M."

Caught off guard, I stared at my partner. "Who's Ace Morgan?"

"He's the leader of the Challengers of the Unknown, a team of purple-garbed comic book adventurers. They have an intriguing origin tale."

Where the heck was he going with this?

Mr. O'Nelligan continued. "Having survived unscathed a horrific plane crash, the Challengers believe that they're living on borrowed time and conduct their lives accordingly. An interesting concept, isn't that, Mr. Mazzo—living on borrowed time? The knowledge that, at any moment, one's fate may catch up with one. That fate could be, for example, the revelation of a secret."

The Grand Mazzo wasn't looking so grand. "I don't know what you're—"

"Come now, sir." Mr. O'Nelligan leaned in toward him. "You obviously have something you wish to unburden yourself of."

"If you mean being gay . . ."

"You know that's not what I'm referring to." My partner reached over and tapped the note. "*This* is what we're interested in."

Mazzo ran a hand through the bomb-induced streak in his hair. "Okay . . . Okay . . . Yeah, it's from me. To Lorraine."

"It was found in an envelope with no address," I said. "Which suggested it was hand-delivered. We're wondering why."

"I'd tried stopping by Lorraine's a couple times earlier that week," Mazzo said, "but she was never home. I couldn't reach her by phone, either. That Saturday I typed this up to slip under her door, in case she wasn't there again when I stopped by—which, as it turned, she wasn't. So I left the note."

"Your rendezvous was for ten P.M.?" Mr. O'Nelligan asked.

"That's right."

My partner smoothed his beard. "How was Miss Cobble to know you intended to arrive at ten in the evening, and not in the morning? Your note didn't indicate which you meant."

"Lorraine would know I wouldn't be up and about before noon. I'm a night owl. Everyone knows that about me."

I didn't debate him on that. "Okay, but why'd you type the note? So you couldn't be identified?"

"I type everything, man. Even grocery lists. It's a mania with me."

"But why use initials? Why not 'Mazzo' or 'Tony'?"

"It's just how I've always signed my letters. What's next, are you going to ask how many licks I used to seal the envelope?"

"Sure, make jokes," I said. "You're a regular Jackie Gleason, aren't you?"

Mazzo chose not to answer.

"All right," I continued, "assuming everything you just said is true—"

"Which it is."

"*Assuming* it's true, what's the reason you were so anxious to talk to her in private?"

"It was something, well, of a sensitive nature, dig?"

"No, I do not dig," I said. "I do not dig at all. Your note says you wanted to meet Lorraine on the evening she died. The evening she died . . . That's pretty interesting."

Mazzo's eyes narrowed. "Sure, that's how it turned out, but there's no way I could've known that's what it would be. Her last day, I mean."

"No?" I fixed him with a stare. "We're wondering if, in fact, you didn't have something to do with it being her last day."

Mazzo shifted uncomfortably in his chair. "That's what I was afraid you might think. When I found out that Lorraine was dead, I figured it was best not to have my name mixed up in things. I mean, her death was a suicide, so what good would it do to have anyone know I'd been at Lorraine's that night?"

"Then that was your place of rendezvous?" Mr. O'Nelligan asked. "Lorraine's rooftop?"

"No, her apartment. Anyway, all of a sudden you guys show up in town, poking around and suggesting that Lorraine's death was murder. It made me nervous."

"So what did you do to calm your nerves?" I asked. "Try to gun me down in the street, maybe?"

Mazzo leapt to his feet, and his chair crashed backward to the floor. Instinctively, I threw an arm across Audrey.

He glared down at me. "Nobody comes into my place and accuses me like that!"

Mr. O'Nelligan spoke slowly and calmly. "Perhaps my associate expressed himself too stridently just now. Please take your seat, sir."

As usual, my friend's genteel brogue proved persuasive. After exercising his glower for another few seconds, Mazzo righted the chair and reseated himself.

He exhaled loudly. "Look, Plunkett, you're crazy if you think I'm out to kill anybody. I had enough of that in the war. It's Bad-news-ville that you and Byron got shot, but I had a lot of pals who stopped a slug back in the Pacific. The world's a dangerous place."

Reluctant to compare myself to the dead of Guadalcanal, I simply said, "Tell us why you needed to see Lorraine that night."

Mazzo looked away; he seemed to be weighing his options.

Mr. O'Nelligan nudged him toward honesty. "It will be best for all concerned if you address that query."

"All right, but there's no reason for this to become common knowledge. You're professionals, right? You don't need to go blabbing this around the Village." Mazzo looked over at Audrey. "And that means you, too, babe—whatever *you're* doing here."

Audrey cocked her head toward me. "I'm Plunkett's bodyguard."

I groaned under my breath.

Mazzo, equally unamused, sighed and folded his hands on the table. "Lorraine had threatened to reveal something about me from a few years ago. Back when Joe McCarthy was dragging people over the coals looking for Reds."

"Yes, you've shared that episode," Mr. O'Nelligan said. "How you stood up to your interrogators."

Tony Mazzo stared at his hands. "Well, maybe it wasn't exactly like that."

"You didn't face down some government witch hunters?" I asked.

"I *faced* them. I wouldn't really call it facing down."

"So that stuff about giving those guys the names of Shakespeare characters . . ."

"That was true up to a point. Yeah, I was cocky to begin with, but those bastards wore me down. They called me a 'lavender lad' and said they'd turn my life into a nightmare. Back then I was still hiding who I truly was, not like now. In the end, I gave them what they wanted. I gave up my friends."

Mr. O'Nelligan furrowed his brow. "It seems odd that you should then go on to promote the fact that you'd been interrogated. Why not simply remain silent about it?"

"Somehow word had gotten around the Village that I'd been hauled in by those guys. I couldn't deny that, so I made up the version where I told them to go to hell. That made me sort of a hero around here. I guess the more I told the lie, the more it seemed to me like that's what really happened. The Village is full of myths and delusions."

"Another thing intrigues me," my partner said. "You went so far as to call your establishment the Café Mercutio . . ."

"One of the friends I gave up—the one I'd first told them was named Mercutio—just couldn't take it when the federal guys went for him. He was a lavender lad, too, a sweet, noble kid. He, well . . ." A look of pain crossed Mazzo's face. "He ended up taking his own life. To honor his memory, I named this place after him in a roundabout way. Of course, nobody knows that but me—and now all of you."

Audrey was the first to respond. "It's like an act of penance in a way, yes?"

Mazzo looked at her gratefully. "That's it. Yes, penance . . ."

I needed to move us forward. "So Lorraine Cobble somehow got hold of this information."

"Yeah, though I'm not sure how," Mazzo said. "One day last month, she told me she knew the true story and might someday get the urge to share it around town."

"So we're talking blackmail?" I asked.

"Sort of like blackmail on layaway. She was just dangling

the thing over me, hinting that she might want something from me someday in order to stay quiet. Once she'd put that out, I felt like I was living under the Sword of Damocles. I started trying to contact Lorraine to resolve things, to get her to promise to keep her mouth shut. Like I've said, that's what eventually led me to leaving this note."

"Bring us back to that night," Mr. O'Nelligan said. "Did you follow up on the note and arrive at Miss Cobble's apartment at ten P.M.?"

"I did."

"Then what?"

"I knocked, but there was no answer," Mazzo recounted. "I knew there was a possibility that Lorraine might blow me off and not be home. After knocking for a while, I tried the door, and it opened. I thought it was odd that she'd left it unlocked if she wasn't there, so I went inside. I was wondering if maybe she was sleeping."

"Did you close the door behind you when you entered?" my partner asked.

"I left it opened a crack. Anyhow, her apartment was empty, so I sort of lingered there, thinking maybe she'd just run out for a second and would be coming back to meet me. At one point, I heard voices in the hallway and thought it might be her. I stood next to the door and listened but realized it wasn't."

"Voices?" Mr. O'Nelligan leaned forward. "Who did they belong to?"

"One I'm pretty sure was the hundred-year-old guy who lives down the hall."

"One hundred and five," my partner amended.

"Right. The other voice I couldn't make out."

"Could it have been a young guy with a Puerto Rican accent?" I asked.

"An accent sounds right," Mazzo said tentatively. "Anyway, by the time I left, there was no one in the hallway."

I followed up on that. "What time would you say this was?"

"I got there around ten and left maybe a half hour later."

"Without having seen Lorraine," Mr. O'Nelligan clarified.

"Yeah, without having seen her. Ever again, actually."

"Which is to your benefit, right?" I pointed out. "Since you no longer have to worry about her giving you away. You must feel like a real lucky cat."

"That's one way of looking at it," Mazzo said edgily.

I matched his tone. "There are a lot of ways of looking at everything you've just told us. A lot of strange, funny, suspicious ways."

"The Mercutio's closed right now," Mazzo snapped. "No coffee, no music, no poetry. You posed your questions, and I answered them. It's time you all vacated."

He stood and gave his plush mustache a final twirl, looking very much like the villain from an old melodrama.

"Thanks for the hospitality," I said, rising.

"Go to hell, my friend." Mazzo somehow managed to sound well-mannered and menacing in the same breath. Like a graceful acrobat cavorting with growling lions.

CHAPTER TWENTY-EIGHT

ACK OUTSIDE, I THANKED our uniformed guardian, slipping him a couple of bucks for his trouble. The cop's scowl made me think he might arrest me for bribery, until I realized that his displeasure wasn't with the act but with the amount. I reluctantly forked over a fiver, which seemed to satisfy him. As the pride of the force sauntered off, Mr. O'Nelligan and I began reviewing our encounter with Mazzo.

"If the man's to be believed, this focuses our aim considerably," my partner said.

"Who says he *should* be believed. Mazzo seemed to have a fast, handy answer to every question."

"Is that not what we were seeking?"

"*Too* handy for my taste."

"When one decides to unleash the truth, it oft comes swiftly."

"Sure, maybe everything he said about the Red-hunters and Lorraine's threats is true, and about him sneaking into her apartment. To me, the logical conclusion of all that is Mazzo somehow coaxing Lorraine to the roof, heaving her off, and eventually gunning down the PI who's on his trail."

"I feel the need to point out that until recently, you weren't even willing to admit that there *was* a trail that required pursuing."

I indicated my bullet-kissed temple. "Well, that's changed."

"And you're convinced Anthony Mazzo was your attacker?"

"Let's just say I'm not convinced otherwise. If I'd felt we had an ironclad case against him, I would have thrown him to our cop pal."

Audrey joined in. "Mazzo seemed sincere to me. After all, he didn't have to share that he'd been at Lorraine's that night."

"Oh, yes he did," I said. "Remember, I'd already connected him to the note."

My fiancée's eyes widened playfully. "Golly, Lee, *you* connected him to the note? I guess I missed that part of the deductive process."

"I mean *you* did," I muttered.

"What's that? Louder, please."

Our Irishman intruded. "Let us, for the moment, assume that Mazzo's account is truthful. One part of it struck me as quite significant. For the first time, we have confirmation of Cornelius Boyle's claim that he spoke to Hector Escobar in the hallway. Again, we are brought back to the grocery boy and his refusal to admit his presence there that night."

"Which, of course, doesn't even matter if Mazzo is our culprit," I said.

"True, but if Mazzo is blameless here, then Hector's denial

may have great import indeed. I suggest that I follow through on yesterday's task and pay the boy a visit."

"Okay, maybe it'll prove worthwhile," I admitted. "I'm coming with you, though. I don't want to divide our forces right now. Don't forget, as far as we know, whoever shot down Spires and nicked me is still out there, whether it's Mazzo or some other gunman."

"So we presume," Mr. O'Nelligan said. "Although the gendarmerie is now in pursuit of him."

"Yeah, well, pursuit isn't the same as capture. I'm not sure how effective Smack's cronies will be. Anyway, we'll drive over to the grocery." I turned to Audrey. "But not you."

"That's where you're wrong," she said matter-of-factly. "There's no way you're shaking me loose."

I stood my ground. "Did you not just hear me say there's a mean person with a pistol running about?"

"And did you not just hear me say I'm sticking with you? If you try to march off on me, Lee, I'll just follow behind, determined and devoted."

"Like a cocker spaniel?"

Audrey gave me the evil eye. "No, dearest. I was thinking more like a guardian angel. You are such a chowderhead sometimes."

I turned to Mr. O'Nelligan. "Talk to her, will you?"

My partner smiled. "I fear that no eloquence on my part would suffice to avert our young lady's obstinacy."

"What in God's name are you saying?" I asked.

Audrey matched Mr. O'Nelligan's smile. "He says I'm coming with you."

* * *

TWO DAYS BEFORE, Mr. Escobar had been the one stationed outside the grocery overseeing the produce stands. Today, conveniently for us, it was Hector. The kid's focus, though, plainly wasn't on fruit and vegetables but on the petite, pretty girl whose hand he was holding and whose eyes he was locked into. Once he saw us approaching, Hector released the girl's hand and stared us down.

"Why are you here?" His defiant tone was clearly meant to impress not only us but his girl as well. "I already talked to you people."

"We enjoyed it so much the first time, we came back." I was feeling fairly defiant myself, especially with no Toro in sight.

Hector turned back to his girlfriend, and they shared an exchange in Spanish. Without understanding a word of it, I think I caught the gist: Hector wanted Rosalia—that's how he addressed her—to leave him to his enemies, but she refused to do so. I glanced from the girl to my fiancée. Apparently, Rosalia was a small Puerto Rican version of Audrey.

Once he realized that his young lady was immovable, Hector faced us again. "So, what do you want?"

Mr. O'Nelligan took on the narrative duties, explaining how Cornelius had once again insisted he'd seen the teenager that night and adding Mazzo's confirmation for good measure.

Hector took it all in, then shook his head vigorously. "No, no, no! I told you, that was not me."

I started to lay into his denial but was promptly cut off by Rosalia.

"Can't you see he's telling the truth?" Though obviously upset, she kept her voice steady and strong. "Hector is not someone who likes to make lies. He has a very good heart. Hector! Swear on your cross. Then they'll know you're speaking the truth."

Rosalia reached over and drew out a thin silver chain that was hidden under Hector's shirtfront. She placed its tiny crucifix into his palm and nodded at him.

Hector looked at us, quietly said, "I swear," then kissed the cross and slid it back under his shirt.

"It belonged to his *abuela,*" Rosalia told us. "His grandmother. He loved her very much and would never swear on it if a thing wasn't true. He just wouldn't."

I didn't know how to respond to that, but apparently Mr. O'Nelligan did.

"Of course he wouldn't," my partner said gently. "Thank you for clearing that up. We'll leave you young people to this lovely spring afternoon."

He gave them a little bow and led us away.

AUDREY AND I were leaning against Baby Blue, about two blocks from the grocery, as Mr. O'Nelligan paced slowly before us, his brow knit and his hands folded behind his back.

"So, what's going on in that multilayered brain of yours?" I asked my colleague.

"All brains are multilayered," he answered absently. "Mine need not be singled out."

"Fair enough. What rollicking thoughts are filling yours right now?"

Mr. O'Nelligan stopped in his tracks. "I'm attempting to arrange the particulars of this case in a useful order. To separate the wheat from the chaff, as it were."

"Well, I don't know if Hector's the wheat or the chaff here," I said. "Just because your girlfriend defends you doesn't make you a worthwhile person."

Audrey turned to me. "I feel like I should say something biting. I'm just not sure what."

"Please don't overexert yourself."

"Anyway, I think Hector's being truthful," she stated firmly. "That's my opinion."

I was on the verge of asking Audrey when exactly she'd obtained her private investigator's license, but, for the sake of my health and well-being, I didn't.

Instead I said, "If Hector is on the up-and-up, that means it's Cornelius who's lying."

Suddenly, Mr. O'Nelligan made an announcement. "I'm going for a stroll. Lee, may I borrow the list of phone numbers pertinent to this case?"

"Sure, I suppose." I handed the list over. "Why do you—"

"Everyone we've spoken to is accounted for here?"

"Yeah, I've been gathering numbers since we started."

"Excellent, excellent." My colleague gestured across the street. "Over there's a pleasant-looking—though oddly named—little eatery, Trenchard's Tomato Tavern. Why don't you two take your lunch and I'll meet you there in an hour or so's time?"

With that, he spun on his heel and strode away.

Audrey seemed somewhat shocked. "What just happened? In the middle of an investigation, Mr. O'Nelligan goes off on a private little promenade? I thought he'd be much more dedicated than that."

"Don't knock those promenades. It's when he gets his best deducing done and earns his dime—so to speak."

"Speaking of dimes, Lee, when are you going to start paying Mr. O'Nelligan for his work?"

"I've tried! Time and time again, I've insisted he take

something, but he refuses. He just prattles on about quests and knights and all his usual quackery. So don't blame me."

Audrey laughed. "You're no match for that old rapscallion, are you?"

"I certainly am not."

OVER SOUP AND sandwiches, I quickly brought Audrey up to speed on the investigation. Since she was refusing to abandon me, she might as well know what we were up against. Once I'd gotten the storyline up to today's events, Audrey leaned back in her chair and brought her fingertips together in a contemplative pose.

"Lorraine Cobble certainly seems to have been a contentious woman," she observed. "With many enemeies."

"Many enemies, one killer," I said.

"What is that, an old Eastern proverb?"

"Yes, one I just made up. Maybe I should perch myself on some mountaintop and dispense wisdom to truth seekers."

"Maybe you should confine yourself to just babbling to your fiancée. At least I'm used to it."

I wagged a soup spoon at her. "You know, some people consider me quite the wit. I'm not sure exactly who those people are, but I'm positive they exist."

Audrey giggled and shook her head. "Oh, brother . . ."

The restaurant owner, gray-haired and congenial, approached our table. "Are you Lee?"

"I am."

"A friend of yours just called." He glanced down at the scrap of paper he was holding. "O'Nelligan. He said he was in a rush but wanted to get a message to you. I wrote it down."

"How'd he reach you?"

"Not many Trenchard's Tomato Taverns in the phone book, I guess."

Of course, Mr. O'Nelligan wouldn't likely forget such alliteration. Mr. Trenchard of the Tomatoes passed me the note and departed.

I read it aloud. "'Meet at Mrs. Pattinshell's apartment as soon as possible.' Mrs. Pattinshell's? Why there?"

"She's the ghost chanter, right?" Audrey asked. "Maybe she's got another song for you."

I moaned a little. "Lord, I hope not. Getting sung to by dead people is not my idea of entertainment. I'll take Nat King Cole over Casper the Friendly Ghost any day. You sure you still want to keep going with this?"

My fiancée grinned and slapped the table. "Aye, aye, Captain! Where thou goest, I go, too."

CHAPTER TWENTY-NINE

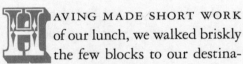AVING MADE SHORT WORK of our lunch, we walked briskly the few blocks to our destination. Just outside the building, we encountered Cornelius Boyle, dressed in his usual white and leaning on his gnarled walking stick. Apparently, he was setting out on one of his life-lengthening jaunts.

"I already talked to your pard," Cornelius told me. "He says he's got things all figured out."

"Mr. O'Nelligan?" I must have looked surprised. "What things has he figured out?"

He gave me a dismissive wave of the hand. "Not sure. Go talk to him. I'm off for my constitutional." Then, taking notice of Audrey, he added, "You're welcome to join me if you'd like, young lady."

My fiancée declined with a smile. "I think I'll stick with this fellow here."

Cornelius nodded. "I understand. 'You've got to dance with them what brung ya.' That's what my grandpap used to say." With that, he began making his way slowly down the block.

Watching him go, Audrey half-whispered to me, "You know, as old as he is, his grandpap could have danced with Dolley Madison."

"I heard that, missy," Cornelius called over his shoulder. "Like I tell everybody, I've got good hearing."

PAUSED IN THE hallway outside Mrs. Pattinshell's apartment, we were greeted by a man's voice raised in anger. Without bothering to knock, I flung open the door and entered. The lights were all on—no candlelight this time—and there before us stood Mr. O'Nelligan facing off against Patch Doonan. Patch, unsurprisingly, was the one testing his vocal cords. His two brothers were also in attendance, as usual attempting to calm their combustible sibling.

"For the love of God, Patch." Neil had on his patented look of exasperation. "Leave the man be."

"Not when he's catapulting his threats at me!" The barrel-chested Patch was all but shouting into my partner's face. "Don't provoke me, O'Nelligan!"

The oldest Irishman in the room stood his ground, staring calmly and unflinchingly into his confronter's eyes. "If you would only hear me out—"

"Bollocks to that!" Patch answered.

"No more of this." Tim slapped a firm hand on his brother's shoulder. "Mr. O'Nelligan wasn't threatening you at all. If you'd just let him finish—"

"Bollocks!" Patch shook Tim loose and took a step closer to my partner.

Compelled to act, I moved forward and grabbed Doonan by the arm. "You need to relax, chum." I expected to smell alcohol on his breath but was spared that.

He broke from my grip. "Ganging up on me, are you? I heard about you getting wounded, Plunkett, but that won't stop me from defending myself."

His hands became fists, and he looked ready to pounce on me. At this point, Mr. O'Nelligan apparently had had enough. With a forcefulness I'd never before seen him display, my partner seized Patch's shirtfront in both hands and pulled him close.

"Hear me well, young man," Mr. O'Nelligan hissed into his face. "You will cease this coarse behavior at once. In a moment, I'll continue the account I was presenting before you so preposterously overreacted. First, though, you'll hear this."

"Let go of me," Patch said weakly, clearly shocked by the older man's controlled fierceness.

Mr. O'Nelligan tightened his grasp. "Shut your mouth and listen. You're a young fellow, Doonan, surely still finding his way in the world. You're full of vigor and wit and song, all estimable things. Alas, you're veering dangerously close to becoming the very parody of an Irishman that you've mocked. The sort one sees in inferior stage productions—the drunken, brawling lout whose blood overheats at the smallest perceived slight. I'm convinced that you're a better man than that pitiful stereotype. The question is, can *you* be convinced."

He released Patch and took a step back. Doonan started to say something, some denial or rebuttal, but the words died on his lips.

"You are the oldest of your brothers," Mr. O'Nelligan said softly now. "Your strength and sturdiness will, no doubt, be appreciated in the course of time."

Patch just stood there, saying nothing for a very long moment. Then he simply nodded.

Mr. O'Nelligan now addressed me. "As you'll soon see, Lee, things have fallen into place quite marvelously. I made a series of phone calls and was very fortunate in reaching all the desired parties. More company is expected, but I'll begin to lay out some particulars right away."

"So you've unraveled this tangled jumble?"

"That remains to be seen. I do hope so."

Audrey looked eager. "And I get a ringside seat to see you work your magic."

"Trust me, dear girl, it may not be as entertaining a diversion as you would desire. Tragedy and Sorrow are the main players here."

"Where's Mrs. Pattinshell?" I asked.

"She's in her boudoir, having vacated the room when things grew hot. I'll fetch her momentarily." Mr. O'Nelligan turned back to the Doonans. "Shall I continue with what I was telling you?"

It was Patch who answered, his temper now sapped. "Have at it."

"Not an hour ago, I managed to reach a man named O'Hallmhurain who clarified some things for me. According to what he's heard—and he hears quite a lot—there indeed was a Doonan involved in the New Year's attack on the Brookeborough police barracks. Here's where you interrupted me before, Patch."

"This time I'll not," Patch said contritely.

"Mr. O'Hallmhurain says that this individual was neither your Uncle Michael nor yourself but rather a man named Mykolas Doonan. Have any of you heard of him?"

The three brothers exchanged looks of uncertainty.

Tim spoke for them all. "I guess we haven't. After all, there's a whole flock of Doonans knocking about Ireland. But what breed of Doonan goes by the name Mykolas? There's nothing remotely Celtic in that."

"Apparently he's of mixed Irish and Lithuanian descent. His involvement in the barracks incident was not central, but enough to be mentioned in certain quarters. The similarity between 'Mykolas' and 'Michael' may well have led to the confusion." He turned to the elder Doonan. "Additionally, Mykolas has a son Patch, which might account for your name being brought up."

"He knew all this?" I asked. "Your man O'Whatshisname?"

"O'Hallmhurain," my friend corrected. "As I've stated, he makes it his business to stay informed."

"So I'm no longer under suspicion in your eyes?" Patch asked Mr. O'Nelligan.

"If I thought you suspicious in this matter, it was due chiefly to your refusal two nights ago to firmly deny your involvement."

"Well, a man doesn't like to be trounced with accusations," Patch said without much passion.

"I see," my partner replied flatly. "Tell me, did Lorraine Cobble ever suggest to you that she thought you were connected to the barracks attack?"

Patch looked perplexed. "No, but why should she? Why would she even be aware of events over in Ireland?"

"Miss Cobble was aware of many things," Mr. O'Nelligan said vaguely.

"So is this why you asked us to come here?" Tim asked. "To hear Patch be exonerated?"

"In part." Mr. O'Nelligan pulled out his pocket watch and consulted it.

Tim pressed on. "But why here? Why Mrs. Pattinshell's place?"

My colleague replaced his watch. "I presume that in this relatively small community the local musicians are all familiar with her and her reported abilities?"

"The ghost chanting?" Tim shrugged. "Sure, everyone knows about it."

"So I suspected."

"Not to say, of course, that everyone believes in it," Tim added.

"I understand. We have two more guests expected, and one will be arriving quite soon. I should summon our hostess before he arrives."

Mr. O'Nelligan stepped to the side of the room, lifted a black drape that covered an entrance there, and called for Mrs. Pattinshell.

Presently she appeared, her gaunt face fairly radiating displeasure. "More people? How many bodies do you intend to wedge into my living space?"

"Not many more," my partner said.

"I've had enough, do you hear me? This is my home. Get out! Get out, all of you!"

Mr. O'Nelligan positioned himself in front of her. "As I've explained to you, madam, your acquiescence is required. We must see these events through to their end."

"Not with me you won't!" She thrust a bony finger toward the door. "Go! Go! Practice your chicanery elsewhere."

"Chicanery?" Mr. O'Nelligan's face hardened. "Need I remind you, my good woman, that it is *you* who have actively practiced subterfuge here? I think it would be to your advantage to comply with my requests. After all, you've attempted to misdirect a murder investigation, haven't you?"

Audrey whispered into my ear, "Misdirecting the investigation? What's he mean by that?"

"You'll see." By that I meant *I'll* see, because I really didn't know where Mr. O'Nelligan was going with all this.

My partner's reprimand seemed to have put Mrs. Pattinshell in her place. With a grunt and a grimace, she dropped herself into her upholstered chair behind the lace-covered table.

A knock sounded on the door. Being the closest to it, I took on the doorman duties and found myself staring at a short, well-dressed man with a trim, graying Vandyke beard. His fedora was worn at a jaunty angle, and the white carnation in his lapel gave him added dash. For a befuddled moment, I wondered if Mr. O'Nelligan had brought in an uptown lawyer, or perhaps some ritzy gangster.

"Hey, you must be Buster's punk." The voice was familiar, though its owner was certainly not. "Yeah, I can see it around the eyes. It's me, kid. Smack."

I gaped at him. The Smack I'd imagined on the phone was a burly hulk in a cheap, wrinkled sports jacket. The version before me was a dandy in a double-breasted suit.

"Uh, yeah . . . hi, Smack," I sputtered.

My partner was at my shoulder. "Detective Wilton, please enter."

"You gotta be O'Nelligan." Smack studied him with a crooked grin. "I tell ya, Lee, this assistant of yours could talk Churchill out of his cigars. He calls the station forty minutes ago, convinces me he can prove the Cobble dame was a homicide, and gets me to drop everything to show up here. You should put that tricky brogue of his in a can and sell it. You'd make yourself a fortune."

Smack entered and assessed the gathering. "I recognize most of this crew from my investigation last month. Okay, so what's the deal here?"

"Please have a seat, Detective," Mr. O'Nelligan instructed. "All will be made clear. Everyone, do make yourselves comfortable."

"Didn't you say we're expecting someone else?" I asked him.

"Our present assemblage is adequate to start things off."

Smack whistled. "Listen to this guy! Yeah, Brogue-in-a-Can. A guaranteed fortune."

"Alas, our present business has nothing to do with fortune," Mr. O'Nelligan said somberly, "but everything to do with *mis*fortune. Grave, woeful misfortune . . ."

CHAPTER THIRTY

SMACK, TIM, AND NEIL SET-
tled into wooden chairs, while
Patch leaned against the wall
under the creepy painting of figures writhing in the mist.
The dispossessed queen, Mrs. Pattinshell, remained in her
plush high-backed throne. Audrey and I wound up standing
to the right of Mr. O'Nelligan, who'd placed himself in the
center of the room—the lead actor commanding the stage.

He began. "With my superior's permission, I will now put
forth the findings of our investigation."

My friend glanced over at me to indicate that I was the
referenced superior.

"Sure, proceed." I felt foolish uttering the words, well aware
that my superiority was a charitable illusion he'd conjured for
my benefit.

Mr. O'Nelligan straightened his necktie and cleared his
throat, indicating the presentation was under way. "We accepted

this case on behalf of Miss Sally Joan Cobble, the deceased's cousin. Since that young lady is presently in Pittsburgh, several hours away, she will not be joining us this afternoon. Our findings will, of course, be passed on to her in due course. Detective Wilton, we thank you for coming here as a representative of the law. Your patience is matched only by your panache."

Smack's Vandyke twitched in either amusement or annoyance; I couldn't tell which.

My partner continued. "We entered into this with precious few facts. All we had was two brief pieces of correspondence, a history of Lorraine's strained relationships, and Sally Joan's strong doubts that her cousin died by suicide. At the start, our agency was not fully convinced that this was a case of murder."

By that, I knew he meant that *I* wasn't fully convinced. From the get-go, Mr. O'Nelligan had been the one who smelled foul play.

He pushed on. "Several days ago, Minnie Bornstein, Lorraine's fellow song collector, shared with us an interesting analogy: the idea that although many versions of a ballad may exist, the main narrative remains intact—what she called the spine of the tale. It occurs to me that our investigation might be seen in such a light. Our task was to sift through the variations, the numerous plotlines that arose for us, and identify the spine of this tale. That is, the core truth of Lorraine Cobble's death."

"So you're stating that she was indeed killed?" Neil asked.

"I am. Lorraine did not die of her own volition."

Patch was wide-eyed. "No lie? You know that for a fact?"

"I believe I do," said Mr. O'Nelligan. "Now, over this past weekend, the variations I speak of came fast and furiously. I'll enumerate them here. First off, we had the two notes—one of unknown origin indicating that Lorraine had a rendezvous on the day she died, the other from a man named Cardinal Meriam, whose acrimony Lorraine had earned this past winter. Then we had the account of the long-lived Cornelius Boyle. Cornelius swore that he'd encountered a grocery boy, Hector Escobar, in the hallway near the time of Lorraine's death, a claim which the boy has denied. Also complicating things was a rumor circulating in regard to Patch Doonan."

"A discredited bloody rumor!" Patch chimed in.

"Correct. Although it was only today that it was fully dispelled. Another variation to our tale concerned the alleged abilities of our hostess here."

"They are *not* alleged," Mrs. Pattinshell asserted, her nose in the air. "They are *actual*."

Mr. O'Nelligan ignored her. "Specifically, we were faced with her claim that the spirit of Lorraine Cobble had offered a song from beyond the grave. A song that seemed to implicate Cardinal Meriam in her death."

I noticed that Mrs. Pattinshell glanced away at the mention of Lorraine's ghost ballad.

"A song from Lorraine?" Tim straightened in his chair. "Can that be true?"

"I'll address that matter momentarily," my partner promised. "Yet another thread, a most distressing one, presented itself last evening when an unidentified gunman attacked Byron Spires and Lee here."

Smack started to say something, but Mr. O'Nelligan cut him off. "Detective, I know via our phone conversation that you have information to impart. In a minute, I'll ask you to provide it." He turned to me now. "Is there anything I've left out, Lee Plunkett?"

I appreciated being consulted, though I guessed it was

mostly a gesture of benevolence. "Well, we also had multiple accounts of Lorraine's quarrels and run-ins. They turned up pretty frequently."

"Yes, the woman seemed to flourish on conflict," Mr. O'Nelligan said. "We can certainly add those accounts to the mix. So, my friends, as you see, we were presented with several different versions of the tale. In one, the person requesting the rendezvous had a hand in Lorraine's death. In another, Cardinal, the mysterious magician, became an ominous figure. In yet another, young Hector Escobar came under suspicion. And so forth. At different steps in our investigation, one or another of these variations would catch our attention, drawing us toward it as a possible explanation of why Lorraine was killed. Regarding the rendezvous note, for example, Ruby Dovavska's name emerged at one point as the possible author, then Cardinal's, and finally—"

"It was Mazzo!" Audrey blurted out. At once, her face reddened. "Sorry. Didn't mean to interrupt."

Mr. O'Nelligan smiled back at her. "No apologies required, dear girl. Credit where credit's due. Yes, Miss Valish here deduced that it was the Grand Mazzo who requested the rendezvous that day. Mazzo wanted to meet Lorraine for his own private reasons. Reasons which, I believe, had nothing to do with her death. As for the rumor concerning Patch Doonan, we've already noted that it proved false. Ultimately, few if any of these threads had a direct connection to Lorraine's death, and yet—and here's the intriguing part—all of them in some way factor into our solution."

"Okay, so what *is* that solution, O'Nelligan?" Smack demanded. "I'm here against my better judgment 'cause you said you could deliver the goods."

"And delivered they shall be," my partner insisted. "If I may continue, perhaps the most prevalent version of the tale was the one concerning the shadowy Cardinal Meriam. Over the last few days, his name has recurred with great frequency, continually demanding our consideration. I am brought to mind of an incident from my boyhood in Ireland . . ."

Now I was the one whispering into Audrey's ear. "I was nuts to think we'd get through this without one of his Old Country Chronicles."

Audrey shushed me. "I happen to like his stories."

"When I was a lad, it came to pass that one of the exhibits escaped from the Dublin zoo." My partner smiled at the memory. "A scarlet ibis, a rather exotic bird of South American origin."

"You're right!" Patch called out. "I remember our da telling us about that."

"Yes, it was quite the event," Mr. O'Nelligan said. "For a week after the bird fled its confinement, sightings of it were reported throughout Ireland. From east to west, north to south, people swore on scripture that they'd beheld it in flight or perched on some high branch off in the distance. Even in my own County Kerry—as far from Dublin as geography permits—a schoolmaster, several farmhands, and a convent of nuns reported seeing it. Several prominent ornithologists tried to debunk these claims, yet still the reports continued."

"The ibis was eventually discovered, wasn't it?" Neil asked. "In a shed not a mile from the zoo, if I remember Da's story right."

"That is so," Mr. O'Nelligan said. "Apparently, the bird had developed a fondness for Dublin. The thing is, for that unaccounted week, the allure of seeing an exotic, red-plumed, almost mythological creature winging across the heavens was so strong that many succumbed to the fantasy. Thus, Erin's Scarlet Ibis became, in its way, legendary."

"Which brings us back to Cardinal Meriam," I jumped in, actually getting the point of the story. "He was our own little red-plumed legend. Cardinal seemed to pop up for us at every bend in the road."

"Exactly!" My colleague shot me a fond look, no doubt delighted that I'd managed to follow along. "Although Mr. Meriam's whereabouts remained a mystery, he persistently drew our focus. And the focus of someone else, as we'll presently see."

"Presently see?" Patch threw up his hands. "When the hell do we reach the end of all this?"

"Very soon." Mr. O'Nelligan paused to regard us all, the practiced actor evaluating his audience. "More on Cardinal in a moment. In recently sharing an anecdote with my comrade Lee, I suggested that the number three has a certain power to it, as seen in literature and history."

"Oh, for Pete's sake!" Smack wiggled impatiently in his chair. "If I wanted long endless lectures, I'd have run for Congress."

Mr. O'Nelligan didn't stop to argue. "The number three, sacred and significant in many traditions, has here again shown itself. In our investigation, three unknown individuals have needed to be identified—the one who wrote the rendezvous note, the one who shot Plunkett and Spires, and the one who killed Lorraine Cobble."

"Of course, two or more of those could be the same person," I reasoned.

"They could be, but they are not," my partner said. "We know now that we're speaking of three separate individuals. It's already been revealed that the note writer was Anthony

Mazzo. As for last night's gunman, Detective Wilton can address that issue. When I called him earlier to request his presence here, he shared the welcomed news that the assailant had
been captured."

"Captured?" Audrey sounded both shocked and relieved
(as was I). "The awful bastard who shot Lee and Byron?"

Audrey wasn't one for profanity, but at the moment she
seemed well within her rights to let loose. She reached over and
gave my hand a quick squeeze.

Mr. O'Nelligan gestured toward Wilton. "Detective, will
you illuminate us?"

"It's about time," Smack grumbled. "Yeah, he's behind bars.
Seems that some passersby saw him racing from the scene of
the crime last night. Our guys picked him up a couple hours
ago, and I was there when he got hauled in. Seedy little twerp
by the name of Loomis Lent."

"Loomis! Sweet Jesus!" Patch Doonan pushed himself away
from the wall. "I always knew he was a wrong one. Why'd he
do it?"

"Yeah, why?" I pictured the small rumpled man with the
rumpled mustache and rumpled ideas. "Was it because he
killed Lorraine and thought I'd picked up his trail?"

"It was the opposite," Mr. O'Nelligan said. "He was attempting to avenge Miss Cobble. If I understand Detective
Wilton correctly, you were not the intended target, Lee."

"That's right, kid," Smack agreed. "Lent was gunning for
Byron Spires. You just got in the way."

Audrey caught her breath. "Why Byron? Is *he* the one who
pushed Lorraine off the roof?"

"He is not," Mr. O'Nelligan said. "Although Loomis believed
he was."

"But why?" I asked.

Smack answered that. "Seems Lent saw you Saturday night when you were shaking Spires down. He heard you telling Spires how you knew about what he did to Lorraine Cobble."

"What Spires did? But I never——" I flashed on the young musician pinned against the outer wall of the Mercutio, with me shouting in his face *I know what you did to her; I know what you did* just as Loomis stepped out onto the sidewalk. "Wait, I wasn't talking about Lorraine then. I was referring to——" I glanced over at Audrey. "Someone else."

"Well, that's not how Lent took it," Smack said. "He thought you were accusing Spires of killing the Cobble dame, who I gathered he took a shine to. Next day, he figured you'd have arrested the guy, but when he heard on the street that Spires was still free, he concocted his little plan. He waited last night outside the coffeehouse—him and a Smith and Wesson—figuring Spires might show up, which he did. Lent didn't shoot at first, on account of Spires having some doll on his arm."

Beside me, Audrey stiffened slightly. Byron Spires' goatish leanings were no doubt becoming clear to her.

Smack kept going. "According to Lent, Spires went inside but came right out again, this time with both the girl and you, Lee. She went back in immediately, but you were still standing close to Spires. Not wanting to kill more guys than he had to, he waited for Spires to walk away from you. Didn't matter. Lent's shooting was so sloppy, he ended up creasing you anyway. And that's the scoop. By the way, looks like Spires is going to pull through. The docs dug a slug out of his chest and sewed him up proper."

Audrey sighed softly, and so did I. After all, it was because of me—or at least Lent's misconstruing of my words—that Spires had gotten shot.

I attempted to summarize. "All right, we have Mazzo as the note writer and Loomis as the gunman. And for Lorraine's killer . . ." I looked at my partner, my eyebrows raised in good old-fashioned bewilderment.

Mr. O'Nelligan again extracted his pocket watch, studied it for a moment, and nodded to himself. "It's almost time. The person in question should be here any minute." He looked over at Mrs. Pattinshell. "I trust you conveyed my instructions precisely, madam?"

Our ghost chanter, who had maintained a low-grade scowl throughout the proceedings, now broke her silence. "I fulfilled your request as specified."

"Hold everything!" Audrey, judging by her own raised eyebrows, had contracted my case of bewilderment. "Are you saying Lorraine Cobble's murderer is coming here now?"

"Yes," Mr. O'Nelligan said simply.

If the topic hadn't been homicide, the punctuality of the knock on the door would have been almost comical. Again I played the doorman, but this time my heartbeat was in overdrive.

Staring at the person in the hallway, I can say that I truly wished it was someone other than who it was. Almost anyone else—Mazzo or Hector or Ruby or even Spires, risen miraculously from his hospital bed. Or maybe a man I'd never seen before, with incriminating bright red hair.

Sadly, you don't always get what you wish for.

CHAPTER THIRTY-ONE

IMLA THORPE LOOKED AT me with wide, startled eyes. Maybe as startled as my own.

"Mr. Plunkett? Why are you—?" Then she noticed the roomful of people behind me. "Oh God . . ."

For a moment, it seemed that she might turn and flee, but Mr. O'Nelligan came forward and took her by the arm. "Come in, Miss Thorpe. We've been waiting for you."

He led her inside, and I closed the door. All three Doonans were now standing, though the youngest seemed unsteady on his feet.

"Kimla!" Tim had gone ashen. "What are you doing here?"

Patch didn't look much better. "Ludicrous! O'Nelligan, you can't mean this."

My partner released Kimla and offered her a chair. Refusing it, she moved past the Doonans to stand near the wall at the spot that Patch had vacated. Beneath the ghostly painting, she wrapped her arms tightly around herself and stared forward blankly, avoiding everyone's eyes—most notably Tim's.

Smack Wilton, who like our hostess had remained seated, looked Kimla over and frowned. "So this is your murderer, O'Nelligan? This stick of a girl?"

"Unfortunately, yes," my partner said softly.

"Deny it, Kimla!" Tim cried out. "For God's sake, deny this nonsense!"

Kimla said nothing, denied nothing.

Tim turned to Mr. O'Nelligan. "It's plain to see you've intimidated her. I don't know how you pressured her into coming here, but obviously you've blundered in a big way. Kimla's a quiet lass. A fine, peaceful young lady." He spun back toward his girl. "Jesus, Kimla, why don't you say something? C'mon! You never touched Lorraine, did you now?"

Kimla remained silent, her jaw clenched and her eyes unfocused, but a single tear traced its way down her cheek. It seemed like an answer.

"Aw, no." Tim thrust a hand through his dark hair. "No, no, no, no . . ." He staggered a little, and Neil eased him back into his chair.

Mrs. Pattinshell now rose. "All right, you have her. I've fulfilled my part of the bargain. Now take her away and return my home to me."

"In due course, madam," Mr. O'Nelligan said. "But it's important that everyone here understand what came to pass."

Smack grunted. "You bet it is. If you expect me to slap the cuffs on somebody, I'm gonna need more convincing."

Mrs. Pattinshell, seeing that her wishes were to be ignored, moaned and slid back into her chair.

Mr. O'Nelligan continued. "I should explain that our hostess was instructed to call Miss Thorpe and tell her to arrive at precisely this time. Miss Thorpe was expecting to find no one here but Mrs. Pattinshell. All has gone according to plan."

"Okay, but why here?" Smack asked. "We could have done this down at the station."

"To address that and other points, I'll explain now how we identified Miss Thorpe as Lorraine's killer."

"Yeah, how *did* we identify her?" I wondered aloud.

"Earlier this afternoon, I took a fine long walk." Mr. O'Nelligan's answers were nothing if not roundabout. "This allowed me to ponder and prioritize the facts that we've gathered these last few days. In the course of our quest for truth, while various threads played themselves out, one lingering problem could not be ignored—Cornelius Boyle's claim that he spoke with Hector Escobar near the time of Lorraine's death."

"Coupled with Hector's counterclaim that he wasn't there," I put in.

"Indeed. Apparently, one of them had to be lying. And yet, after repeated interviews, it became apparent that neither was."

Audrey joined in now. "Hector swore on his grandmother's cross that he wasn't there. He seemed in earnest."

"He did," my partner agreed. "Mr. Boyle seemed equally sincere in his own assertions. Of course, his eyes and ears, though a source of pride for him, bear over a century of usage. Then, this morning, we heard from Tony Mazzo that when he himself had been in Lorraine's empty apartment, he heard the exchange between Cornelius and another person. What Cornelius saw that night was a slender individual of dark complexion, at a bit of a distance and obscured in shadow. Based on who he had seen earlier that day, he guessed it to be Hector the grocery boy. Cornelius called out—first in English, then in Spanish—and that individual answered, briefly but convincingly. Thinking no more of it, Cornelius returned to his apartment. Sometimes one sees what he believes to be true, even if the reality is false."

"But it was never Hector, was it?" Audrey asked.

"I came to believe that it was not," Mr. O'Nelligan said. "Especially after our encounter with the lad today. The question now arose, if this figure in the shadows wasn't the grocery boy, then who could it be? If it was a stranger, then of course, there was no way to guess. But what if he was one of the men in Lorraine's circle? Who of those we'd met resembled him? Going over the possibilities, no one seemed a likely match. Perhaps the closest was young Tim Doonan."

"What *now*?" Patch barked. "So it's Tim you're accusing?"

"I am not. Tim is fair-skinned and more solidly built than Hector. Additionally, Cornelius' youth spoke Spanish, a skill I wasn't sure Tim possessed. I added up our hallway lurker's known traits—the slenderness, the complexion, the ability to speak Spanish—and an unexpected possibility arose. Miss Kimla Thorpe. True, she was the wrong sex, but with her thinness and her husky voice, perhaps disguised, she could quite possibly be mistaken for a teenaged male. Especially by ancient eyes in a shadowy hall. As for the Spanish, I recalled that when we heard her perform Friday evening, she sang one of her songs partially in that tongue. A love ballad from Madrid. While that did not necessarily indicate fluency, it did suggest that she knew enough of the language to toss out a few words to Cornelius."

Neil Doonan cut in. "Surely, though, that's not enough to be certain it was her."

"There was, in fact, more to go on," Mr. O'Nelligan said. "I'd been reflecting on Mrs. Pattinshell's latest ghost song. While I'm very open to the world's metaphysical possibilities, I was not convinced that the song presented to us genuinely came from Lorraine's spirit. Obviously, we were being steered toward believing that Cardinal Meriam was her murderer. Earlier, Lee here had suggested the possibility that Mrs. Pattinshell herself created the song. Surely that would be the simplest explanation. After all, having read Cardinal's letter to Lorraine, Mrs. Pattinshell was aware of its threatening tone and could infuse those sentiments into the lyrics. Conversely, it could also be that another party had written the ghost song and somehow coerced Mrs. Pattinshell into saying that it came from the late Lorraine. In reviewing the lyrics of the ghost ballad, one line echoed for me—*none can brave the storm*. I realized that I'd heard it recently in a different song, again one from Miss Thorpe's repertoire."

I looked over at Kimla. She was still hugging herself tightly, staring off at nothing at all. I thought I saw her lips silently forming the words "brave the storm."

My colleague went on. "Although not a completely unique phrase, it was distinctive enough to be taken note of. As I've mentioned, I was already considering Kimla to be that person in the hallway, and the echoed lyric further elevated her as a suspect."

I tossed in my two cents. "Also, she was one of the few people we showed Cardinal's letter to at the Mercutio."

"Meaning she was privy to its menacing tenor," Mr. O'Nelligan said. "Taking in all these things together, Kimla Thorpe seemed a valid choice. The question was how to confirm it. I devised a plan to confront our hostess about Lorraine's ghost song. Arriving here an hour ago, I secured her admission that she'd lied to us regarding the song and, in fact, had been paid to do so." He addressed Mrs. Pattinshell. "It might be best, madam, if this portion was given in your own words."

She glared bullets at him but, after a moment, obeyed his request in her clipped, formal manner. "Yesterday morning I awoke to find that an envelope had been slipped under my door. The unsigned letter within had been penned in a strained hand, as if the writer were attempting to disguise his or her identity. The letter consisted of two sheets, the first being the lyrics to a song, and the second being a set of instructions. Additionally, some cash had been included, not an ungenerous amount. The instructions told me to call up Plunkett and O'Nelligan, inform them that I'd received the song from Lorraine's spirit, and sing it to them in whatever tune I fancied. If I complied with this, more money would be forthcoming. As it turned out, the investigators insisted on coming here to hear the song, so I was forced to memorize the lyrics. That is all." She turned now to Smack Wilton. "As you see, Detective, I've done nothing illegal. Unorthodox perhaps, but not illegal."

"Unorthodox!" Smack snickered. "That's just another word for no-holds-barred batty, ain't it?"

Mr. O'Nelligan took over again. "In order to draw Miss Thorpe out into the open, I had Mrs. Pattinshell phone her earlier to say that she'd figured out Kimla's identity and demand she come here to sort things out. No doubt feeling cornered, Kimla, as we see, did indeed comply."

For the last several minutes, Tim Doonan had been sitting in silence, appearing deeply shell-shocked. He now looked over at his girlfriend and managed to rasp out a question. "Is it all true, Kimla?"

Still avoiding his eyes, she gave a barely audible "Yes."

Something between agitation and anger drove Tim's words. "But why? Why did you kill Lorraine?"

Instead of answering, Kimla looked over at Mr. O'Nelligan. "*You* tell him." There was bitterness in her voice. "You seem to know everything."

"I certainly don't know everything that occurred," my partner said, "but I can speculate. While I had identified you as Lorraine's killer, it was hard to imagine someone of your gentility in that role. I wondered what could possibly have compelled you to such an extreme act. What did you hold so close to your heart that you would fight to protect it? The answer was Tim."

"Yes," Kimla said under her breath.

Mr. O'Nelligan kept on. "My guess is that events began to unfold that evening at the Café Mercutio when Patch played his jest on Lorraine and Loomis Lent, sending a bottle of wine and a provoking note to their table. Lorraine was enraged at this presumed mockery, but perhaps even more so at Patch's subsequent comments ridiculing her song gathering."

"That she was," Patch agreed.

"The accusation—made in public—that she had pilfered tunes from poor hobos and farmers must have struck Lorraine to her very core. Remember, her role as songcatcher was her greatest source of passion and pride. Here was a woman whose anger could be searing when she felt herself wronged or insulted, and that anger was now turned toward Patch. We know that Lorraine would often depend on Loomis for dark gossip about others, and we know that Loomis may have been privy to a rumor concerning Patch and a barracks attack in Ireland."

"Because we'd been in *Deirdre of the Sorrows* together?" Patch guessed.

"Most likely," my partner agreed. "Now here I take a leap, but I propose that Lorraine, upon learning of Patch's possible involvement in the attack, decided that she'd use the information to malicious effect. Additionally—and here again I speculate—she perhaps planned to extend that fate not just to the eldest Doonan but to his brothers also. Well, Miss Thorpe, might this be the case?"

"Lorraine swore she'd get them deported!" It came rushing out of her now. "Arrested and deported! She said that if Patch was involved, then probably all the brothers were, or at least that's how the authorities would see it. That meant that Tim—" Kimla stopped to catch her breath.

My partner nodded. "Yes, as I've said, I felt that it must all come down to Tim. To your affection for him."

Tim bowed his head and let out a low, pathetic groan. Standing beside him now, Patch reached down and rested a hand on his shoulder.

Kimla couldn't seem to stop. "She'd come by the Mercutio that morning. I think she was hoping to find Patch, to rub it in—what she'd learned and what she was planning to do. But Patch wasn't there, and neither was Tim or Neil. I was the only person in the room, just having coffee and reading a book. I guess Lorraine figured telling me would have to do. That's when she made her threats about getting the boys jailed and deported."

"It could have been a bluff," I said.

"I don't think so," Kimla insisted. "Lorraine was clever enough and vindictive enough to carry through on her threats. I had to believe she could do what she promised to do. I tried to talk to her, but she was out the door before I could get a word in. Tim was away for the weekend, so I couldn't go to him about it. I had commitments for the rest of the day, way into the evening. It wasn't till very late that I made my way to Lorraine's."

"This was close to ten P.M.?" Mr. O'Nelligan asked.

"Something like that." Kimla's voice was becoming distant and trancelike; she unfolded her arms and let them fall to her sides. "I'd decided that I was going to reason with her. I was going to get her to promise to leave Tim alone, to leave all of them alone. There was no answer when I knocked on her door, but then I heard someone singing on the roof, and I knew it must be her. I climbed up. There was a half-moon that night, just bright enough to see her by. She was singing 'The Wild, Weeping Heather.'"

"The song she said Spires stole?" I asked.

"Yes, that's the one." Her trance seemed to be deepening. "Lorraine was standing by the edge of the roof. I went over and began pleading with her, begging with her not to bring any harm to Tim. I told her that he was such a good person, that she had no idea what a good person he was. Maybe Patch had done what she claimed or maybe he hadn't, but not my Tim. She told me that getting Tim and Neil into trouble, too, would make Patch's suffering all the worse."

"Jesus," Patch muttered under his breath.

"I told her that Tim had a pure, true heart. That's when she laughed. She said that I was talking about him like he was someone out of a ballad, but that people were never as moral or worthy as the characters in songs. She said that people were shameful and foolish, and that I was a fool for thinking Tim was something special. Then she laughed again and said she hoped they'd lock him away till he was withered and broken. That's when I pushed her."

Those last words hung over the room like a storm cloud, and no one spoke for a long interval.

Finally, Kimla continued, her voice barely audible now. "I couldn't believe what I'd done. It just didn't seem possible. It felt like I was in some dream, and if I hurried home quickly enough, none of it would really have happened . . ." She faded out, lowering her eyes and again wrapping her arms protectively around her slender form.

Somewhat to my own surprise, I was able to take up the narrative. "Then you descended to the fifth floor and paused near the stairwell. That's when Cornelius stepped into the hallway and called out to you. You must have been hugely relieved when you saw that he'd mistaken you for Hector. From your earlier visits to Cornelius, maybe you were aware of Hector and his grocery runs. When the old man started speaking in Spanish, you knew enough of the language to answer, probably altering your voice to sound more male. That's why Mazzo didn't recognize you. You convinced Cornelius it really was Hector there, and he went away. Does that all ring true?"

"That's how it happened," Kimla answered quietly. "In the days after, I drove it all from my mind. Lorraine's death was declared suicide, and I think, in a way, I made myself believe that's what it truly was. Maybe I hadn't even been there at all."

I was reminded of Mazzo saying that the more he told the lie about lambasting McCarthy's minions, the more it seemed like the truth. It's peculiar what the human mind can do.

"Then you two came to town." Kimla looked at my partner and me. "And I couldn't pretend to myself anymore."

"No, you could not," Mr. O'Nelligan said. "With our arrival, homicide was now being considered, and you were put

on guard. Two nights ago, when you observed us accosting the
Doonans about the barracks attack, you realized that we were
getting closer to the source of Lorraine's killing. Having seen
Cardinal Meriam's foreboding letter to Lorraine and knowing
of Mrs. Pattinshell's ghost songs, you fashioned your plan of
misdirection and set it in motion. You hoped to have us believe that Cardinal had killed Lorraine and that he was beyond
our reach."

"That's why I went to the Mercutio last evening." Kimla
wasn't holding anything back now. "To see if you two might
show up and say something about the song. I needed to find
out if you believed it was really from Lorraine. You came in,
Mr. Plunkett, but you didn't say anything about it."

"I did think it was a little strange that you asked me directly about our investigation. Before that, you'd kept a low
profile and didn't seem to want to talk about it. Anyway, you
decided to give us Cardinal . . ."

"No one really knew what had become of him," Kimla
said softly. "Or if he'd ever return here. So it seemed like there
was no harm in aiming you toward him."

I reworded that. "No harm in sacrificing him, you mean."

"I'm sorry," Kimla said, though it wasn't me she was staring at but Tim.

The youngest Doonan looked like hell. He now got to his
feet, and he and Kimla met each other's eyes for the first time
since she'd entered the room. She had given way to heavy trembling, and he looked on the verge of collapse. They moved toward each other. Finding myself unable to watch, I turned away,
and I saw that Audrey had done the same.

When I looked back, Smack Wilton, now standing, had

parted the couple and was pulling a pair of handcuffs from his jacket pocket. "Okay, miss," he said without his usual gruffness. "It's time we got going."

The skittish Siamese, up to this point unaccounted for, leapt into its mistress' lap and let out a long plaintive *meow*. It was a sound both chilling and mournful.

CHAPTER THIRTY-TWO

E EXITED MRS. PATTIN-shell's in waves. Smack led Kimla away, followed a minute later by Mr. O'Nelligan, Audrey, and me. We left the Doonans behind us, as Patch and Neil gathered up their devastated brother.

When my party reached the street, we were met by cries and chaos. Down the road to our left, Smack lay sprawled on the sidewalk, his fedora beside him. He was gripping his shin and yelling out, "Stop! Stop!" He tried to get to his feet but was obviously hobbled.

Kimla, her hands still cuffed before her, had broken free and was racing our way, not directly toward us but into the traffic-filled street. Horns blaring, several cars barely missed her. It quickly became apparent that her intention was to be struck down. From our right, a wide delivery truck came hurtling toward her. Clearly, it couldn't stop in time. Without thinking,

I shot forward and caught Kimla by the arm. I realized at once that I hadn't run out alone: Audrey was beside me, gripping the girl's other arm. The truck's horn screamed fiercely as we flung ourselves backward. Then the vehicle flew by, its loud wail fading into the distance, and the three of us were lying together on the sidewalk. As Kimla dissolved into tears, Audrey and I, on either side of her, locked eyes. Something unspoken passed between us.

Mr. O'Nelligan crouched down beside us. After assuring himself of our well-being, he whispered, "Thank God," and helped us lift Kimla to her feet. Smack Wilton and the Doonans converged on us at the same moment.

Smack took his prisoner firmly in hand. "Whadda ya say, sister? Are we done with the shin kicking and traffic dodging?"

Kimla Thorpe, her face smeared with tears, nodded and then turned to Tim to offer a parting glance. Smack led her away, this time without incident.

Mr. O'Nelligan placed his hands on Tim's shoulders and looked deeply into his eyes. "I know this is an unimaginable burden, lad, but you are young and will prevail. There's a certain quotation you might keep in your heart—'By virtue and energy, by wisdom and right action, you shall overcome the sorrows of life.'"

Tim nodded and got out a fragile "Thank you."

Neil stepped forward and put an arm around his brother's waist. "Come along then, Timothy." They moved off together down the street, in the direction opposite to the one Kimla had been taken.

As Patch turned to follow, Mr. O'Nelligan reached out and caught his arm. "As I said before, you are the oldest and your strength will be needed."

Patch nodded. "I understand, sir." Then he, too, headed off.

As we watched them move away, Audrey asked, "Where was that quote from?"

"It's from the *Dhammapada*," Mr. O'Nelligan answered. "The teachings of the Buddha. If Kimla cannot benefit from it, then perhaps Tim can."

SINCE WE'D COME to the Village in two cars, Audrey took Mr. O'Nelligan with her back to Thelmont, and I drove myself. I was glad, actually, to be traveling alone, grateful for the silence after so much talk and commotion. We reunited at Mr. O'Nelligan's house, and from there I called Sally Joan Cobble in Pennsylvania. While providing a basic account of what had happened, I didn't share every single twist and turn. It seemed enough to confirm that someone had indeed killed her cousin, to identify that person, and to give a basic explanation as to why. In describing the final moments on the rooftop, I tried to be as subtle as possible, but I think Sally Joan grasped the image of Lorraine standing there, scheming and taunting to the end.

"Lorraine was more than that, you know," she said softly. "More than that angry, bitter woman. There was something else in her, something good and passionate that maybe only I saw. I wish you could have known that part of her."

"So do I," I said, and I think I meant it.

She thanked me for our work, expressed her dismay that I'd been wounded in the course of it, and promised to send my fee immediately. I told her there was no rush.

I hung up and said to no one specifically, "I wish we could have provided her with a kinder version of her cousin."

"That was not our lot." Mr. O'Nelligan was seated in his

easy chair. "We were summoned to deliver truth, and so we have. Besides, Sally Joan has her own memories of Lorraine to succor her. That will be her own private truth. In the end, Lorraine Cobble was, like all of us, a complicated being. She encouraged people in pursuing the music in their lives, and yet she also enraged and alienated them."

"There's one thing I'm wondering," I said to my partner. "Why did you set it up so that Tim and his brothers were there for Kimla's confession? It seemed sort of cruel."

"That was certainly not my intent," he answered. "As painful as the episode was for young Tim, I felt it was important that he witness it. Otherwise, he might never have fully accepted the dark reality of what happened that night."

Audrey was seated beside him. "It's all so strange. When it comes down to it, it was love that brought Kimla to that terrible moment. Her love and Lorraine's hate."

"Well expressed, lass," my colleague said quietly. "Perhaps sometimes a love ballad can also be a murder ballad."

"Then there's Loomis Lent," I noted. "He also acted out of misguided love."

Mr. O'Nelligan nodded. "Yes, his affection for Lorraine. Without question, much tragedy has arisen from the human heart."

Audrey turned to him. "What was that Yeats poem you quoted yesterday? The one about the heart longing?"

"It's actually not a poem," our Irishman answered. "It's a bit of prose from *The Celtic Twilight,* his book of folktales and faery legends. The full lines are thus: 'Let us go forth, the tellers of tales, and seize whatever prey the heart long for, and have no fear. Everything exists, everything is true, and the earth is only a little dust under our feet.'"

Audrey smiled to herself. "I like that. It's kind of lovely and kind of frightening."

"As is the world around us," said Mr. O'Nelligan. "Lovely and frightening and worthy of our best songs."

AFTER DECLINING OUR host's offer of tea and sandwiches, Audrey and I said good night to him and headed out the door. Standing in between my Baby Blue and her Buick, with the Thelmont Twilight settling over us, we embraced, holding on to each other tightly.

When we finally stepped apart, she said, "It's been a long day, hasn't it?"

"Several long days."

"Yes, several." Her face registered something between calm and weariness. "I didn't get to tell you, Lee, but yesterday afternoon I got a call from my friend Delores Polk. Remember her?"

"The travel writer, right? Your one wealthy pal."

"She's not wealthy, but she's doing nicely for herself. Anyway, she's working on a new book and wants an assistant. A travel companion."

"You mean . . ."

"She wants *me*, Lee."

"But . . . for how long?"

"A month, at least. Maybe more."

"Five months? Ten? A few years?" There was no agitation in my voice. I was too bone tired for that, but her words had left me off kilter. "What about us?"

"*Us* doesn't change," Audrey said firmly. "But you know I've been feeling the need to get out and explore. This is my

chance to see something besides the streets of Thelmont. Delores says we might even go to Europe."

"Europe . . ."

"I talked to Mrs. Jerome. She has a niece who can fill in at
the five-and-dime right away. So I could leave soon. Very soon."

Then there was silence. Not an awkward silence; not an angry one or a sad one; not a silence that comes from confusion or
mistrust. It was the silence born of a long, disorienting day—
one day and many days—that had left us in an odd new place.
A place where we didn't quite recognize ourselves or each other.

And, strangely enough, maybe that was a good thing.

I was the one who finally spoke. "I hope you get to see the
Eiffel Tower, Audrey."

"Yeah?" She smiled; there was relief and gratefulness there.

"Yeah. And the Taj Mahal and the pyramids and the malt
shops of Mars. *Especially* the malt shops of Mars."

"You *know* there are too many calories in Martian ice cream,"
she scolded. "What are you trying to do to me?"

"Just trying to expand your horizons."

"More like my waistline. I much prefer Saturn sherbet."

"Oh, you would."

I reached out and pulled her to me. Our kiss was long and
deep, accompanied by the trilling of a bird in the distance.
Maybe it was a cardinal. Or a scarlet ibis.

Maybe it was better not to know.